McCarren's Rules ~ Angel Falls

by

DeeAnna Galbraith

McCarren's Rules, Book 1

McCarren's Rules ~ Angel Falls

COPYRIGHT © 2020 by DeeAnna Galbraith

Cover Art by *Abigail Owen*

The Wild Rose Press, Inc.
PO Box 708
Adams Basin, NY 14410-0708
Visit us at www.thewildrosepress.com

Publishing History
First Crimson Rose Edition, 2020
Trade Paperback ISBN 978-1-5092-3309-0
Digital ISBN 978-1-5092-3310-6

McCarren's Rules, Book 1
Published in the United States of America

Dedication

For my favorite grandson,
Reed Douglas Galbraith

One person is sitting at the conference table. A man of about thirty-five, business casual dress, nice build, with dark, close-cropped hair and beard. His eyes are worth a second look. Espresso brown and I can tell from the emerging crows' feet he either spends more than average time outdoors or laughs a lot. His gaze makes me want to hold up my hands in surrender, whether I'm guilty or not. That is one handy stare.

We sit, and Rippa leans in. "Spanish Inquisition at ten o'clock."

Even as tired as I am, I grin at her remark.

Fletcher comes in and looks like I feel. "Thank you for coming, Julianne. I didn't know you'd be bringing the kids."

"They're adults and know what's going on."

I don't ask where Mitch and Veronique are. Too afraid if I do, it will cause them to appear.

The attorney tips his head toward the stranger. "This is Macklin Pierce. Head of McCarren Multinational Security."

Mr. Pierce pins me with that handy stare. "When was the last time you saw Angel Falls?" No preamble or "Nice to meet you." His voice is deep and authoritative. Not James Earl Jones deep, but in a similar register.

I push out a breath. "Maybe Fletcher hasn't already shared, but I didn't take my own necklace, have it copied, and replace it. I mean, how stupid would I have to be to do that, then fly across the country and sign papers to have it examined?"

Praise for DeeAnna Galbraith…

She is the award-winning author of *DELTA ON MY MIND*, *GAMBLING ON THE GODDESS*, *CHASING GLORY*, and *THE CROWN OF EVERYTHING* (children's book).

~*~

…and for *GAMBLING ON THE GODDESS*:

"In this compelling story of a 'high roller' financial genius/poker player and a beleaguered club owner, Galbraith deals a complex plot, sympathetic characters and an unusual setting. Makes one wish to be lucky enough to vacation in beautiful Lake Tahoe and spend quality time with these exciting people. The reader can't lose with this story."

~Melinda Rucker Haynes, Author

Chapter One

The red-eye is aptly named. Then again, I suck at flying any time. Low lights in the cabin and comfy seats notwithstanding, the flight from Seattle to New York in the middle of the night will leave me wobbly-eyed and fuzzy-brained.

Not so, my niece Rippa and our house guest, Ben Brown. They both doze and wake to the airline breakfast snack in time to *oooh* and *aaah* at the famous skyline.

The purpose of our trip is two-fold. I've been asked to approve the loan of my one-of-a-kind blue diamond necklace, Angel Falls, to a tour of custom pieces created by iconic Argentine designer, Carlos. The necklace is in my safety deposit box in a New York bank. The tour organizer, a Mr. Barone, has requested I sign the tour contract in person. Rippa and Ben, recent high school graduates, are coming as tourists, on me. And having closed my most recent insurance fraud case, I have the time.

We land at LaGuardia and pick out our limo driver. Easy as he's holding a sign with my name, *Julianne McCarren*. From his accent, he's local and proves it by navigating the Lincoln tunnel and Manhattan traffic with ease. Our hotel room reservations have a start date of yesterday, a trick I learned when I used to travel with my husband to avoid having to wait until three. I yawn my way through check-in.

Poor Cara, you still can't rest on a flight.

And there he is. My dead husband Raif commenting on my life. Cara, an endearment. His words aren't part of a conversation, but observations inside my head. They are in his voice and crystal clear. He may be there because of unfinished business. I don't know. It's been three years since he died in a skiing accident. Grieving is a possibility, too—but I did that up nicely. Checked out of normal for nearly a year. Guess it's a gift of sorts. Part of the healing process, as the remarks are becoming less frequent.

That has a downside too. If he stops altogether, it would be like losing him again. I don't dwell on it.

It's barely nine a.m., and my appointment to meet with Fletcher London, McCarren Multinational's corporate and family legal counsel, and Mr. Barone, the tour representative, is three hours away. I want nothing more than to unpack, grab a shower, and take a power nap. Rippa and Ben pore over the hotel menu and order from room service. Of course. Food first.

****

We arrive at McCarren Multinational offices to find Mr. Barone has been delayed. Fletcher's assistant shows Rippa, Ben, and me to a conference room adjacent to his office. I thank her, walk in, and stop. Mitch and Veronique McCarren are inside. Mitch is Raif's half brother, and Veronique is Mitch's wife. My response is ruder than intended. "Um, why are you two here?"

Mitch hasn't changed. Still taking the first bullet in case his rude, greedy wife offends someone. "Veronique's idea, I'm afraid. She likes to stay on top of family matters."

The only thing that makes us family is the McCarren surname, but I bite. "What does my necklace have to do with family?"

Veronique shifts a shoulder, and the action slides her double strand of pearls under the collar of her green silk dress. "Is McCarren family heirloom." Although she's been in America for over twenty years, Veronique clings to her Russian accent. She also clings to the belief that Angel Falls should be hers.

I correct her with what I hope is a pitying smile. "Nope, just mine." I hold a hand toward the teens. "My niece, Rippa Parkes, and our friend, Ben Brown. Kids, this is Raif's half brother, Mitch McCarren, and his wife, Veronique."

Veronique may be frowning. It's hard to tell since she's fond of Botox. Mitch, however, shakes hands with each of them and gives me a quick hug.

I step out of the hug, still disconcerted. "How did you find out about my meeting?"

"That's my fault, Julianne," confesses Fletcher, entering the room with a dark-complexioned man dressed in a well-cut navy-blue suit and dazzling white shirt. "I mentioned Mr. Barone's offer to Felicity, and she told Veronique."

It's hard to be angry with Fletcher. Not so hard with his wife, Felicity, and her pal, Veronique.

Introductions all around, then Barone opens a leather folder and pulls out some papers. "Here are the documents allowing insurance evaluation and loan of Angel Falls."

Veronique examines her nails and responds, *sotto voce*, "It should have been left to the only *real*

McCarren."

I ignore her and grimace at the half-dozen pages until Fletcher comes to my rescue. "It's been vetted by my office. Take a look, initial the dates, and sign by the stickered arrows."

This is good news for my tired eyes. I sit in one of the banker-green upholstered leather chairs at the dark cherry conference table and scan the paperwork, sign where necessary, then stand and hand them to the Argentine. "The tour should be well received."

His eyes crinkle at the corners. "I met your mother-in-law once. She was a beautiful as well as generous woman. Giving your share of the tour gate to the McCarren Multinational Foundation was my idea. Good, yes?"

An excellent idea since the foundation was created by Raif's mother to help parents of children with debilitating diseases get the expensive treatments they need and can't afford. Plus, the necklace was originally hers. "Yes, it is."

Veronique picks up on the talk of money right away. "What are you saying? Any proceeds for the display of a McCarren family heirloom should be split amongst the family."

Little sleep and a greedy woman who has inserted herself into something that is none of her business has made me cranky. I give Veronique the most withering look I can muster. "The foundation will get much better use out of the money than your plastic surgeon."

She steps toward me, her face a red mask, but as much as I would like to have a reason to smack her, Mitch surprises me and grabs her arm, holding her back.

Barone's eyebrows return to their normal level, and he smiles, giving me a clipped bow. "You will be present for the verification tomorrow when the insurance expert is available?"

I haven't seen the necklace since I wore it to the annual foundation gala last fall, and having mixed feelings about not seeing it for another year, I shake my head. "Not necessary, thank you."

Besides, this trip is for the kids.

Fletcher rubs his temples with his thumb and middle finger. He's familiar with Veronique's personality and turns to me. "May I take you three to dinner while you're here?"

"That sounds nice. I'll let you know when we've worked up a schedule. Let's go, kids."

Outside the building, Ben waves his hand in front of his nose. "Does that Veronique person always wear so much perfume? My eyes were starting to water."

It's true. My sister-in-law tends to wear her perfume at maximum saturation. Which results in the fragrance entering a room and taking up residence before she does.

Rippa is nodding. "And what's the deal with her and your necklace and money?"

I glance behind us at the entrance to McCarren Multinational Headquarters. "Veronique comes from a poor, lower-class background. Money and social status mean a lot to her."

Rippa tilts her head. "Don't she and Uncle Mitch already have plenty of money?"

I laugh. "Our definition of plenty of money and hers differ wildly."

Ben looks up and down the sidewalk. "Where to

now? You said before we left we could see that famous Bronx Zoo if we had time. Can we go now?"

I did say that, but lack of sleep has me regretting it. The look on two hopeful faces urges me to pull up my big-girl pants. I smile. "Great idea."

Six hours later I collapse on my hotel room bed.

****

Ben and Rippa are fascinated by the practice of stepping off the curb to hail cabs and agree to take turns while we're in New York. They're disappointed the next morning when several are available in front of the hotel.

The agenda for this week includes visiting museums the kids have picked out. This morning is one of Rippa's choices, the Cooper-Hewitt Smithsonian Design Museum. Then lunch in Little Italy at either Parm or La Mela. Afterward, if we can still walk, it's the New York Hall of Science, for Ben. I've never been to either museum. Raif and I loved The Frick, with its beautiful, quiet galleries containing some of the most wonderful art and statuary in the country.

By the time we get back to the hotel, we're beat. Rippa and Ben flip through the room service menu before I even take my purse off. I notice I forgot to turn my phone back on after leaving the last museum. I have three messages from Fletcher, the last one an hour ago. "Please call as soon as you get this. A serious situation regarding Angel Falls has come up."

Fletcher answers my call-back on the first half ring. "Julianne. Thank goodness I caught you. I need to talk to you right away."

A frantic edge strains his voice. Something I've never heard from the normally unruffled attorney.

"Okay, talk."

"Not over the phone. I can meet you in your hotel lounge in fifteen minutes."

"Fletcher, I'm tired and hungry. What's the problem?"

He sighs. "I know this sounds dramatic, but I'd rather speak to you in person. Please. And get a table with some privacy."

More drama and still way out of character. "Fine. I'll order food and a drink there."

"See you soon."

I share my plans with Rippa and Ben, promising to let them know what's going on when I return, then leave them to wait for their dinners.

The lounge has appetizers, and since the after-dinner drinkers haven't crowded the place yet, it's quiet. Fletcher arrives and orders a drink to be sent to the table. He sits on the front part of his chair and leans forward. "In addition to being the McCarren family attorney for twenty-two years, I hope you've come to see me as a friend."

Oh my God, Cara, he's never this freaked out.

I've only known him for six of those years, but Raif trusted him, so I do too. "I do. And in the spirit of friendship, please tell me why we're here."

The server brings Fletcher's drink, and he takes a gulp, his mouth puckering. "Did you or Raif have a copy of Angel Falls made? I mean it's okay if you did. It's your property. I'm just saying you could've come to me if you needed money."

The hair rises on the back of my neck. "Copy? What are you saying? No."

"Then we have a problem. Mitchell offered to use

his key to access your box, and Veronique invited herself. They met Mr. Barone and the tour's insurance evaluator at the safety deposit vault area of the bank this afternoon. The necklace was produced, and shortly after examining it, she announced that the stones were moissanite."

Angry tears bank behind my eyelids. "How…how can that be? There's a process for giving access to those boxes. Only three keys are assigned to mine. I have one, and Mitch, and you."

Having delivered the bad news, Fletcher taps our table lightly. "I don't know, but the head of McCarren Multinational Security is going to be in my office at eight a.m. tomorrow to discuss the theft and replacement. Veronique insisted she and Mitchell be there too." He pats my hand and takes another swallow of his drink. "You don't have to be present if you don't want to."

Cara, we need to get your necklace back.

The hot tapas I ordered smell rich and spicy. I swallow reflexively, and my stomach cramps, so I take a calming breath. "I haven't *done* anything with Angel Falls. I wore it to the charity gala last September and put it back in the box the next day. That's the last time I saw it."

"Are you sure it was the genuine Angel Falls?"

The question generates the threat of tears again, so I close my eyes and concentrate. "Yes. Raif had the clasp engraved. I look at it every time I put it on."

Fletcher finishes his drink and leans back. "I'm glad you'll be there. Dealing with Veronique is never a prospect I look forward to."

I sigh. "Veronique is a drama queen and only

happy when she's the center of attention. It's no secret she thinks Angel Falls should be hers. If she didn't take it, and I'm not ruling that out, I'm not staying away while she trashes Raif and me. Besides, if I can't recover the original before the tour, the replica can show in its place. Most people won't know the difference."

Fletcher's eyebrows threaten to join. "*You* plan on recovering it?"

"I may need help, but yes, I do."

Chapter Two

My six-thirty wake-up call comes too early for the amount of sleep I got last night. I'm destined to spend another day with gritty eyes. I told Rippa and Ben what was going on, and she shoots me an occasional worried look at breakfast, but I'm trying to avoid panic until I find out more. When I do, I intend to get involved as much as my investigation skills and the McCarren name permit.

It's Ben's turn to hail a cab, and we arrive a few minutes early. This time we're shown into a larger conference room. One person is sitting at the conference table. A man of about thirty-five, business casual dress, nice build, with dark, close-cropped hair and beard. His eyes are worth a second look. Espresso brown and I can tell from the emerging crows' feet he either spends more than average time outdoors or laughs a lot. His gaze makes me want to hold up my hands in surrender, whether I'm guilty or not. That is one handy stare.

We sit, and Rippa leans in. "Spanish Inquisition at ten o'clock."

Even as tired as I am, I grin at her remark.

Fletcher comes in and looks like I feel. "Thank you for coming, Julianne. I didn't know you'd be bringing the kids."

"They're adults and know what's going on."

I don't ask where Mitch and Veronique are. Too afraid if I do, it will cause them to appear.

The attorney tips his head toward the stranger. "This is Macklin Pierce. Head of McCarren Multinational Security."

Mr. Pierce pins me with that handy stare. "When was the last time you saw Angel Falls?" No preamble or "Nice to meet you." His voice is deep and authoritative. Not James Earl Jones deep, but in a similar register.

I push out a breath. "Maybe Fletcher hasn't already shared, but I didn't take my own necklace, have it copied, and replace it. I mean, how stupid would I have to be to do that, then fly across the country and sign papers to have it examined?"

Pierce scribbles a note on the tablet in front of him, then speaks without looking up. "Doesn't sound too rational. Maybe he shared that you were the last one to access your safety deposit box before yesterday. Something about this scenario doesn't work. I'm here to help."

Fletcher lifts a shoulder. "I was told you were the last to open your box after our meeting last night. I thought you'd rest better if we tackled that bit of information this morning."

Nice of him, but it didn't work. I focus on Macklin Pierce. "I appreciate the offer, Mr. Pierce…"

"Do you mind calling me Macklin or Mack? I'm not big on formality."

The "let's be friends" approach? "All right, Mack. Call me Julianne. Here's where I stand. My husband gave me the necklace as a wedding gift. I want it back, and if that means I don't play nice, so be it."

His eyes hold what looks like a glimmer of respect. "The last entry requesting access before yesterday was signed by you about ten months ago."

I do the math in my head. "That's true. I wore it to the McCarren Rescue Foundation Gala last September and put it back in my safety deposit box the next day before my flight home."

He looks up, a grin in place. "Want some help with that hole you're digging?"

Damn. The grin works almost as well as the stare. What is it with this guy? "It's not a hole. I'm just tracking with the bank records."

He glances at Fletcher. "Sounds like a hole to me."

I ignore him and address Fletcher. "When does the bank open? I want the investigation to start as soon as possible, and as I told you last night, I'm going to be involved."

Fletcher rubs his hands together. "Mitchell called me from the bank after they discovered the switch. I asked him to hold off notifying bank security and the police until you saw the duplicate for yourself and checked to see if anything else was missing from your box."

I hadn't thought of the other things in my box, but it's a good place to start. "Thank you."

Mack slides a card across the table. "This has the numbers where you can reach me, and my office and home addresses on the back, in case we'll be working together."

I nod and calm a bit. I should be grateful Fletcher has thought of getting me some help since I don't intend to drop this in the laps of the police and hope for the best. I reel off my cellphone number. "I'm serious about being involved in the recovery. I have an investigator's license and am pretty good."

Fletcher turns to him. "Can you take Julianne to the bank this morning?"

I realize I haven't introduced the kids and hold my hand toward them. "Sorry about my manners, Mack. This is my niece, Rippa Parkes, and our friend, Ben Brown. They'll be coming too."

Mack doesn't get a chance to respond to either Fletcher or me when the door opens. Mitch and Veronique have arrived.

Veronique looks at me, tilting her head back. "Mitch told me to be civil. That's very hard to do when I know you've stolen a priceless piece of jewelry that's been in the McCarren family for decades. You couldn't wait, couldn't give it to someone who would appreciate…"

"Stop. Talking."

Mitch puts a hand on his wife's arm. This time she shakes it off. Frost forms on her words as Veronique starts toward me. "What did you say to me?"

Jet lag, more lack of sleep, and my missing necklace have generated a doozy of a negative mood. I don't intend to deal with Veronique's cheap shots. An uncivil word crouches on the back of my tongue, but I refrain from uttering it. "I said stop talking. I'm a McCarren, the same as you. This situation is none of your business. Angel Falls is mine, and I intend to find out how it was stolen and who is responsible. We can do without posturing and drama."

Veronique curves a blonde wing of hair behind her ear and looks around the silent room. "I see no gentlemen are here to take my part." She folds her arms, and the heat in her look would melt Russian tundra. "I stand by my accusation."

Fletcher clears his throat. "We were initially going to discuss how to handle the release of information, now that it's been determined that the Angel Falls in Julianne's box is a copy, but she's suggested we loan the replica. It's done all the time with priceless art pieces on tour. She's pointed out very few of the public would know the difference."

"That is ridiculous assumption," blurts Veronique. "Besides, it does not belong to her. She cannot loan it out."

I find it interesting that Veronique is concerned about the ownership of the replica, but before I can speak, Mack cuts her off with surgical precision. "Julianne's right. Loaning a replica is a common practice." He smiles. "And after the police check it over for evidence, technically it's hers since it was in her personal box. Unless you know who the real owner is and how it got there."

My sister-in-law's face pales. However, she's not done. "Be careful how you speak to your boss."

From the glare he sends Veronique's way, the head of security's had enough. "I report to the board of directors for McCarren Multinational, not you or your husband. I also agree with Julianne's assessment of your presence. Why are you here? I get it that you're a McCarren, but the necklace isn't or wasn't yours, and the tour of Carlos' best designs doesn't include anything that belongs to you. So I'm asking again. Why are you here?"

Cara, I like this guy. I met him when my parents' plane crash was investigated.

I'm beginning to too.

Veronique almost quivers with indignation. "I—" A side glance at her husband. "—we're here, Mr. Pierce, to protect the interests of the McCarren name."

Pierce gives it an extra beat, to let her squirm I'm betting, before responding. "Protection is part of my job description. I'd be interested in your plan for protecting the McCarren name. Or why it needs protecting."

My sister-in-law rolls her eyes and spreads her hands. "Once media finds out…"

He cuts her off again. "That'll only happen if you decide you want your name in the news."

Rippa leans in to share again. "Busted."

Fletcher addresses Veronique. "I've abjured Mr. Barone and the insurance evaluator against releasing any information regarding Angel Falls. They've signed nondisclosure agreements."

Veronique's gaze skitters around for a place to land. "Of course. Unless it has already slipped out."

Rippa is hot on her smartphone. "Busted again. Does she ever talk without putting her foot in it? What does abjured mean? Wait. I'll look it up."

I pin Veronique with a pointed look. "Fletcher can release a statement if that happens. Mr. Pierce was about to take me to review the bank records and start an investigation. That includes *anyone* with a key to my box. One of us will let Fletcher know the results as it progresses. You can check in with him."

I turn to Fletcher. "Please contact Mr. Barone and see if he's interested in touring the replica, then let me know."

The attorney nods, a hint of a smile hovering.

Ben, who's walked to the window, comes up

15

behind me. "Um, we only had time for coffee and a pastry this morning. Can we have a real breakfast before the bank opens?"

I laugh. Food can only improve my mood. "Sure. Mack probably knows a good place nearby."

Mack stands, says a few quiet words to Fletcher, then tips his head toward the door. We follow. My last glance at Veronique is met with nearly tangible poison darts. Luckily, half are aimed at Mack.

The elevator doors *whoosh* closed, and Rippa says a dramatic, "Whew, is she ambitchous or what?"

Mack produces a combination bark of laughter and cough. "Great observation, though."

I hold in my own laugh. "Rippa."

"Okay, okay."

Ben's gaze stays on the elevator doors. "I know she's your relative and everything, but that is one messed-up lady."

Strong language from Ben. "Calling her a lady is generous."

"Me-ow," says Rippa, then giggles.

Mack pulls his head back to take her in. "Nice shirt."

He is now Rippa's friend for life. She loves vintage bowling shirts with names from the fifties and sixties like Georgia, Kitty, and Liz on the pockets and team names like Fillies or Alley Cats. Her most prized shirt has an embroidery of the famous Vegas cowboy on the back. Her giggle escalates. "Thanks."

Ben rolls his eyes.

****

The restaurant Mack chooses is surprising for its location in the heart of New York City's financial district. It offers a large selection of bacons, German sausages, hash browns, porridges, egg dishes, juices, and regular coffee. No green shakes, lattes, wheat grass, probiotic yogurt, or hot lemon water in evidence. Ben loves it.

Mack watches in amazement as the teenager digs in to a piled-high platter. "My mother used to say I had a hollow leg."

I like him. Mack seems like a straightforward, no-nonsense guy, with no metrosexual tendencies. Qualities that make him comfortable to be around.

No wedding ring, Cara.

Raif's comment surprises me. He's never made an observation like this before.

Breakfast over, Mack makes a call, then turns to me. "Investigating or hanging out as tourists, especially as a McCarren, calls for a driver. They're martial-arts trained and when on duty, have access to weapons. I'm making one available to you for your stay. For safety and my peace of mind when I can't go along." He hands me another card. "Here's the number to call."

I narrow my eyes, not sure if I'm insulted because I believe I can take care of myself and the kids, or grateful because, well, it's New York City. "Does Veronique have a driver?"

His eyebrows threaten to collide. "Okay, same subject, different cast. If she does, it was not approved, nor provided by, McCarren Multinational Security." He tips his head to the side as a short, black limo with tinted windows slides to the curb. "Feel special now?"

I nod, thinking any mugger with half a brain wouldn't take on Veronique anyway. "Thanks."

Our driver is young and fit, dressed in a black suit,

snowy white shirt, black tie, and serious expression.

"Trainee for Men in Black." Ben grins.

Mack chuckles and gives the driver an address not too far away. The banks and other financial institutions surrounding us are impressive. Marble and carved limestone exteriors in styles from Art Deco to ultra-modern. The bank we stop at possesses a three-story lobby with chandeliers and inlaid marble floors. Rippa and Ben stand goggle-eyed.

Ben's gaze slides upward. "This is your *bank*?"

Same way I felt the first time I saw it. "Sort of. It's the bank McCarren Multinational uses and where the family safety deposit boxes are located."

We go upstairs, and Mack speaks to the receptionist. She taps her headset and makes a connection. A few minutes later, a tall woman wearing a business suit and semi-bored expression walks out and introduces herself as Ms. Barrick. She briefly glances at Rippa's bowling shirt with the name Polly and a patch of a seven-ten split on the sleeve. The woman smiles at Mack. "I understand you want to review the records for your box due to an access problem?"

I step forward. "That's me. I've been told something was removed from my box illegally."

A mild expression of surprise. "That's not possible."

"Nonetheless, it has happened."

She starts to turn. "I'll pull your records in my office, and we can sort this out. Name, please?"

"Julianne McCarren."

The surname makes her stop mid-turn, square her shoulders, and face us fully. The question on her lips dies as I smile brightly.

"Yep. One of *those* McCarrens."

Out comes the serious banker. "I'm sure we can lay your doubts to rest, Ms. McCarren. Can we get refreshments for you and your friends?"

I shake my head. Even Ben can't want anything.

She bestows a managerial nod. "Then we'll get right to it."

Fletcher gave me an envelope with pictures, insurance information, and other documentation regarding Angel Falls. My key is in an envelope with the box number on it in my purse. I get it out when we're seated.

Banker Barrick starts tapping on her keyboard, then asks for my ID. I show her, and she holds it up to her screen. "Box in the name of Julianne and Raif McCarren, Raif McCarren deceased. Keys also assigned to Fletcher London and Mitchell McCarren." She looks at me. "Is that correct?"

"Yes."

"Your box was last accessed yesterday at 1:07 p.m. by Mitchell McCarren. Is that correct?"

"Yes. Will you please go back to the one previous to that?"

More typing. "September 18, 10:13 a.m. Correct, also?"

"That sounds right. Can you verify it was me?"

She swivels her screen to show me the sign-in document.

"Yes. That's my signature."

"According to the entry, this has already been verified. May I ask for the details of your concern?"

I try a different tack. "How long do you keep

camera records of vault access?"

She cocks her head as if trying to remember something. "Tapes were replaced by digital recordings a year ago. The records are intact as far back as the installation of that system."

Well, damn. The trade has to have happened within the last ten months, but no access record means no picture. Another thought occurs. "Are you the person who escorts clients to the vault? I remember a young blond guy."

She glances at her screen. "Three others have those qualifications in addition to myself. That escort would be Ian Ward. He's still employed here, but on personal leave. His fiancé passed away unexpectedly."

I sigh. "Oh. I'm sorry. That being the case, I'd like to open my box now."

"Of course. Your friends can wait in the public room adjoining the vault."

I agree and sign the access card. I'm escorted into the vault and look around. Nothing has changed. No upgrade to single key or digital entry. Opening a box still requires a master and a renter's key. After Ms. Barrick uses her master, I'm left alone.

Cara, we'll figure this out.

I open my box. The replica is very good. If I didn't know better, I'd have to take the expert's word that it's not the original. I pick it up and for a wild minute, entertain the thought that Veronique and the expert are in this together and this is the real necklace. I turn over the intricate platinum clasp. No inscription. That's weird and poses another question. It's not an exact duplicate without the inscription. Did whoever had it made only care if it *looked* like Angel Falls to the casual observer? I lay it back in its velvet box, sort through and verify the paperwork is undisturbed, and leave.

The banker is waiting for me with Mack and the kids. "Everything as it should be?"

I shake my head. "My diamond necklace has been replaced with a forgery." I nod toward Mack. "This is Macklin Pierce, head of security for McCarren Multinational. I'd like to have him meet with the bank's security team. Now." I turn to Mack. "I left the forgery there. Aside from the stones being moissanite, Raif's inscription to me on the clasp is missing. Interesting that the duplicate has everything perfect except that."

Mack nods. "Good to know. Somebody not interested that it was personalized."

Rippa's glance bounces toward the vault. "Really sucky too."

My stomach clinches, and I turn to an unhappy Ms. Barrick. "Let's wait until the police need to pick it up to turn it over."

The confident banker façade slips, and the woman standing there is shaken. She pulls a business card from her suit pocket and hands it to me. "I'll call our chief of security. Can you come back to my office and help me with some information for an initial report?"

Now that I've determined the real Angel Falls is gone, my energy is sapped. I take her card and hold the envelope out to Mack. "Will you meet with them and get the ball rolling? Police report and all that?"

He takes the envelope. "I've worked with Comstock, the bank's chief of security, before. I'll catch you up later."

The banker tries one more time to break down my

assertion. "You think the necklace was stolen, copied, and the copy put into your box sometime in the past ten months?"

"Yes."

"You're aware that each box has a list of those authorized to access it. That part of our security process makes your claim next to impossible."

"Next to, but not impossible. I did some research online last night, and safety deposit box break-ins are more common than people think."

A curt nod. "Unfortunately. But this is the first in my tenure as the manager here."

Shortly into our acquaintance, Raif brought up McCarren's Rules. I laughed at first, but they really seem to apply. *Don't hang out with bears. If you come across one, don't poke the bear. If a bear pokes you, outthink it.* Bears being a metaphor for something or someone you don't want to deal with. My missing necklace falls under rule three.

Chapter Three

The driver picks us up for a ride back to the hotel. I was so freaked out about my necklace I didn't check my voicemail. There is one, from Fletcher. He apologizes for not being able to take us to dinner while we're in town, but offers tickets to the Broadway show of our choice. Rippa and Ben go to his room to catch up with their online friends and argue about which show they want to see. I take a much-needed nap and am awakened when room service delivers lunch.

Afterward, Ben, Rippa, and I spend hours in the American Natural History Museum. Doubly happy we have access to a driver, as the hotel address sounds close by but is many blocks away. I turn my phone back on, and Mack has left a call asking me to dinner to discuss the case. He suggests Chinese, which is fine with me.

The kids order dinner and a couple of action movies. They're in for the night. I give my newly appointed driver the evening off and grab a cab to Shun Lee Palace in Chinatown.

Mack is waiting out front and looks very nice in a navy shirt open at the neck, khaki slacks, and casual loafers.

He eyes the cab as it pulls away. "Your driver unavailable?"

I give him my stubborn face. "No apology. I'm not

comfortable inconveniencing people. They must be bored to tears hanging around waiting for some prima donna to call and be whisked around town. Besides, I come to New York every year and have not needed a security driver yet."

"Good to know, but not the point. My job and my peace of mind are at stake. Besides, that driver is going for a doctorate in chemistry. Aiming to work against bio-terrorists. He needs all the time on the clock he can get."

He's right. Please use the driver, Cara.

I hold up one hand. "Half of me surrenders. The other half is withholding full acceptance. Now, can we eat?"

Mack shakes his head and opens the door. "Am I having dinner with the half that surrenders?"

Cute.

As much as Raif and I traveled, I'm not much of an adventurous eater and order crispy orange beef and sticky rice. Mack says a few words to the waiter in Mandarin. The man smiles and bows before leaving.

I'm impressed. "Not an easy language to learn."

Mack's gaze is mischievous. "I know about enough to order food."

His admission makes me laugh and relax. "How'd it go at the bank?"

"The paperwork has been filed with the bank and NYPD robbery unit. PD took the replica and will release it to you after it's examined. Bank security is notifying the feds."

Guilt at laying all of that on Mack's doorstep creeps in. "Wow. I didn't realize the ripple effect would spread that far. Thank you."

He smiles. "Most interesting thing I've been involved in for quite a while. Where do you want to go next?"

Already thought about that. "Since nothing else in the box was disturbed, I think the necklace was the original target. And as much as Ms. Banker wouldn't like to think, I believe there may have been duplicity from someone inside the bank."

"I agree. Any other questions?"

My sense, so far, is that I'll get an honest answer. "Just wondering. I have no investigative authority in the state of New York, yet you're letting me slide right into the thick of things. How come?"

No hesitation on his part. "Two things. First, I checked on your reputation as an investigator, and you're good—thorough and relentless. Second, the necklace is important to you, and I don't think there's any way I can keep you out. Better safe with me and my resources."

He's right on both counts. "Nice way of saying you don't want a loose cannon messing with your investigation. Even if her surname is McCarren."

A chuckle from Raif. *He's got you figured out, Cara.*

Mack doesn't even blink. "Batting a thousand. What next?"

Our server brings egg-drop soup, a small carafe of tea, and two cups.

I can taste a hint of ginger. The soup is really good. "Three keys and ten months leave a lot of options. We start with the key holders. Did the bank security guy admit that anyone in the bank could be involved?"

He shakes his head. "He knows every employee

can't be squeaky clean and agreed to do some discreet checking. Said he'll let me know if he turns up anything hinky."

The soup bowls are cleared, and our orders come. Mine is delicious. Mack's has lots of noodles and sauce. He shows off his dexterity with chopsticks. A huff after his first bite confirms his order has a several-star rating for spicy.

I wrinkle my nose. "You always liked hot food?"

He laughs. "Grandmother on my mother's side is Puerto Rican. She's a great cook, and I grew up on heat in Spanish Harlem."

I would not have guessed. We have polar opposite backgrounds, but he's remarkably good at staying inside my comfort zone. "What's that like?"

"Spanish Harlem? It's whatever you want it to be. Like growing up inside a noisy kaleidoscope. Color, music, nonstop voices, mostly at the top of the register." He grins. "Very matriarchal."

"They did a nice job."

"Thanks. They've made me their life's work. When I was small, my mother and grandmother would take me to the area of Central Park where the nannies for the Upper East Side kids sat. I didn't get to play, though. We'd sit on the same bench, and I was made to listen and repeat the way they spoke. Knocked the edge off the Spanish-English I heard at home."

"They wanted a lot for you."

Another grin. "Still do. I have to make scheduled appearances at Sunday dinner and spill my guts about my social life."

I laugh outright.

His relaxed posture doesn't change, but his

expression turns serious. "I was prepared not to like you, you know. I did a little cyberstalking before our first meeting. Pretty, rich, world-traveling woman loses a necklace valued at half a mil. A necklace she almost never wears."

I stiffen at his summation but realize that's the picture I present to people who don't know me, and I'm surprised at how much I want his picture of me to have changed. "Actually, I'm a homebody. Live on a beautiful lake with Rippa and Ben and my sister. And although Raif and I traveled for his work, this trip is the first I've taken this year."

He tips his head to one side. "Perception updated. That necklace doesn't have a monetary value for you, does it?"

"None," I say, gratified that he gets it.

His grin returns. "Except for wimping out when it comes to spicy food, you're okay."

"Thanks for the exception."

He winks. "More for us."

"Us being people who like their food crazy hot?"

He slurps a noodle and nods.

Yesss! Sounds inside my head. Raif loved five-star heat.

I have no room for dessert but see a favorite, fried ice cream, on the menu. While we're waiting, I feel comfortable enough to ask Mack a question. "How does a guy with your heritage, raised in Spanish Harlem, get a name like Macklin Pierce?"

"The world is small," he quips. "My straitlaced grandfather Pierce graduated from Princeton in 1950. He and some friends decided to go to New York and celebrate. Their first night in town, they landed in

Spanish Harlem. Grandfather asked a pretty Puerto Rican girl to dance, and the rest, as they say, is history."

"That's a great story. How did the folks take it?"

He grins. "Shock and betrayal on both sides. Grandmother Quintana's parents were enraged she wasn't going to marry a good Catholic Puerto Rican boy. And Grandfather Pierce's parents thought their world had come to an end. I still have to spend a week with them every summer to prove I have Pierce roots."

"Well, you're here, so your parents must have prevailed."

"Named after my Yankee grandfather."

"I am impressed."

I really am. He seems to handle his opposing backgrounds with ease.

The fried ice cream is delicious, and as I finish the last of it, Mack pays the bill. "Can I give you a lift back to your hotel?"

"Depends."

"On…?"

"On how far out of your way it is."

He pulls in his chin. "You are definitely not a New York woman. I live between McCarren Towers and your hotel. Close enough?"

I nod. "Then I accept. Thanks."

It's mid-June, and a muggy haze greets us on the empty sidewalk outside. It's still light out, and Shun Lee Palace is in a retail shopping area, but many of the stores around us are closed.

Mack tips his head. "I'm parked in a garage a half block down."

We're close to the large structure when the sound of running feet approaches from behind.

I hear a man say something like "pole chet ick."

We stop and turn, then Mack pulls me back and to one side. This surprises the two men coming at us. The larger of them can't stop. He draws back his head and makes a clumsy attempt to swing at Mack. He has no room to get momentum, and I hear a loud clunk as his lower jaw gets rammed into his upper jaw by Mack's elbow. The man sinks to the sidewalk. It's also too late for the other man to change his trajectory. His eyes widen as his partner drops. His second of inattention allows me to stomp on his instep and bring the heel of my hand up hard under his nose.

Mack grabs my hand and we run. No thumping footsteps echo behind us, but we don't slow until we reach his car.

We're exiting the garage on a side street when Raif speaks. *Close call. Please be more careful, Cara.*

Seriously good advice.

My adrenaline infusion is clearing. I take a breath and turn to Mack. "Proves your point about using the security driver. Random?"

"Don't think so. Did you hear what one of them said?"

I nod. "I'm good with Spanish and some French, but this was more guttural. Slavic maybe. Sounded something like *pole chet ick.*"

He checks his mirrors. "You have a good ear. I think he said '*Poluchit' ikh.*' Loosely translated Russian for 'Get them.' "

"Russian muggers?"

"Could be. But Russians with that tendency don't usually operate this far into Manhattan."

For a corporate security guy, he has a good grasp

of ethnic boundaries. "Not good news."

"Nope. On the other hand, this could get us a step closer to who took the necklace. Your sister-in-law is Russian. Your brother-in-law has a key to your safety deposit box and teaches Russian Literature. He's also involved with his student assistant, who is Russian."

No surprise there. Veronique was Mitch's first assistant, and Raif told me his half brother's choice each year depends on the student's looks and *charming ways*.

A nervous giggle escapes. "You did your homework on the New York McCarrens too."

"I like being prepared."

I hike my thumb in the vague direction of the restaurant. "You were more than prepared."

"You held your own too. I like your style, more and more."

He likes you, Cara.

"Speaking of handling," I say, not comfortable with compliments from Mack yet, "do you think we should report the attack?"

He stops at a light and turns to me. "And say what? Two guys who may or may not have been speaking Russian came at us. We defended ourselves and got away?"

Chapter Four

No way can Fletcher London knowingly be a part of what happened to my necklace, but he doesn't live in a vacuum and has to be crossed off the list. I left a request with his assistant, and she put us first on his calendar.

Mack is waiting for me outside Fletcher's office. "Where're the kids?"

"They signed up for a half-day tour. We parted ways after breakfast."

His eyes widen a bit. "Do you think that's safe?"

I grin. "Called the driver. He sounded horrified at acting as an escort to teens but agreed to show them around. If the people who live and work here are like those in most big cities, he's never seen most of his own tourist attractions."

He gives me a thumbs up. "He's a good sport. Also a good call on your part."

We enter, and Fletcher is waiting for us at his neat-as-a-pin desk. He looks resigned. "You want to discuss access to your vault box?"

I sit in one of two chairs facing the desk. Mack occupies the other.

I push out a breath. "Thought we'd start with the obvious. Everyone who has a legal key."

Fletcher stops squaring a stack of papers and tilts his head. "You think there's an illegal key out there?"

I shift a shoulder. "It's worth considering. I also thought a vault box in a bank was a safe place."

The corporate attorney slides a key with my box number stamped at the base across his desk. "I think you're entitled. Here's mine."

Mack has his fingers interlaced on his lap and doesn't reach for the key. "No need for that. Do you keep it here in your office?"

Fletcher shakes his head. "Too high a security risk. I keep it in my personal box at the same bank. I took it out when the replica was discovered."

No response from Mack for a few seconds. He pulls in his lips before forming a difficult question. "How many keys to your box? And who else has access?"

Fletcher looks genuinely surprised and a little chagrined. "It's my personal box. Only my wife Felicity and I have keys. Is that a problem?"

Mack gives a slow nod. "Anytime there's more than one way to get at something valuable, it's a potential problem."

I need to share Felicity London and Veronique's pal status with Mack.

Tired lines radiate from the sides of Fletcher's eyes. "I assure you there is no connection, but I'll ask my wife if she has ever been approached about the key."

Mack reaches for the key and slides it back. "Thanks."

I nod. "Yes. Thanks for your time."

A hint of the smile we saw yesterday emerges from the attorney. "Guess this means you'll be talking to Mitchell and Veronique."

I make a face. "Bearding the lion."

His smile becomes full blown, his enjoyment at the thought evident.

"Now you're just being mean."

He nods and makes a shooing motion. "Better get to it."

Mack is thoughtful on the elevator ride down. "We need to consider the ripple effect. Somebody brags about having a connection to a priceless object or artwork. Next thing you know, they're pressured into putting up or shutting up."

That seems to be a reach. "You think that's what's happened? Theft and copy based on what? Bragging?"

A half frown emerges. "Maybe not exactly that, but we can't rule out anything. The more people who can get their hands on the keys, the more strings there are to follow. Best deal would be if we could narrow down the time frame. Unfortunately, if the necklace has been missing for a while, it's probably been deconstructed, the diamonds sold, and the platinum melted down."

This hasn't occurred to me, and my heart squeezes at the thought. Not so much at losing a beautiful and glamorous piece of jewelry, but the idea that it was my wedding gift from Raif. To destroy it for the diamond and platinum value seems sacrilegious.

We don't know that yet, Cara.

I become aware Mack's watching me.

His expression softens. "Or it could have been stolen on spec."

This is a new kind of investigative trail for me. "What does that mean?"

"A wealthy collector in Hong Kong or Dubai or even someone attending that gala you wore it to last

September. *Someone* saw the necklace or heard about it and paid to have it stolen for their private collection. It *is* a one-of-a-kind piece."

I get it that he's trying to lay out some options, but this is another thought that hasn't occurred to me. "How common is that?"

"You said it yourself. Safety deposit boxes are robbed more often than people think. It only takes one weak link. A bank employee who needs money or buckles to some outside threat. Any number of reasons."

I close my eyes in frustration.

****

Mack and I find a coffee shop, get our drinks, and grab a recently vacated table. It's mid-morning near Wall Street, and the place is packed. Seattle has a reputation for being coffee crazy, but these finance-types could provide a challenge for caffeine consumption.

He blows across the top of his cup, watching me. "What do you think about the security of your key in Fletcher's care?"

I don't have a definitive answer. "I trust that he thinks he's doing his best to protect my interests, but he might be naïve where his wife is concerned."

An eyebrow rises, and he leans forward. "Is that an observation from listening to him, or do you have some information you can share?"

I liked it that he asked if I could share, knowing it might be personal. "Not sure how relevant it is, but Raif pointed Felicity London out at a McCarren family function once. She spent most of her time in conversation with Veronique. They looked very chummy."

A grin lifts the corner of his mouth. "Chummy?"

"It's a good word. Expand your vocabulary, Pierce."

"Fair enough. And Fletcher's wife being 'chummy' with Veronique could prove helpful." He studies me. "What's wrong?"

I squelch a big sigh, hoping I'm not about to paint a target on Veronique because I don't like her.

"It's bad enough that the necklace is gone and I might never see it again, except as a copy, but it bothers me that what we have so far points suspicion squarely at Mitch and/or Veronique."

He nods. "In a way, that's a good thing."

I taste my caffè macchiato and as much as I don't want to add fuel to the fire… "You know she tried to buy it?"

He shakes his head. "When?"

"An indecently short amount of time after Raif died."

This is bringing up sad memories, Cara. I'm sorry.

Mack makes a face of distaste. "Tacky."

"No one I know has ever accused her of being sensitive. I turned her down, but she came back two more times, offering obscene amounts of money. I had to get rude."

He grins. "I'd like to have seen that. You'd think with all their money she could afford her own one-of-a-kind piece."

"Several times over, but she has this fixation for Angel Falls. Raif told me once it had to do with jealousy. Mitch's dad left his mother when Mitch was ten. Dad remarried within a year, and Raif was born

35

when Mitch was twelve. Their father spent all his time with his new wife and son. When Mitch married Veronique, his jealousy colored their relationship. After the plane crash that killed his parents, part of Raif's inheritance included Angel Falls. Mitch got an equal share plus a vineyard in Tuscany. Veronique has always claimed the necklace should have gone to the oldest son. She was the first person I thought of when this came up. Mainly because of her obsession."

He snaps his fingers. "Reminds me of something. About five years ago, a request for a security check came across my desk. The person making it was Veronique. She wanted a Russian jeweler named Ansel Fuhrman vetted. Under 'reason,' she put 'personal.' I turned down the request, citing inappropriate use of McCarren Multinational resources. She went to the board, and I got a call from the CEO asking us to do the work as a 'personal favor.' "

Not such a long shot if she's still dealing with him. "What was the result?"

"On the border of shady, but no glaring legal hassles." He leans back. "I'll do some research to see if anyone else pops and check my contacts at Interpol and other agencies. Are you willing to offer a reward for information that leads to an arrest and recovery?"

Wow. "Um. What's the going rate?"

"$50,000 should do it. That's ten percent of the insured value."

Nearby heads crane in at the sound of money, so I lower my voice. "I'd prefer not to pay a criminal to catch another criminal, but if that's what it takes. Does that work?"

He takes a sip of his drink. "Lots of variables.

What's the relationship of the squealer to the thief? Is the reward higher than what the thief got paid to steal it? If the thief blows the whistle, will they still face prosecution? What if gangs or family are involved? What price does the squealer put on his or her own hide? Variables."

I shudder. "I'll let you do your thing and coordinate the reward offer with the police. I'm going to spend the afternoon with the kids, then do some online snooping. Catch you later?"

Mack nods. "Gotta take a look at my in-basket and see how other projects are playing out. Call me if you find a juicy detail? Otherwise, we can meet day after tomorrow for breakfast. Same place as before?"

****

The kids arrive back at the hotel, and I *oooh* and *aaah* over the kitschy souvenirs they've purchased. We take a walking tour of St. Patrick's Cathedral, which is stunning but crowded with tourists like ourselves, then Rockefeller Center where Rippa takes dozens of pictures.

We make use of our driver and go back to Little Italy for an early dinner because Ben wants another go at meatball sandwiches. My mind is on Angel Falls.

Rippa interrupts. "Earth to Jules."

I smile at her. "Sorry. I've been too immersed in my missing necklace to give you guys the trip you deserve."

Ben pipes up. "Not so fast. I'm having a great time." His gaze skips past me. "Just that one more place where I want to shop."

Rippa casts a wrinkled nose at Ben. "Can't forget that. Jules, however, is having a sucky time due to her stuff being stolen."

Stuff puts a teen perspective on my mood. "Point taken. What'll we do tomorrow?"

"Ben and I have talked it over, and we want to help."

I start to object but reconsider. I'm good at online research, but these two are excellent. They *live* online. "I need to find some mention of blue diamonds or Angel Falls. Boring, but necessary."

"In," they chorus. They jabber on about how they will try to sniff out word on underground jewelry deals and fences.

Ben frowns. "Wish I could access the dark net."

"Whoa. No illegal stuff. I mean it. Why don't you start by looking for private sellers of estate and designer jewelry? I'll look into the publicity angle."

Mack calls as we're on our way back to the hotel. "I made an appointment with Mitch for ten a.m. day after tomorrow in his campus office. Veronique won't be there. She has a charity brunch to attend and refuses to miss it. Just as well. She tends to get defensive."

I laugh. "And loud about it. By the way, Rippa and Ben want to help, so I've got them doing online research. They're my secret weapon."

"Great. I haven't turned up anything, but I have private agents I can tap who specialize in high-end stolen artwork. See if their sources have anything. I'll do that tomorrow and get out the word on the reward."

****

Back at the hotel, Ben wants to dig into the cannoli we brought from La Bella Ferrara. I sigh. It *has* been a half hour since dinner. The creamy pastries taste amazing.

As we polish those off, my cellphone rings. It's Mitch.

"Hello, Julianne. I'm sorry the way the meeting ended. Veronique can be very focused and is sometimes hard to, um, convince of the merits of another opinion."

Fancy way of saying she's pigheaded. "Not disagreeing, Mitch. What do you want?"

"I thought as long as the main purpose of your trip was for the kids, I'd offer a tour of NYU tomorrow morning. It's a beautiful campus, and who knows? Maybe after a year or two in a western university, one or the other might want to try out New York. Family here after all."

That wouldn't be a selling point for me, but the offer seems nice. I put my thumb over the cellphone speaker. "Hey guys. It's Mitch. He's offering a tour of NYU campus tomorrow morning. I've never seen the campus, but I hear it's pretty nice. Afterward we can review our research at the New York Public Library as planned. Okay?"

Two nods indicate acceptance.

"That would be fine, Mitch. Where and when?"

"I'll meet you at the Gould Center on West 4th at nine, and we'll go from there."

"Okay. See you then."

The kids and I settle in to our electronic zones and start working. I enter Mitchell and Veronique McCarren in the search engine. They must be on every charity hit list in the city. Dozens of photos and write-ups appear, but I narrow it down to the past ten months.

I scroll through the entries, not sure what I'm looking for. Besides charity events, I also find a number of university functions, no doubt fundraisers. Most of the pictures feature Mitch and Veronique, until I see one where they are mentioned but in the background. The photograph catches Mitch almost full-on beside another couple. Veronique is partially turned away. Not enough, however. The flash freezes the dazzle of diamonds at her neck.

My first instinct is to grab a cab to the Upper East Side and throttle her.

It will be easier to get the truth from Mitch, Cara.

Raif is right, but it really pushes my buttons that Veronique thinks she got one over on me. Maybe more than once. I'm guessing this wasn't the only time she *borrowed* it.

I text Mack along with a link to the picture. He calls me. "Very interesting. We can take the picture to our meeting with Mitch. Doubly glad Veronique won't be there."

"I'm not. Since Mitch was in the picture, he's aware of what went on. I don't think he'll go toe-to-toe with his wife over this, but I also don't want it to be minimalized. My necklace is gone, dammit, and right now I wouldn't mind roughing up a certain arrogant Russian blonde to get some answers."

The soft sound of keys tapping comes across. "Um, did you notice this picture is dated about seven months ago? If it's the real Angel Falls, that gets us closer to the time when it was taken and copied."

"The *real* Angel Falls?"

"Can't tell by the picture. I interviewed Barone, though. He swears the surprise shown by Mitch and Veronique in the vault seemed genuine. She might have worn the fake, thinking it was real."

If Veronique has nothing to do with the replica, I

get a momentary charge out of her prancing around in moissanite thinking she has the real thing, but still hope the seven-month date is relevant. "How long would it take to make a copy good enough to fool everyone but an expert?"

"I can check, but I don't think it could be done with a picture alone. They'd probably need the original."

Part of the original insurance on the necklace included pictures. Lots of them. "How about the appraisal? It had pictures from all angles, including the back. It also had a list of size and color for each diamond and its placement in the necklace. Could a talented jewelry designer or goldsmith duplicate it from those?"

A pause on his end. This is probably not a question for a corporate security specialist. "I suppose. They'd need a high-resolution smartphone camera to take pictures, and the original could remain in the box until they were ready for the switch."

"It's a theory. Could you follow up on that?"

"Narrowing your focus?"

Good question. "I think of it as sharpening. For now."

"You're the boss."

I like his late-night voice. "How come I'm the boss? You told Veronique you didn't work for them. I'm a McCarren too."

Mack laughs. "Has to do with my low tolerance for PITAs. Good night."

I smother a laugh in return. "Good night."

Chapter Five

After breakfast, the kids and I call our driver and head to the Gould Center. It's information central for NYU. We're near the entrance when we hear the tappity-tap of heels gaining on us. We have barely enough time to move aside before a blonde girl closes in. She passes in a jangle of bracelets, and Ben jerks his head in her direction, wide-eyed.

The girl is wearing a pencil skirt, a fuzzy, short-sleeved sweater containing a truly awesome chest, and five-inch heels. Her hair is long and dip-dyed, her mouth, pouty.

I pluck at Ben's sleeve and shake my head as he veers toward her. "Barracuda," I say, pointing at her. "Little fish," I say, pointing at him.

He shrugs to lope along with us while Rippa laughs.

Jangle-bracelets swings through the door just ahead of us. I see Mitch and start to catch his eye, but his attention is riveted on the girl. Not the "wow, here's an eyeful" kind of attention, but the "hey, lucky me, I know you personally."

Rippa, Ben, and I stop. My guess is she's Mitch's assistant and happy place.

The girl slides her hands up the front of his jacket and leans in. Mitch squares forty-five-year-old shoulders and looks at her with mixed adoration and lust. He ends the moment and turns her when he sees us waiting. "Julianne, kids, this is Nadya Vasilyeva, my assistant. She knows the campus even better than me and has generously agreed to help us tour."

Oh, Cara. Nothing good can come of this.

Mitch takes her hand and pats it. "I'm hoping this will provide a distraction. Nadya's brother, Timur, a bicycle messenger, was recently killed in a hit-and-run accident."

Sympathy noises from the three of us. "We're so sorry," I offer.

No one has called for a close-up of the grieving sister, but Nadya wears a brave face, tremulous smile and all. What Mitch can't see is the calculation. Heck, he probably couldn't see it if he were looking directly at her.

"Thank you," comes her soft reply. "Timur will be greatly missed."

Ben steps forward and holds out his hand. "Ben Brown."

Nadya's face morphs into a coy smile. She wraps his hand in both of hers, and the bracelets add harmony as she shakes. "Nice to meet you. After tour, let Mitch and me take you all to my favorite Russian restaurant. The food is authentic."

His eyes widen, but my brother-in-law doesn't hesitate. "Sure."

Mitch and I fall in step behind the others as we start across campus. I tip my head toward Nadya. "She's very pretty."

His forehead creases, then smooths. "And young. Same age as Veronique when we got married."

Twenty-two going on thirty, I'd guess. "Not sure

where you're going with this."

"Nowhere. She just graduated and is leaving for Russia next week."

"Ouch. Sorry."

"Me too."

The restaurant is not what I expected. Rose-covered wallpaper and mismatched tableware, furniture, and linens create a shabby, cottagey feel. But the food looks good. Although it's crowded when we arrive, we're seated right away. Mitch pulls out chairs for Nadya and me. Rippa and Ben seat themselves. I sit across from Nadya and discern a couple of things. She is wholly in charge of her relationship with Mitch. And as a twenty-something student, she wears a heavy, patchouli-based perfume and seriously expensive jewelry.

Raif liked to buy me jewelry. I don't wear it much, but I have some beautiful things. His mother came from a wealthy family in Argentina. His grandfather had invested heavily in Argentine gold mines as part of the McCarren holdings and his father traveled there yearly where he met Raif's mother and later, the jewelry designer, Carlos. The bangles that clink as Nadya talks are high-karat gold.

I feel sorry for my brother-in-law, but only for a moment. He's made poor choices for life relationships and will no doubt continue to do so. His money and family name allow him to withstand public censure. His mother is still alive and lives with her second husband in East Hampton. She detests Veronique and only sees her son when he is by himself.

Mitch talks to the kids about the campus, and Nadya takes my measure. "You were married to

Mitch's brother?"

I nod. "For three years."

"Mitch's father and your husband died in accidents. McCarren name is unlucky?"

Not this McCarren, Cara. I had you.

"No. They were lucky enough to have the lives they wanted." I glance at Mitch, but the restaurant is noisy, and he either doesn't hear our conversation or doesn't care.

Nadya continues her tactless line of questioning. "But no children to inherit."

Blunt, and a little painful. Raif and I wanted kids but agreed to wait five years. Rippa will inherit from me, and since Mitch and Veronique have no children, McCarren Multinational will be run by whoever's running it now, for the benefit of the stockholders. I return Nadya's bluntness with a smile. "Are you looking to get adopted?"

She seems thoughtful and doesn't smile, so I change the subject. "Mitch says you're going back to Russia soon."

"Student visa will expire. Mitch can get me hired on at campus, but…" She shrugs. "I can always return other ways."

I'm thinking she doesn't mean via *Beautiful Brides from Russia* dot com. The situation with my necklace and Nadya's wide-open relationship with my brother-in-law makes an almost full-circle connection. I look up to catch him making moon-eyes at his assistant. Damn.

Lunch ends, and we say our good-byes to Mitch and Nadya.

****

We pack our tablets to share what we've found in

the Rose Reading Room of the New York Public Library. Quietly, of course. That way we get to see a famous landmark and trade information at the same time.

Upon arrival, I'm struck dumb. Having lived in New York at one time, I can't believe I've never been in here. The space is over one hundred years old, huge, and stunning. Definitely a room for scholarly research. We wander a while, pointing out beautiful finds, then head for an unoccupied table.

I open my tablet to the newspaper article with accompanying picture and position it for Rippa and Ben to see.

"I knew it," Rippa says in a harsh whisper. "She's a liar."

Ben points at the corner of the photo. "True. But look at the date, Rip. She might be wearing the fake."

My niece huffs a breath and slumps. "She's still a phony."

I tip my head in agreement. "Don't paint her in prison garb yet. Veronique's a selfish woman. What I don't know is if she's focused enough to put together the theft and reproduction. Why would she steal it and have a copy made if she had the original? Especially knowing the replica would eventually be discovered and all of New York society would learn of it?"

Damn. I'd just answered the main question I had for my sister-in-law. That didn't mean she was off the hook for wearing my necklace or its facsimile, without my permission.

"Okay," Rippa says. "What else you got?"

"Nothing that points anywhere. Mack is using his contacts to look for anything professional, and I've been thinking about a Russian connection ever since night before last."

Rippa shudders. "Lucky you were with Mack."

"Hey," Ben says. "Jules held up her end."

Rippa shoots him an eye roll. "I just meant it might have been really bad if she'd been alone."

Their voices were drawing looks from nearby tables. I hold my hand out flat and lower it toward the tabletop. "Not a competition. What did you two come up with?"

They look at each other, grinning. Then Ben taps his tablet. "A Russian connection."

This should be interesting. "To my necklace?"

Rippa gives a half nod. "Close. We did Facebook searches on Veronique and Nadya."

Social networking is something I wouldn't have thought of right away. My online research into insurance fraud cases usually involves tracking false identities and financials. "Anything good?"

"Not for Veronique," Ben says, looking around like he's about to reveal a state secret. "She's got a sad page and sadder friends." He grins. "Nadya's not very security minded. Plus, she's mobbed up."

"Excuse me?"

Rippa elbows him. "So drama. He means Nadya isn't very smart when it comes to Facebook security. Her page is wide open. And she has lots of *friends* who are Russian gang members."

"Show me."

Rippa flips open her laptop and pulls up Nadya's Facebook page. On the left are pictures of some of her hundreds of friends. Not all of them are students or family members. Some of them do look like mug shots.

"Give me a for instance."

Ben points to a picture. "This guy."

His name is Kolya Vladimirhoff. He has an abundance of facial piercings and was glancing to his left when the picture was taken. Possibly to make sure his gang tats are seen. "What makes you think he's Russian mob?"

"We pulled up his page, then ran him and some of his *friends* through Mug Shots USA and the state criminal database." Ben looks around again. "He's got a record. Mostly for theft and mugging old people. Sometimes with weapons. And those are just his recent arrests. Since he's nineteen, he's probably got a sealed juvie record."

Eager faces wait for my response to their sleuthing. "Okay, good work. But reality check. True, they're Russian friends of Nadya's; how close we don't know since it looks like she accepts anyone who asks. True, they're on the unsavory side, but unless you haven't told me an important detail, young Russian thugs don't equal the theft and replacement of a necklace valued at over half a million dollars from a bank vault box."

Ben's shoulders slump.

Rippa, however, looks determined. "I think there's a connection. We just need to dig deeper."

I nod. "Go for it."

The smiles return.

"But online only. Subject change. Tomorrow's our last day here."

Dual groans only teenagers can produce. "You said we were helping," Rippa accuses. "Besides"—wheedling now on board—"we haven't seen the Statue of Liberty yet."

Ben looks pained. "And that one place I wanted to shop."

They're right. Most of my time and thoughts have been focused on Angel Falls. Which freak-out shouldn't totally interfere with their one big graduation gift. "New plan. I'll see if they can extend our room stay for another four or five days." I hold my index finger in the *shhh* position, then wiggle it at the fist pumps. "That is the last of the negotiations."

I wait for that to sink in. "And just to show I mean it, we're going to the Statue of Liberty today."

Ben grabs his cellphone. "I'll call my dad and tell him about the new dates. Do they sell food at the Statue of Liberty?"

Rippa takes out her cell too. "I'll do the same. Piper won't care."

Chapter Six

I didn't invite them, because of the blunt questions I intend to pursue with Mitch, but the kids pass on leaving the hotel anyway this morning. They're determined to uncover more on the Russian gang connection.

Mack picks me up at nine thirty. "How'd your secret weapons work out?"

I give him a sideways smirk. "As a matter of fact, great. They went the social networking route. Tapped into Veronique and Nadya's Facebook pages."

An eyebrow tilt yields a comic mask. "Smart. Anything interesting?"

"Not for Veronique, but Nadya's page is wide open, and she has quite a few friends who are low-echelon Russian gang members."

Good thing we have a driver, because Mack turns his full attention on me. "How low?"

"Older teens. With records. Rippa and Ben stayed at the hotel to build their *case.*"

"Not just smart," he says, a frown forming. "Very smart. Keep me updated. In the meantime, none of you act on this information. Okay?"

I peer at him from the tops of my sunglasses. "Didn't I hear you use the word smart? We have no intention of taking on Russian gang members."

The driver drops us at the NYU campus and agrees

to pick us up in an hour. We find the building, and in it, the second floor where Mitch's office is located. It isn't fully closed, and Mack holds up his hand as I reach to knock. "Listen."

Nadya's voice is breathy. "Puhleeeze, Mitchie. It's a very small favor. If they ask, say no. That's all you have to do. They won't question your word. If you tell them the truth, they'll come after me even though I haven't done anything. If I am investigated, your government might not let me come back. Ever."

My lips disappear over my teeth. I'm here hoping to get information on my missing necklace, and my brother-in-law's little hottie wants to make sure he lies for her. Great.

"That's an exaggeration," Mitch soothes. "No one will blame you for doing as I asked."

There's a rustle of clothing and whispering, then Mitch's muffled voice. "They're due right now, so no. Maybe later."

Mack crooks his finger and tips his head toward a nearby hallway. I follow him on tip-toe. He peeks back around the corner. "I think Mitch would be more vulnerable to our questions alone. Let's give Nadya a few minutes to leave."

I glance at Mitch's office door and keep my voice low. "Agreed. Miss Vasilyeva holds too much sway over my brother-in-law. I especially want to know if she is asking him to lie to us about the availability of keys to my box."

I hear high heels descending the stairs. When they die out, we walk back to Mitch's office. I put on a sunny smile and knock on the door, swinging it inward.

Mitch finger combs his hair. "Right on time."

He'll never learn, Cara.

Raif's sad tone makes me sad too. He and Mitch weren't close, but they still cared about each other.

The air in the small office is thick with Nadya's scent. Mack takes a shallow breath before speaking. "Thanks for setting aside time for us."

"Glad to. Although I don't think I'll be of any help."

"It *will* help narrow down the number of people who have access to my box."

Mitch leans his head to the side. "Don't you already know that?"

"We know who the primary key holders are. But not who might *inadvertently* have access to those keys, and thus, to my box."

Mitch rolls a pen between his fingers. "Considering their name also has to be on the access list, that sounds pretty random."

Mack shakes his head. "Not as random as you'd think. For instance, Fletcher keeps his key to Julianne's box in their personal box at the same bank. His wife, Felicity, knows it's there and has access to it. All they would need is help from a vault escort."

Mitch does not have a good poker face. His gaze darts around the room, then settles back on his pen. "I see what you mean, although I'd think Felicity London would be above reproach." His voice transitions to professor-lecture mode. "Your box key is on my personal key ring, and Veronique has no need for my keys."

Good point. "Who said anything about Veronique?"

Mitch backpedals after throwing his wife under the

bus and lifts a shoulder. "I thought you were looking at anybody *inadvertent*."

Mack holds his hand palm out. "Can I see your key ring?"

"Of course." Mitch puts down his pen and pulls open his lap drawer to extract a large key ring. He slides it across his desk.

I look from Mitch to the key ring and back. "Not wowed by your security measures."

He shrugs. "It includes personal and university-issued keys. I'm more comfortable sitting without them in my pocket. Perfectly safe."

I'm not convinced. Especially after overhearing Nadya's comments. "And you take them with you when you lecture? In this hall?"

Mitch nods. "Usually. Plus, the office door is locked when I'm not here."

I wonder if his lectures are as pointless as his answers. "Help me understand. If the office door is locked when you aren't here, is the key you use to lock it on this key ring?"

He gives me a pitying look. "There are multiple keys to my office door."

"Then who else can unlock your office door?"

Big sigh. His patience is wearing thin. "Julianne, honey. Veronique and I are family. Don't you think you and Mr. Pierce should be concentrating on security at the bank?"

"We think there *is* a connection at the bank," Mack says. "To someone who also has a key."

Mitch's gaze takes another trip around the room. "That's a big leap with only three keys out there."

"With multiple people who can get their hands on

them," I repeat.

Mack holds up a single key on the ring. "What's this?"

I look closely. It's a safety deposit box key with a different number stamped on it.

Mack's discovery is not greeted with a happy face from Mitch. "That goes to my personal box. Before you ask, same bank."

The way he says "my" begs a question. "Yours and Veronique's?"

Mitch releases a huff of air. "No, mine. And I would consider it a great favor if Veronique isn't told of its existence."

I have respect for Mitch's survival instinct, but he hasn't answered my other question yet. "Okay by me." I look at Mack, who nods. "I'd still like to know who else has a key to your office."

"Security, I imagine maintenance and janitorial services, and me." His gaze rolls up and to the left. "That's it."

"I assume Veronique could lay her hands on your key ring at home."

No hesitation. "Sure, but there's nothing on my key ring she has use for."

Maybe, maybe not. But not once has Mitch mentioned Nadya. "What about your assistant?"

The question seems to annoy him. "I thought you meant now. Um, Nadya used to. All the assistants had keys to the offices of the professors they worked with. Nadya no longer does. Turned it in last week when she graduated."

Mack gives the ring of keys a small toss. "How long did she have it?"

Mitch's jaw bunches, and he holds out his hand for his keys. "The same as the other assistants. About a year."

"Thanks. We appreciate your time." Mack drops the keys in Mitch's hand.

Relief washes over my brother-in-law's face. I'm not done with my questions, but Mack tugs my hand, and I let him lead the way out. "Yes, thanks," I say over my shoulder as we leave.

In the hall, it's my turn to tug. "What the hell? I didn't even get to ask about the newspaper picture. And I was just getting started on Nadya."

Mack holds up both hands. "I know, but Mitch was *done*. We got a couple of pieces of information, and I think we need to be happy with that. For the time being."

He has a point. Mitch's growing agitation was clear. I take a breath. "Okay. We learned Nadya had access to the office and thus to the safety deposit box key. At least until last week. Which gave her plenty of time if she wanted in."

"And?"

"Based on the times I've seen them interacting, I think my brother-in-law would lie to protect her."

He is nodding in agreement. "That's the vibe I got, although I don't think Mitch wanted to make the same connection."

"*Connection* is the key. Now that we have a possible link outside the bank, our next step is to look inside."

"Got someone in mind?"

I nod. "Sort of. I've been thinking about the last time I went into the box before the fake was discovered.

I'd waited until the last minute and was in a hurry to catch my flight. Then I had to wait for an escort to the vault. I remember being ticked that they only had one person available that day. They explained that there are only a few people who act as escorts because of the high security involved. The guy who escorted me last fall still works there. And there are other escorts."

"Doesn't the person wanting to open a box have to be authorized?"

I glance back to the door of Mitch's office. "That's just it. Of the two other keys, there should be only Mitch's and Fletcher's names. That's where the collusion comes in."

Mack looks in the same direction. "Narrows your options to someone at the bank who's allowing an unauthorized person with a key to gain the box."

"Bingo. Since I hope we can eliminate Mitch or Fletcher in person. Which still leaves an unknown, however small, number of people who could be guilty by association. My money is on the people who could get to Mitch's key. And we need to find out if he or Veronique has authorized anyone else to access their box. That information should be available at the bank."

"Agreed. Do you have the card of that safety deposit box manager? She or someone with authority can let us know."

I slip the card, and my cellphone, out of my pocket and dial as I walk. "Appointment today if we can get it?"

He glances at his watch. "Sure."

My call is transferred immediately. "Hello, Ms. Barrick. Would it be possible for Mr. Pierce and me to come interview any vault escorts available today?"

There's a slight pause, then a sigh I assume is weary resignation. The price she pays for her title. "That's problematic. Ian is on personal leave, and of the other two escorts, one is on vacation. Which means we can't have our only available escort gone. However, Ian has asked for a couple more days. He's coming in after lunch to sign some papers in HR. I'll ask him to take a few minutes to talk to you while he's in."

"One o'clock?" I ask my question on the phone and toward Mack.

He nods, and Ms. Barrick says she'll arrange it.

He scrolls on his phone. "Meantime, I'll visit the police team who've been assigned to your case. They're not supposed to give out info on a case in progress, but I've worked with one of them before. Maybe they'd be willing to trade information. At the least, I'll find out who they plan to interview. Want to come with?"

"Can't. The kids have been hard at it and stuck in their rooms. I'll bring what they have, and you can fill me in on what you have after the meeting at the bank if that's okay."

"Sounds good."

I've been thinking about Nadya's plan to leave the country and decide to try and get one step ahead of her. "One more thing. Can you find out Nadya's home address?"

Mack tips his head. "A woman who reads my mind. You're spooky."

Good to know he's still on my wavelength. "I get that from Rippa."

"She seems like a special kid."

"You have no idea."

Chapter Seven

Ben and Rippa are nearly bouncing off the walls when I get back to the hotel. Neither is any good at holding on to news, so I don't even have to ask.

Rippa gives a fist pump. "The front desk called and agreed to extend our stay."

Probably a good thing as empty food and drink containers abound in the room. "Wow. That *is* exciting."

Ben gives a well-practiced chin tip. "That's not all. You're gonna love what we found."

Again, I miss the nanosecond of opportunity to ask what.

Rippa stands shoulder to shoulder with Ben, nearly vibrating. "More connections to the Russians. We've been cyberstalking Nadya."

"I hope it's not the kind of stalking that could result in anything that bites you on the butts."

Ben's gaze skitters to the corner of the room. "Not if you know how."

I move on. "What have you discovered that I'm gonna love?"

Rippa rises to the balls of her feet. "Nadya has a rich sponsor who pays her bills."

I don't know about love, but if true, this is certainly interesting. "All her bills? Like which ones?"

I hope this isn't about Mitch, Cara.

Me too.

"First, this morning she got a Facebook request asking her to *like* a new condo complex near NYU campus. Contractor is a Kalashnikov Construction."

"And?"

"And we thought she might have contacted them about moving into one."

Probably not. "Don't think so. Mitch told me she was going back to Russia."

"We thought she couldn't afford one until we read her comment. 'Thinking about upgrading. Will keep in mind.' "

I think it sounds more like bragging. "Maybe she has long-term plans to return. If the new units are geared toward first-time owners, they could be reasonable in price."

Rippa shakes her head. "Not these units. We took the virtual tour, and they are uber expensive."

Nadya is many things, but financially able to buy an upscale condo is probably not one of them. "Then she might be kidding. And what does her comment have to do with a 'sponsor' paying her bills?"

"Getting to that." She cuts an impish glance at Ben. "One of her Russian *friends* posts, 'So are you going to work at The Gypsies after you graduate?' "

"What does that mean?" I ask.

Ben jumps in. "This is where the decoder ring comes in. We went to the Kalashnikov Corporation website. It lists all the associated businesses. The Gypsies is a restaurant in the building this Kalashnikov guy owns and where he has his office. There's also a night club and some kind of computer training center. Anyway, the website had a link to the manager for

Nadya's building."

"Wait. How do you know where she lives?"

Rippa tilts her head. "An address?"

Silly me. What was I thinking? "Kinda getting off track here."

Is it possible to pace in one spot? Ben shows that it is. "Almost there. So the manager's website, which has a password a ten-year-old could crack by the way, has a spreadsheet showing the occupants of Nadya's building and details of this past twelve months' rent payments. Nadya's apartment isn't on there. It's blank like the whole year was paid for in advance."

"Online chatter with some Russian teens? She might not even know these guys. You said she has a wide-open page. One of those people who says yes to any friend request. As for living there rent free, she might assist the manager."

Rippa's mouth twists. "Have you met Nadya? Plus, we checked into what else she gets free."

I can see they want to buy into the Nadya connection and take me with them. It's valuable information, and I'm glad they're enjoying the challenge. Just not there yet. "Did you find anything?"

Ben grins. "Yep."

Rippa lets loose her famous eye roll. "It was my idea."

"Only the tuition and lab stuff. I found the food."

Of course he did. "One at a time, please. Rippa?"

"There are sites where prospective employers, banks, and other loan institutions can check an applicant's Fico score and their payment history. Nadya has no outstanding student loans, tuition, or labs. She also has several credit cards at high-end department stores with zero balances. And she doesn't have an employment history outside her student assistant's job with Uncle Mitch. Which in itself couldn't begin to cover her expensive tastes."

A pattern's emerging. I turn to Ben. "You?"

"Food," he crows.

"Like at that restaurant?"

"More like nice food from home. I Googled Russian grocers and found a place not far from her apartment. I called and asked how much to pay off Nadya Vasilyeva's outstanding bill. The guy said it had already been taken care of. Then he laughed said it was okay if I wanted to pay it twice."

"Did you ask who was paying the bill?"

Ben drops his chin. "No. I should've."

"No harm, no foul. It's still useful."

Our girl Nadya certainly has her hooks into someone. It may or may not be related to her access to Mitch's key and thus to my safety deposit box, but it's interesting. "You guys rock. Can you send copies to my email?"

They nod in unison, and Ben speaks. "Can we order lunch now?"

Rippa elbows him. "Yeah, 'cause it's been a whole hour since you polished off those snacks we bought at the bodega on our way back to the hotel yesterday."

I laugh. "I asked the concierge about the best burgers and fries outside the hotel kitchen. She's having some sent over. That okay?"

Not only okay, Ben turns so quickly he knocks a nearby chair over. He rights it and tips his head. "Going to my room to wash up."

Rippa gives one of her best eyebrow hikes.

"Smooth, Brown."

I try not to laugh out loud. "After lunch, Mack and I are going back to the bank for an interview. You guys want to keep on this?"

"Definitely," Ben says over his shoulder.

"On a roll," Rippa agrees.

****

One o'clock and Mack comes through the bank's doors. His punctuality is an asset in my book. I hate waiting, but a lot of guys think if they're "reasonably close" to the time promised, it's all good. I'm glad Mack's not one of them.

We go to the vault sign-in desk and are about to announce our appointment when the manager comes toward us. In her wake is a man about my age who is in bad shape. He is pale and thin, and as they draw closer, I see deep blue eyes. They would be beautiful if not rimmed in red with puffy lids. Also a look of surprise is in the tilt of his head when he sees me. His mustache grabs my attention next. It's sparse and looks as if all his facial hair effort went into producing it. I force my gaze away to his blond-tipped hair. He's the same escort from ten months ago, but I hardly recognize him. Stress, illness, or some dark emotion has taken hold, and he looks like he might shake apart.

"Scared?" Mack's low-voiced question upon seeing the man.

"In part. Walk softly."

The manager nudges the guy forward. "Ian, this is Ms. McCarren and Mr. Pierce."

Ian bumps a nod and allows a hello through a throat that sounds like he's speaking over wet sand. His gaze travels to the floor.

I reach for his hand, and my touch makes him quiver. "I don't know if you remember me, Ian. It's been since last fall."

His shoulder jerks, but he gives no verbal response.

The manager steps to the desk and speaks to the girl. "Is Conference B occupied?"

She taps a few keys. "Open for another twenty minutes."

"Book it to me," she says, then turns to her employee. "Help them any way you can."

Ian doesn't seem so sure. He takes a half step back, almost losing balance, and still not accepting eye contact.

I'm beginning to think this is a terrible idea when he shifts forward in defeat.

Mack and I follow but move aside at the room's entrance.

The young escort glances at his boss.

"Would you like me to stay?" she asks.

His gaze lifts, and he moves his mouth sideways. "I'm okay."

Either he might not want her to hear his side of the conversation or he's determined we aren't a threat. I'm betting on the former.

He sits angled forward, looking as if he's ready for a quick departure if necessary. I mirror his posture, which seems to alarm him into sitting back. I copy that too.

"Thanks for seeing us. We heard about your loss. I'm so sorry."

This visibly surprises him, and tears well. I carry tissues and offer him one. He dabs his eyes, takes a breath, then swallows before responding. "Thank you.

Timur and I were engaged. We were going to get married and buy a house in Connecticut. You know, something with a garden. Then adopt."

My attention snags on the name. Nadya's brother? If so, this is quite a coincidence. "Timur Vasilyev?"

He wipes away remaining tears. "Yes. Did you know him?"

"Only by his reputation for kindness." A big fat lie on my part, but I want to give my brain time to make some connections.

Mack takes the reins. "How long were you and Timur together?"

Ian's tissue is sodden. I hand him another.

"Six months."

"When was the accident?" Mack asks.

Ian dabs at his eyes again. "Sorry. The so-called *undetermined event* happened ten days ago."

"Then we really appreciate your taking the time to help us." I pause. "Are you okay to go on?"

"Yes." Barely audible.

I lace my fingers and straighten. "In the lobby I got the impression you weren't expecting us. Or at least me. Do I make you uncomfortable?"

He shakes his head quickly. "Not at all. When Ms. Barrick said I was going to talk to Ms. McCarren, I thought it was another one. She's always carrying things in and out of her box, and she's kind of rude." A sardonic smile. "Always wants 'the manager' to escort her. Like the rest of us aren't good enough."

"Would that be Veronique McCarren?"

The escort's head dips a little. "Yes. If you're related, I'm sorry I said she was rude."

"I am, and you're not wrong. No offense taken."

He sniffs and smiles.

Indeed. I wonder why Veronique makes frequent visits to her box. In the same vault as mine. "To continue, how long have you worked here?"

Easy question. Nothing to get worked up about.

Relief washes Ian's features. "Almost five years."

Mack and I wait a beat. It's surprising the number of people who feel they have to fill the silence.

Ian screws up his mouth. "He was the best bike messenger in the city and a wonderful man. He didn't deserve to die."

Which meant what? Now we have an answer to an unasked question. Is this another lead? Or is his fiancé's death the only thing occupying Ian's mind? Maybe this coincidence has nothing to do with Angel Falls.

"Deaths often don't make sense," I say, hoping to close the subject.

Anger swamps his eyes. "You don't know."

I sigh. "Yes, I do. I was married for three years, and I loved him very much. He died in an accident." *And it still feels like someone took a scalpel and sliced off part of my soul.* "The item that was stolen from my vault box belonged to his mother and was his wedding gift to me."

We were lucky to have three years, Cara.

"Oh," Ian says, then pulls back his shoulders in a stubborn set. "It was ruled undetermined, but no way was what happened to Timur an accident."

Okay, so we're not done talking about Timur. Could be worth a look at the police report. It's also interesting that Nadya wasn't nearly this upset. At least in public. I took a chance on a direct approach. "You think he was killed on purpose?"

Too much. Ian snaps out of his self-pity. "Yes, but can we talk about something else?"

Back on track. "Sure."

His shoulders curl inward again. "My manager said you think your box access is an issue. What kind of issue?"

I think my necklace being stolen should be plain enough, but I let that stew for a minute. "My necklace was stolen and replaced with a replica within the last ten months."

He's still nervous and tries for concern but can't quite manufacture it. "You think that happened with help from someone here?"

Since I had a picture of my sister-in-law wearing the necklace within the past seven months, I wasn't, but Ian doesn't know that. "Yes."

"Have you talked to the other escorts?" Tight and defensive.

From Mack. "Someone in particular?"

Ian's gaze slips to the reproduction art on the wall behind Mack. "Not really."

We've used up five minutes on not a thing we came here for. "Then let's get your opinion on how this could have happened."

Ian shrugs. "I can't imagine."

Mack cuts him off. "You've been an escort for five years, and you've never imagined or considered how the robbery of a vault box could be pulled off?"

Ian is prepared for this question. "We don't know what's in any of the boxes. How would any of us know to pick one with a diamond necklace in it?"

The hair on the back of my neck prickles. "I didn't mention it was a diamond necklace."

There's no change in his demeanor. "Ms. Barrick told me."

So he did know what the issue was. "Fair enough. However, Nadya knew."

Ian's expression registers shock. His slender hand slaps the table. "I hate her. She's mean and selfish and greedy. Timur was nothing like her. He was smart and real, and I loved him."

Not a direct answer but helpful and sustains the connection.

A tap on the door interrupts us, and a young woman in a gray suit pokes her head in. "Hi, Ian. I need to set up for my one-thirty meeting. Your boss said it was okay."

I check my eye roll. Of course she did. Her baby chick might be saying something to make the bank look accountable.

Ian springs up. "We're just finishing."

Mack and I make no move to leave. We've used up very little of our allotted twenty minutes, and most of our time has been spent on another matter. I tap the table. "Have you contacted, or been contacted, by the police?"

Ian glances at the doorway. "About what?"

"The stolen necklace." I pause. "Or Timur's death."

"Not about the necklace." Barely a whisper.

The girl at the door arches an eyebrow and backs out, closing it softly.

I slide a pencil and small tablet across the table. "We'd like to talk to you again. After you've had more time to heal. Can I have your personal contact information?"

His gaze pings around the room, then he scribbles on the paper. "Okay, I guess."

I know he's hurting, but Ian is a good lead. "We're going to find out what happened to my necklace. Think hard about how the theft could have happened. You might come up with something."

He sucks in a short breath, then leaves.

We stop by Barrick's office on our way out. I nod at the conference room across the hall. "Thanks for the opportunity."

"He's a good kid," she responds. "A little emotional, but that's natural given what he's going through. Was he able to help?"

"Probably more than he realizes. We didn't finish, though. We'll be talking to him again."

Her look is definitely one of surprise. "Is that really necessary?"

I cut a glance to Mack. "We had a tough time getting Ian to focus on our vault questions. He kept straying to the topic of his recent loss."

Her gaze drops to her desktop. "Go easy on him. Sudden loss of a loved one, by accident or other means, tears away at the mental balance of those left behind." She splays her hands and looks up. "Sorry to get maudlin. It's just that it's so soon for Ian. His personal leave's been extended for another week. Maybe you can catch him at home after a couple more days."

Her assessment of feelings for those left behind after an unexpected death is very perceptive. "We plan to. Thanks again."

Sorry you went through that, Cara.

Mack turns to me on the sidewalk outside the bank. "If he *is* involved, he could be a weak link. And as unsportsmanlike as it sounds, I think we need to play him while he's still grieving."

If his grief is anything like mine, he'll need a lot longer than a few days to bring himself back to a righted world. Rippa says I still get this look around my eyes when death or funerals are mentioned within earshot. I try to roll past it but sometimes don't succeed.

Mack tilts his head. "I didn't know your husband other than meeting him on a couple of occasions. He was a nice guy. You okay staying close to Ian while he's vulnerable? Sometimes circumstances require harsh measures, and I don't want you to be uncomfortable."

Nice of him, Cara.

I swing my gaze past Mack. "Thanks for asking. I'm fine. I'd also like to see the police report on Timur's accident. I know it was mostly denial talking, but there was an underlying certainty in Ian's claim. Could be something to it."

"No such thing as a coincidence, everything happens for a reason? In this case, the girl who has access to the vault box key has a deceased brother who was the fiancé of the vault escort."

"I wonder if Mitch is aware of that. Could be worth another chat. If only to bring him up to date."

A smile settles on his mouth.

"What?"

"You want to confront him about the charity event picture."

Avoiding his dead-on comment, I take out my cellphone and turn it back up. I hadn't wanted to be interrupted during the interview. "Mitch lives in Mitchland. He's protected by money, name, and the community of his campus. Veronique gets her way by agitating his personal space until he caves. Otherwise he stonewalls. I think it's time to go all Veronique on him."

His smile is replaced by an all-out grin. "I like that."

I scroll until Mitch's office number appears and tap it.

"You have reached Professor Mitchell McCarren. This is Thursday, June twelfth, and I will be in my office until three. Please leave a message."

I click *End*. "Not going to give him a chance to hide."

"Good choice," Mack says, hanging up his phone. "Car's on its way. We can be there by a little after two."

Chapter Eight

Manhattan traffic bested us until almost two forty-five. Climbing the stairs to Mitch's office, we find we're not alone in wanting to see him.

I stop and stare. "Geez. Looks like a Russian brothel sprang a leak."

Mack tries, unsuccessfully, to choke back a laugh.

Outside my brother-in-law's door is a gaggle of blondes, close enough in appearance to be matryoshka dolls. As we approach, a girl on the fringe, with an amazing chest, looks us over. "No men," she says in a thick accent, then leans in to inspect my hair. "Expensive job but is too short, and you are too old."

This pronouncement irks me. First of all, it looks expensive because I'm a natural blonde. I stand straighter. "Too old for what?"

"You are not here for pre-interview?"

I glance at Mack, who grins and shrugs. He, of course, is garnering admiring glances from the gaggle. "No. Pre-interview for what?"

"Next year assistant to Professor Mitch."

That was quick. Nadya's chair isn't cold yet, and Mitch is busy backfilling her position.

A groan from Raif. *Talk to him, Cara. Please.*

I would, but Mitch is too deeply entrenched in his home-away-from-home lifestyle.

A carbon-copy pre-interview candidate opens

Mitch's office door and steps through, followed by my brother-in-law. The girl turns and holds out her hand for a dead-fish handshake. Mitch obliges, and the girl shudders at his touch. It's a happy-all-over wiggle you might see in a puppy, and I almost laugh. Mitch clearly revels in his rock-star status.

"Thank you for coming, Marta. I'll post my decision next week." He looks past the others and sees us. His smile wanes. "Julianne, Mack. What can I do for you?"

Five pairs of heavily made-up eyes squint at us.

Mitch addresses the group. "Interviews are closed for today, ladies. Those of you who haven't pre-interviewed, please come back tomorrow at two."

Heels clatter against the textured stone floor as the women change direction, and purses are repositioned on hips as they file past us in colorful, if sullen, silence.

Mitch tips his head toward his office. "Glad for the interruption."

Doesn't look that way, but Mack and I enter and take the two chairs across from his desk. A desk that, knowing his relationship with Nadya, might have been used for some in-between lectures Russian-American détente. "Pre-interviews?" I ask, dying to hear more.

My brother-in-law shuffles files into a neat stack and sits. "Nadya's idea. Student employment jackets only have headshots. She knows all the candidates and thought if I spent a few minutes with each, I could match personal preferences with qualifications. Save time over scheduling full interviews."

Shallow but brilliant in its efficiency. Personal preferences, indeed. I pretend enthusiasm. "That makes sense."

A sound that might be agreement, or a stifled snort, comes from Mack. Mitch doesn't acknowledge it, so neither do I.

"If you have a few minutes, we wanted to talk to you about an interesting fact we learned this afternoon."

Mitch's turn to feign interest. "In regards to your missing necklace?"

"There may be a roundabout connection. Do you know who Ian Ward is?"

I can see the gears turning as Mitch ponders my question.

He shakes his head. "Name sounds familiar, but I can't think in what context."

"Mr. Ward was engaged to Nadya's brother. He's also a vault escort at the bank where our boxes are located."

The barest flash of consternation crosses his face. At least that's what I think it is. Mitch puts out pretty much the same vibe most of the time.

"So what's the connection?"

I stifle a heavy sigh and the urge to tick the points off on my fingers. "Nadya had access to my key via your key ring. Her brother's fiancé had access to my box and possibly my key through her brother."

Not much change to his demeanor, only a slight red flag high on his cheeks. His gaze is direct. "I understand you think you've found something. But look at the people involved. A college student, a bike messenger, and a bank employee. This constitutes a brain trust that comes up with a plan to steal a priceless necklace? How would they go about selling or disposing of it? Be realistic."

Mitch seems sure in his evaluation, arrogant even.

Before I can make a counterpoint, Mack speaks up. "You're giving us their occupations. They also had possible motives. Nadya and Timur were here on temporary visas, both with low-paying jobs. Timur and Ian were in love and wanted to get married and buy a house in Connecticut. The college student lived above her means and planned to come back to this country soon, to live in an upscale residence." He opens his hand. "Not a big leap to think Julianne's necklace would give them all a step toward those ambitious goals."

Mitch's eyebrows rise slightly when Mack mentions Nadya's intent to return to New York soon. Maybe something she hadn't shared? Other than that, he lifts a shoulder. "Young and poor with dreams doesn't mean they're criminals."

I'm getting pissed. Mack and I are lobbing bombshells, and Mitch is pretending there's no war. I stand up. "I have one more scenario. After the bank's master key is used by the escort, the key holder is left alone in the vault. Veronique has lobbied hard for my necklace for years. Did she finally wear you down? Did you have the replica in your pocket when you went in? Slip it in my box, take the original for her, then walk out to the public space and have the replica evaluated? Is that what happened the other day?"

Mitch is on his feet now. "Julianne, honey. You can't believe that."

Mack is up and backing toward the door.

I push my chair back, the legs dragging against the inexpensive carpeting. "We're done here. Thanks for your time."

My brother-in-law's face is pale, his mouth taut.

"Um, sure. Sorry I can't help."

"Won't, Mitch. The word is won't."

Mack is close behind me but wisely doesn't say anything until we reach the concrete and grass that makes up the mini-quad in front of the building. "Didn't get to ask him about the picture again," he says quietly.

I cut him a look, and he presses his lips together hard, which makes me laugh. "What gets me is he doesn't think he could be any part of this. He'd rather suffocate with his head in the sand than admit his girl toy could be involved. It's annoying."

He nods. "I get that. It also might stem from his having to defend himself against Veronique for the whole of their marriage."

No pity from this corner if that's the case. "He made his bed."

He grins. "Or beds as the case may be."

Now *that's* funny.

Our attention is drawn to two girls in attention-grabbing spandex—what other kind of spandex is there—as they blow past us on rollerblades. One flows with a dancer's grace while the other attacks the pavement. Farther down, a guy stands in their path. He doesn't move, doesn't appreciate the view, and doesn't look like a student. He wears tight black jeans and heavy, black, leather-laced boots. His top half is covered in a black T and black leather jacket. His hair is half mullet and half skinhead. The skinhead side is sporting a number of piercings.

He throws down his cigarette, making no attempt to put it out as the girls approach. The graceful one sees and stops a ways behind him. "Hey, trash boy. Wanna pollute the air and dump your garbage back wherever you came from?" She waves a finger up and down, indicating his figure. "Which isn't here."

The guy doesn't say anything. Just takes out a black cigarette and lights it with a cheap plastic lighter, then tosses the lighter to the concrete and stomps on it. Blue plastic shards and lighter fluid squirt from under his boot.

"Whoa," the girl starts, but her friend grabs her by the arm and tows her away. Smart friend. As I watch this play out, I recognize the guy. He's one of the Russian gang members Rippa found on Nadya's Facebook page. What's he doing here?

I pull out my cellphone and turn three-quarters away from the kid's line of sight.

Mack waits, his gaze on the scene.

"I recognize him," I say.

His stance loosens. "Trouble?"

Good question. "Don't know, but it's odd that he's turned up here. He's one of the Facebook friends Rippa and Ben found on Nadya's page when they were cyberstalking her. His name's Kolya something."

"You sure?"

I give him a look that says I pity his weak observational skills. "Haircut's hard to miss."

He tilts his head. "He's sporting a Russian gang tattoo on his neck."

"Yep. Rippa and Ben said he has a record. Small stuff, but escalating violence. His juvenile sheet's probably sealed, or his record would be longer."

"Maybe we can ask him. He's headed this way."

I turn. Kolya is coming toward us in a swagger. Bold choice if he's here to cause trouble.

His inventory of Mack is cursory. Which is interesting. Mack does not look like a lightweight, but the teen shows no outward reaction as he approaches. I don't expect fear, exactly, but maybe a healthy respect. Nothing. Instead he stops in front of me and grins. "I peekchure you as woman who likes to dance."

Goose bumps climb my arms, and my heart hammers. Here's a genuine poster boy for dark and scary. And how does he know I like to dance? "So this is a late invitation to the spring formal?"

A deep guffaw greets my question. "Not interested in older women. I am just messenger. For time being."

"Messenger for who?"

He doesn't answer but reaches in his pocket. Mack stiffens. A move that makes Kolya laugh again. He pulls out a business card with a navy-blue background and a shiny gold embossed bear and offers it to me. "This will get you past security and wave cover charge. Wear pretty dress and diamonds." He smirks in Mack's direction. "Bring friend if you like."

The remark about diamonds shortens my breath and derails the questions I should be asking about his relationship to Nadya. And cover charge for where?

Also something about his eyes Kolya's Facebook picture doesn't convey. For one thing, they are a creepy pale gold-brown color. For another, they reflect a flat greed; he wants to be in control. But no spark of life shines. I suppress a shudder and take the card without comment. He turns, throws down his cigarette, and leaves.

My breath hitches. "He didn't like referring to himself as a messenger but made sure we knew it was temporary. I wouldn't care to be in the way of whatever goal he has in mind."

"*I* wouldn't care for him to take a dislike to me," Mack intones. "Looks like a certified whack job. That tattoo is a gang sign that's he's killed." The farther away the kid gets, the more Mack relaxes. He peers at the card and grins. "Club Bear. Smack in the middle of Russian gang night life. Lucky you."

I click the corner of the card with my thumbnail. "I do like to dance."

His eyes sparkle. "Does that include salsa?"

I have noticed he moves with athletic assurance that leans toward grace rather than jock. But dance? Nice to know. "You salsa?"

"And bomba and cha-cha. Pretty much all Latin dances."

Cara, you haven't danced since Argentina. This is great.

I can't hide my smile. "You're full of surprises, Pierce. What's behind you and dancing?"

"Serious crush on a pretty girl in junior high. She loved to dance, and I couldn't get my grandmother to teach me fast enough."

"Did that impress the girl?"

"For almost two years, then she fell for a guy in high school whose parents owned a dance studio. You?"

I lift a shoulder. "Raif was an Argentine male."

He acknowledges. "Birthright."

Pride in heritage is big for Latin males. If Mack is as good a dancer as Raif was…let's just say, wow.

"You think we should see what's behind this"—I wave the card—"invitation?"

"I'd like to know what he knows and what he

thinks we know. There's a Venn diagram in there somewhere."

"I don't think he knows as much as he'd like to. But whoever wound him up and aimed him at us has an agenda we should know about."

He purses his mouth. "In that case, we should come prepared. Let's set up a meet with the theft team working your case. I'll ask them to bring in someone from the gang unit who's familiar with the Russian element."

I look at my watch. "Can't. I promised Rippa and Ben we'd go to the matinee of *Wicked*. They're excited to see a real Broadway show. At least Rippa is. Ben thinks the flying monkeys will induce nightmares. Then we're going to Tavern on the Green for an early dinner. The concierge made the arrangements for us."

He whistles. "I forget the pull your name has here."

I wrinkle my nose. "That's one of the reasons, besides family, that I choose to live on the other side of the country."

He shakes his head. "I said it before. You are definitely not a New York woman. Okay. I'll make the appointment for first thing in the morning. Pick you up at nine?"

Chapter Nine

The Broadway musical is wildly different from Dorothy Gale's blue-checked dress and pinafore movie adventure. Rippa, Ben, and I spend dinner dissecting Gregory Maguire's prolific interpretation of children's classics, which Rippa believes have been dumbed down and softened so as not to be scary. I agree with her. Ben likes the kinder versions.

He changes the subject. "We've been in town for almost a week and still haven't gone clothes shopping."

Mental heel of hand to forehead. I am such a dud. He's already mentioned this once, and I walked right through it. "Sorry. I totally forgot. Where did you want to go?"

Ben grins and waves a fork that has recently massacred a slab of chocolate fudge cake. "It's this amazing store in NOHO that carries a prime selection of sick clothes. These four Japanese guys are the designers and run only two places. One here and one in Tokyo. They don't have a website, so I shop by proxy."

Ah. Cutting-edge fashion in a real brick-and-mortar store. "Done," I say. "Mack and I are meeting with the detectives assigned to my case at nine. Shopping after that. Okay?"

Rippa wiggles in her chair. "He wants new clothes so he can try to convince those California girls he's not a bone-deep nerd."

Ben, fork still in hand, folds his arms. "At least I have some style and don't look like a bowling alley groupie from the fifties."

Rippa snorts. "Thanks. That's the look I'm going for."

"Then we're cool," he says and polishes off the last speck of cake.

****

Breakfast conversation also centers around more touristy shopping. While I'm out, the kids each want to buy a T-shirt for their parent. Rippa has to find a "socially responsible" T-shirt that has a price which includes a donation to a cause. Ben's only criterion is that the shirt for his dad not be army green. I get a solemn promise from each they won't wander too far from the hotel and an eye roll from Rippa because she doesn't think I'm looking.

"We'll check with the concierge. He'll know the closest T-shirt shops with the best selections."

Seventeen and invincible. Yet kids disappear from the streets of New York every month. I get up from the table and compose my stern adult-in-charge look. "Text me when you get back to the rooms."

****

The building that houses the precinct Mack and I are visiting is straight out of an old Hollywood movie set. Massive stones and smallish windows dominate the arched façade. Steps worn shallow by hundreds of thousands of shoes lead to two heavy doors. Inside, no-smoking signs hang on the walls, but it still smells like a hundred years of used tobacco. The officer on desk duty takes our names and makes a call.

Within a few minutes, a blond guy with the

dimensions of a Seahawks halfback walks down narrow stairs. He's wearing a dress shirt and tie and carrying a manila folder. He grins and addresses Mack. "You didn't say the rich woman was young and pretty."

Mack stretches his arms toward me. "Wanted to see if your keen detective skills would kick in."

He's ignored as the big man holds out his hand. "Bret Hagen."

My hand disappears inside his grip. "Nice to meet you."

"First the beauty. Now the brains." This statement comes from a small woman in a brown suit who must have been right behind him. She is literally in the shadow of the blond. I don't think she's kidding. And from the look on Detective Hagen's face, neither does he.

He tips his head. "This is my partner and, as she said, the brains of the outfit, Susan Pavlycheva. She's also the interdepartmental link to the gang unit. Specifically, Russian."

Following a calculating assessment, Ms. Pavlycheva smiles and inserts herself into our personal space. Her handshake is firm and dry, her gaze direct. "Don't work too hard on the Russian surname. My husband, Ruben, is from St. Petersburg. You suspect Russian gang involvement in the theft of your necklace?"

Her red hair and green eyes having been explained, I like that she comes right to the point. "One of the possibilities."

Pavlycheva nods. "Active cases aren't open to the public, but we'd like to hear what you've run across."

Not what leads you've found or what information

you've mined, but "what you've run across."

I let my annoyance show. "We aren't 'the public.' We also aren't Nancy Drew and Frank Hardy here to waste your time. The stolen property is mine, so I have a vested interest in its recovery. I also have an investigator's license, and Mr. Pierce is head of security for McCarren Multinational. I think we can help each other."

Hagen blinks at my onslaught, and Mack, again, wise man that he is, stays silent.

Detective Pavlycheva pulls back her shoulders. "Your point is taken. We talk." She turns and heads up the stairs.

A mumble from Hagen as we climb. "Young and pretty I could handle. Add brave and smart...?"

Nice hike in my personal stock. Which is a counterpoint to the depressing hallway we're walking down. Areas of chipped paint reveal layers of drab colors on the walls and the door Susan enters. The room itself is small and ugly. It's used for interrogations, evidenced by heavy links welded to the underside of the metal table for handcuffs. The table is screwed to the floor, and the chairs and walls are dented. Like the entry downstairs, a lingering odor permeates the air, this time best described as sweat and desperation.

The two detectives pick up pencils and tablets. Bret flips open the folder. "We've gone over the information gathered by bank security, but there's no apparent Russian connection. What's your theory based on?"

Mack starts with the mugging outside Shun Lee Palace, including the words spoken in Russian.

"Unfortunate," Susan says. "However, it could be an isolated incident."

I wait a beat. "Um, there's more."

An unspoken signal flashes between the partners, and Detective Hagen now has the reins. I change my initial evaluation of these two. Instead of good cop, bad cop, they take turns being in charge.

"Please bring us up to speed," he says. "We have a crushing caseload and can use any information you have."

I outline the connections that include access to my keys, my brother-in-law's Russian wife's obsession, his Russian assistant, and her Facebook interactions with Russian gang members, one of whom, a Kolya Vladimirhoff, now seems to be following me, and the death of the Russian bicycle messenger/fiancé to the bank vault escort. I pull out the card with the embossed gold bear and tell them of the invitation.

Hagen finishes scribbling in his tablet, then just stares at me. Pavlycheva's mouth is slightly open.

The redhead is the first to speak. "That gang member you mentioned, Kolya Vladimirhoff, turned nineteen almost a year ago. I know because I've been keeping track of the little psycho. I was privy to his sealed juvie record due to a case I worked where he was suspected of mugging an oldster who tried to fight back. The victim's permanently disabled. Nothing proved because he didn't have the guts to testify against Vladimirhoff. Plus, his jaw was wired shut. Common knowledge the kid would carve you up like an Easter ham and not blink. He's been escalating to the point where we think he's about to go off the rails. You don't want to be anywhere near when he does."

She continues. "His mother disappeared when he was about eight, and he never spent more than a couple of weeks in a foster home before they kicked him back into the system. His father died in Black Dolphin Prison in Russia a couple of years ago. No one's been able to associate his neck tattoo with a body, but Homicide is trying. Basically, Vladimirhoff makes his own rules as he goes along. He thinks his father was a badass and a role model. He has nothing else to hang on to. We do know he's moved in from the wannabe fringe of Pyotr Kalashnikov's gang and that he's a loner. Which is not to say he doesn't control some of the other members, especially the younger ones. Born at New York Methodist Hospital near Brighton Beach so he's a US citizen. Otherwise, he'd have been up for deportation long ago."

Mack holds up a finger. "This is the first I'm hearing about Kalashnikov. As in the Russian weapons designer?"

Susan nods. "Same spelling, no relationship. The weapons designer was born like a hundred years ago, anyway. The New York Kalashnikov considers himself a mild-mannered businessman. If I were him, I'd watch my back. Kolya's power-hungry."

A tremor camps in my stomach. "That makes him disturbingly real as a threat, so we'll keep that in mind. One question—if he was born in New York, how come the accent?"

Susan again. "He wants you to think he's a badass Russian. It's a scare tactic."

"Works great," I mumble. "But getting back to bodies and associations. Would it be possible for Mack and me to have a copy of the police report on the hit-and-run that killed Timur Vasilyev?"

Detective Pavlycheva's shoulders relax, and she

leans forward. "That's an interesting theory. I skimmed the report since someone raised a big stink about it being a murder and the victim was a young Russian. With no ties to gang activity. You think this is all linked to the theft?"

"Until disproven, yes, that's what I think."

Detective Hagen taps his pencil to his tablet. "Then that's the angle we take."

Pavlycheva nods. "I'll get a copy of the report for you. And thanks. Your information is also worth taking a closer look at Kalashnikov."

A muggy New York June day wraps around us on the sidewalk in front of the cop house. I fan my face. "Taking the kids clothes shopping this morning. Do you have any contacts who are experts in reviewing accidents?"

"Just Janean," Mack says. "A genius at deconstruction." He looks past my left shoulder. "You're not thinking of going to Club Bear by yourself?"

"Tempting, but no. Besides, I don't have anything to wear to a club."

He pins me with a disparaging grin. "And yet you're going clothes shopping."

He has a point, Cara.

He does. But I've never liked shopping for clothes, and I haven't worn a dress since Raif's funeral. I lift a shoulder without making eye contact. "I'll keep it in mind."

Mack's gaze shows a gleam of appreciation. "Actually, you'd be fine in whatever."

"Thanks. Long time since I've received a compliment."

"Mean it. And now that we've covered wardrobe, what do you plan to do next?"

"Concerning?"

His gaze pins me again. "We've turned our findings over to the police team in charge of your case and also to bank security. Your original reasons for coming to New York are wrapping up…"

"You think I should leave the recovery of my necklace to 'professionals?' "

He pushes out a breath. "I thought at first it might be a simple case, but the evidence piling up says otherwise. I'm just not sure a security chief for a corporation and an insurance fraud investigator are the right people to take on a gang who might be determined to have your property…at any cost. And I'm sure as hell not ready for that cost to be you, or possibly the kids, getting hurt."

Wow. He's expressed his personal feelings about me twice in five minutes. I have to admit it gives me a warm fuzzy.

He's a good guy, Cara. Listen to him.

"That's a fair assessment. And without pushing either of us into uncomfortable territory, I'd like to suggest a compromise."

A short nod. "I'm listening."

"While I agree some events point in a direction we're not equipped to handle, I also think we're in a better position than the police to get more information. You heard what Bret said about their overwhelming caseload. I propose we accept the invitation to Club Bear and hope it leads to a conversation with Kalashnikov. If that's a total dead end, I back off."

He pulls his lips in, then out again. "Not much of a

meeting in the middle." The corner of his mouth lifts. "But I shouldn't have expected any different, you being a different kind of McCarren. Okay. I'm in."

I expel a breath and straighten my shoulders. "Thanks again."

Chapter Ten

My reasoning is solid. We take a cab straight to the shop Ben wants to see, then take one right back to the hotel. No wandering around. So I choose to again forego the available driver.

The ride to the address in NOHO is less than fifteen minutes, but Ben is strung tight with only a chink in his superficial cool. We almost go past the little storefront set back from the main street. It's snugged between a custom perfumery and an antiques shop. The setback indicates it must have been a courtyard at one time. As we get out of the taxi, Ben walks unerringly to the shop front. A small inset sign by the door looks almost like a sixth-grade papier-mâché project. The letters look like *kanji*. The small window shows a featureless mannequin with his back to the street. In front of him is a large picture of Shibuya Crossing, in Tokyo. Reportedly the busiest intersection in the world. A whitespace cut-out the size and shape of the mannequin faces the photo. Clever display.

Rippa points to the setting. "That's crazy cool. Where's it?"

Ben and I are in unison. "Shibuya Crossing."

"Raif and I crossed it off our bucket list when we visited Tokyo. It's an amazing place. We also visited some of Raif's friends at a McCarren Japanese Macaque, snow monkey sanctuary. I stay in contact

89

with them and want to go back some day."

Too many things left on that list, Cara.

Ben stretches to see into the store. "My dad took me to the crossing when we went to Tokyo for a military conference. Can we go in now?"

I point to the signage. "What does it say?"

This time it's Rippa who responds in sync with Ben. "Fuji."

I start to ask what the name of a mountain has to do with a clothing store, but Ben has moved on and is walking through the door.

A couple of years ago, he found this guy online who has accounts on auction sites from Japan to London and insider connections to shops that cater mainly to the discerning teen and twenty-something. He charges a nominal annual subscription to suggest and shop for his clients all over the world. This store is one of his destinations.

Rippa and I follow. As we enter, the three of us are sorted, labeled, and boxed by the two young men in attendance. Rippa fares better than me. One of the young men nods at Ben but keeps his distance, and the other is drawn to Rippa's bowling shirt. I am dismissed as an escort and left to wander among the tables and carousels. I don't recognize any of the labels, and only a few of the clothes have a small logo. The prices are in Yen with a discreet translation into USD below.

One of the carousels has about a dozen dresses hanging on it. Raif took me to Paris right after we married and towed me in and out of expensive shops. He pointed out that Parisian women wore more dresses than American women for practical purposes. Homes and even some hotels didn't have air conditioning, and dresses were more comfortable than pants. I gave in and took several dresses to dress up or down from then on. I dropped out of the habit when he died.

A thirty-something Japanese man enters the small shop from the back. He is dressed head to toe and from light to dark in the same tones of purple. He, too, is enthralled with Rippa's shirt and asks to take pictures of it. Rippa obliges, then blushes when he also wants a picture of the two of them. She tries to buy a T-shirt for herself, but the young man tells her she has inspired a new line for their store in Japan and the shirt is free.

I wander to a small rack with only a half dozen pieces where I find a blouse with short sleeves split to the shoulder. It has covered buttons and a small diamond cutout on the back. Flowing pants are in a matching material. The material and pattern are intriguing. It has a heavy, silky feel with an occasional faded line running across. Silk-screened over the two pieces are sections of maps depicting different eras in Tokyo's history.

Rippa walks over and pulls the top off the rack. "This looks like you." She rubs the material between her fingers. "What's it made of?"

"World War Two parachute silk," responds a voice behind us.

I didn't hear the approach of the kid who first spoke to Rippa.

"At the end of World War Two, silk was hard to come by, but torn parachutes and mosquito netting were not. It became a thing to have wedding dresses made from them, especially in Britain. Old parachute silk is still available if you know where to look." He runs a finger over one of the pale lines. "These are the fold creases."

I'm amazed and impressed, quickly glancing at the price tag.

Not bad for a one-of-a-kind outfit with a great history, Cara.

It really isn't. I look around for a dressing room. "It's wonderful. May I try it on?"

He steps back and sizes me up. "It will fit."

I take him at his word and hand him my debit card.

****

We leave Fuji with brightly colored bags. Ben is ecstatic but has enough presence of mind to remember it's his turn to hail a cab. He points to the busy street maybe fifty feet away. "We'll have better luck there."

I start to follow, then stop short. Across the court from the shop, Kolya leans against a building. He's not trying to go unnoticed or hide. He's standing there smoking and watching.

Rippa bumps into me. "Hey." Her gaze follows mine, then recognition lights her eyes. "He's that Facebook friend of Nadya's you told us was outside Uncle Mitch's office. Kolya something. What's he doing here?"

Good question. It creeped me out when I saw him on the NYU campus. My concern was alleviated when he produced the Club Bear card, but this blatant stalking doesn't fall into the same category. My belly wobbles. "I don't like this game."

Cara, please. This kid is dangerous.

Ben turns and glances toward the young Russian. "I think we should ignore him. Just leave." He cuts his gaze to me without moving. "Or I could tell him to shove off if you want."

I shake my head. I don't want, and uncertainty vibrates from Ben. He is way out of his comfort zone but wants to make the offer as the male in the group.

Rippa brings up her chin. "Ben's right. We need to let the creep know we're not intimidated."

Not true. Especially when I see Kolya's cocky grin. Not a cute or silly grin, but one that intensifies my concern. "Stay here," I say to both of them, knowing the tall buildings around this empty court would most likely bounce back any cries for help. Hailing a cab, we'd have to walk past him. Calling the police wouldn't help either. He's just standing there.

I stop outside the teen's personal space. He's dressed all in black again. Even at this relatively safe distance, I wish my Taser was in reach. "Another invitation?" I ask.

His attention flicks past my shoulder. He's sizing up Rippa and Ben. "Pretty girl. She liked witch musical?"

Cold panic sluices into my stomach. Being on this kid's personal radar is bad enough; having him focus on Rippa is terrifying. My claws come out. "Not your business." Words forced past a half-closed throat. How does a nineteen-year-old generate this much power and fear?

He swings his flat, calculating gaze back to me. "I can make my business."

Not on my watch.

Raif and I were cutting through an alley between two busy streets in Amsterdam after an amazing dinner with lots of Spanish wine. A skinny man stepped from a doorway, his hand around something deep in his pocket. "Give me your money, or I'll shoot." Raif looked him up and down, then laughed. "If you ever had a gun, it would have been pawned long ago to feed your habit." He pulled a few euros from his money clip and held them out. "Go away, or I'll find a bully and pay him to come beat you senseless." The addict grabbed the bills and ran.

"I have lots of money," I say to Kolya, my voice sounding calmer than I feel.

A smirk twists his mouth. "Not interested in your money."

I shake my head. "It's not for you. If there are any more threats regarding me or mine, the money will go to hire someone who can make it look like a gang member was killed by a rival."

That's my girl, Raif responds.

Kolya's eyes widen slightly as comprehension, followed by a hint of respect, flashes through. "You can give me name of this someone?"

My turn to be surprised. "Why would I do that? You might see it coming."

He turns to walk away. "You are smart woman. Maybe smart as me, maybe not."

I'm light-headed, and a cold sweat makes me shiver in spite of the humid day. I can't seem to make my feet obey my brain, so I just stand there.

Rippa approaches and touches my arm. "Are you okay?"

I push out a breath. "Will be in a minute."

Ben joins us, his high spirits gone. "What did he want?"

"He didn't really say. We came to an understanding of sorts."

My niece cocks her head. "Sanity on a sliding scale

and he barely registers. Mack's not going to like this."

Yep. He already thinks I should step back and take a hard look at the more dangerous elements I'm stirring up. He may be right. Rippa's safety is way more important than my necklace. Ben's my responsibility too. I have lots to think about.

****

My energy is sapped. When we get back to the hotel, I sit cross-legged on my bed and call Mack. No answer, so I leave a voicemail, then go online to check out Club Bear. The site's amateurish with gaudy, dark photos and smoke-hazed videos. The crowd looks young and the dancing more a flinging off of a bad day than any particular style. My anxiety about sticking out because I haven't danced in a few years lessens.

A chuckle in my head. *You're still better than them, Cara.*

I pull out the dark blue card and click the edge with my thumbnail, scanning the videos for Kolya. After glimpsing his profile twice, I realize I'm hunching my shoulders and taking shallow breaths. This kid is parking in my head, and I don't like it.

My cellphone rings, washing adrenaline through me, my heartbeat galloping. It's Mack.

"Successful shopping?"

I cut a quick breath. "With a twist."

"What kind of twist?"

"Kolya was waiting for us outside the shop. I spoke to him, and he asked if Rippa liked *Wicked*."

His voice drops. "Did your driver see what was going on?"

"Um, we took a cab." I try to save myself. "Which won't happen again."

I feel the digital censure in his pause. "Is everybody okay?"

"Just a little wigged out."

"Do you think he's been sent by Kalashnikov to keep tabs on you?"

"Either that or he's bat-crap crazy and we're in his crosshairs. I'm beginning to think it's the latter."

"Not gonna say that's not possible, but let's start with the first option, Kalashnikov. Can you get away for dinner and dancing tonight?"

Glad someone's putting my nightmare into perspective. "The kids and I had an early dinner at Carnegie Deli on seventh. Don't think I can eat much for the rest of the night, but I'm up for taking a crack at Kalashnikov."

I hear a smile in his voice. "Hope that's figurative."

I smile in return. "As long as you have my back if I get a chance to talk to him."

"Done. I'll grab a sandwich and pick you up. Seven thirty?"

Chapter Eleven

The young designer at Fuji was right. My new clothes fit nicely. Mack must agree. A glint of appreciation appears in his eyes as we meet in the lobby.

"You look great."

"Thanks. I even got a thumbs up from the kids." I take a step back, observing the whiskey-colored shirt that complements his eyes, nicely faded jeans, and soft leather shoes. "You clean up good as well."

He crooks his arm. "Let's show them how it's done."

The drive to Brighton Beach is uneventful, and we pull into a lot next to a multiuse building. The lot is surprisingly well-lit, with security cameras on the building aimed at it. Half the front is a small restaurant with a plain sign in the window. It reads *The Gypsies,* stolen from the title of one of Pushkin's poems about a rowdy band of merrymakers, if I recall correctly from my one college poetry class. This must be the place Nadya's Facebook friend was asking about. Although there's no way my imagination can conjure a vision of Nadya working here.

Next to the closed eatery is the door to Club Bear. It's painted dark blue with a gold bear and what looks like a large statue standing next to it. Nope, it's just the bouncer who turns his attention as we approach.

"Fifty dollars."

I hold out the card, and his eyebrow twitches as he examines it. "Where did you get this?"

"Kolya."

He smirks and opens the door, allowing us entry. The first thing we encounter is the heavy pall of smoke. New York has a no-smoking law for public places with a few exceptions for restaurants that cater to cigar smokers. For whatever reason, that law is not upheld here.

The music's not bad, though, and helped along by a decent sound system. It's not so low that we can't dance without hearing raised voices in the background, and not so high it rattles our back teeth or causes a headache.

Remember that club in Barcelona, Cara?

I do. The flashing lights and pounding bass was enough to induce a seizure. We didn't stay long.

Mack secures a small table and orders what turn out to be very expensive and potent drinks. We're near the entrance to the dance floor, and a knot of guys stands a few feet away. At its nucleus is Kolya, making it clear he knows we're here. Inside my head, common sense says I'm in a public place and Mack's here. Nothing's going to happen. He saw Kolya right away and squeezed my hand. Outside my head I see the same unease I feel coming off in waves from the males around Kolya. I realize they aren't his friends. They are metal filaments drawn to a strong, unforgiving magnet. And young. Some of the younger gang members obviously don't qualify as old enough to be in an adult night club where liquor is served. Yet they aren't approached or carded.

No overt gestures are made toward us, and Mack and I enjoy dancing. He's very good despite the crowded conditions and the fact that we have to take gulps of smoke-laden air. After a few songs, we head back to the table, but a granite-faced guy the same size as the bouncer at the front door intercepts us. He tilts his head toward the club's entrance. "Mr. Kalashnikov would like a few minutes of your time."

Although it's what we came for, I'm not prepared for the sticky feeling of dread the invitation generates. Mack finds my hand again. "Ms. McCarren needs to get her purse." Apparently, that's to be allowed, as the large man stands where he stopped and waits for us. I glance toward the clutch of boys. Kolya is no longer there.

We're led back through the front door, and for an instant I think we're being kicked out. But the bouncer takes a hard right and uses a key to open the restaurant. We go inside, and he closes the door behind us. Visions of mobsters being bumped off in dingy New York restaurants rise unbidden. Everything looks cleaned and ready for the next day, but a fishy smell permeates the air. As we walk deeper, I notice the club's square footage seems larger than the restaurant's, but not by much. Which means some square footage behind the club has another purpose. Maybe storage, but I don't have time for conjecture as at the back we're taken down a short hallway past the restrooms to a plain brown door. My imagination and maybe a few old movies prompts me to expect a heavily jowled, sweaty man with a cigarette stuck in the corner of his mouth.

The restaurant smell doesn't follow us, but a mild fragrance of expensive cigar wafts on the air when we enter. Raif smoked one occasionally, and I can appreciate the aroma. The nicely appointed room also seems contained and quiet, like it's soundproofed. I no longer hear the thump of music. The pale-gray, windowless walls feature dark, iconic Russian art, some of which looks very old. The atmosphere might be meant to inspire ordinary, but my nerves are not calmed.

The occupant of the carved mahogany desk is another surprise. This man is slender and dressed in tailored clothes. His haircut is expensive and conservative, his hands manicured and pale.

Don't trust what you see, Cara.

No kidding.

Mack stops between me and the door. Actually, between me and the escort, who stands in front of the door.

Although I've confronted a few bad guys in my time as an investigator, nothing has ever been this personal, so that gives me some spine, and I stand a little straighter. "You wanted to see us, Mr. Kalashnikov."

"The pleasure is mine, Mrs. McCarren, Mr. Pierce." He shifts his focus to behind us. "This is my associate, Viktor Avakian. He'll remain in the room with us."

I'm not buying the "we're all friends" vibe Kalashnikov is selling.

"And you wanted to see me," the man behind the desk says. "I understand we have a common interest."

If you had my necklace stolen, we do, is on the tip of my tongue, but I bite it back. "How did you come by this *understanding*?"

"Right to the point," Kalashnikov says. "Refreshing. And very American." He lifts a hand toward the door. "People come into my restaurant; they sit, get comfortable, eat, and talk." He lifts a shoulder. "Sometimes we overhear things. Things that can be helpful in my real estate enterprises and *other* business concerns."

A big fat lie as to how he came about his information I'm thinking. "What exactly was overheard?"

"An incident in which a beautiful necklace was stolen. A sad comment on bank security these days. I, myself, trust only my own security measures."

No more real details, but our host isn't an ordinary businessman. "Which leaves us where? Do you know anything about the theft that could help me? And what will it cost?"

"Not at the moment, but I have people who can tell me if any of the rumors are viable."

"Again, what will it cost?"

His gaze flickers. The only sign of his impatience. "American women. Always in such a hurry. I'm sure if I'm able to pass on information resulting in the return of your necklace, we can come to some mutually agreeable terms."

"Terms outside the $50,000 reward leading to its recovery?"

He smiles and reminds me of a cartoon wolf. All teeth and intent. "I would think a more grateful reward would be possible if I were able to put the necklace in your hands personally."

Or, if possible, get his hands on the necklace and cut me out altogether.

I nod and start to leave but decide as long as I'm here to let him know I don't like Kolya's methods. "Part of our exchange has to include your telling Kolya Vladimirhoff to keep away from me, my niece, and our friend, Ben. Following us and making veiled threats is unacceptable. If it continues, I'll notify the police. They're already interested in him, and by extension, you. I'm sure that kind of attention wouldn't be good for your...business."

Lines tighten around his mouth. "Kolya is too impulsive in his desire to make an impression. He was not yet born when the Soviet Union divided and doesn't understand the old ways of his father are far too crude." He casts a glance at the large man behind us. "Although he's been told I don't require a gang enforcer, this is his goal. You have my word his harassment will stop. As for police interest in my business, your warning is unnecessary. I don't deal in drugs or street violence. Too messy and hard to control."

The lines around his mouth and the fact that his hands curl into fists tell me he didn't sic Kolya on us. The teen took it upon himself to do some freelance intimidation. All the more frightening.

I nod. "Thank you. You know how to reach me." He doesn't deny this, which sets my teeth on edge, just a little.

Back in control, Kalashnikov flips his hand outward, signaling the end of the discussion. "Of course."

Mack falls in behind me on our way back through the restaurant. Our escort leaves us at the sidewalk. Guess he figures the reason for our visit is over and stops to say a few words to the statue guarding the door to the club. I hope it has to do with finding Kolya and setting him straight, but I doubt it.

Mack guides me to the parking lot. My curiosity about the building's occupants leads me to the corner where I peer around. The cameras are aimed at the lot, so up next to the building should be out of range. Mack follows. Heavily curtained windows with only cracks of light sit head-high on the back wall.

I whisper, "The kids found out the fourth occupant of the building is listed as a computer training center."

He looks back toward the parking lot, then brings out a penlight. "Want to see?"

"Sure."

He clicks on the tiny beam, and we skirt a dumpster to approach the nearest window. Just enough light in the crack between the frame and the curtain reveals one of several teenage boys with headphones, probably noise-canceling since we can hear the music from the club thump from here. The boys are all focused on computer monitors.

Mack peeks inside. "Seems at odds with the other occupants."

I nod. "And I don't think they'd be here without a solid connection to Kalashnikov's little empire."

We back up and make our way carefully to the car. The door locks snick as he unlocks them remotely. I get in and put on my seatbelt, then rub my arms against a shudder.

Mack starts the car and speaks toward the windshield. "You took a chance bringing up Kolya. Kalashnikov could have decided you weren't worth the risk that he'd get a lead on your necklace, and we'd end up two unfortunate victims in the wrong place at the wrong time. Especially after that trek around the back."

"Sorry. Out of camera range, plus, I remembered Detective Pavlycheva saying how Kalashnikov tries to stay under the radar. That thing he said about Kolya not being born yet at the time of the Soviet Union's division made up my mind. Kolya's tough-guy ruthlessness doesn't fit with the businessman front Kalashnikov wants to portray. I figured that included exposure to the police. And being nosy about what else is going on in his building, well, that just comes naturally."

I'm glad Mack was with you, Cara.

Mack swings a grin toward me. "You are the most excitement I've had in a long time."

I match his grin. "Glad to oblige."

"But…"

"What?"

"We might have shot ourselves in the foot if we were seen sneaking around back by those security cameras."

I wrinkle my nose. "Guess we won't be invited back."

He nods. "About the earlier promise you made?"

I know what's coming. I have to decide if I'm still in or going home.

Chapter Twelve

"Want to go someplace and talk about it?" Mack asks as we head toward Manhattan. "I know a nice bar."

I glance at my watch. Eight thirty. "I'd like that."

It's a pleasant drive, and Mack picks up Lexington Avenue. We drive to an area that's vaguely familiar.

"Where is this place?"

He nods. "Jade Bar at the Gramercy Park Hotel."

Cara, he's trying to impress you.

Nice bar indeed. I've been there with Raif on a couple of occasions. It's very moneyed. "Any particular reason we're going *there?*"

"Sort of."

Um, a bar situated in a hotel? My heart picks up a beat. Is this *sort of,* a hint, suggestion? Can I say, "No thank you," without drooling? *Wait for it before your libido runs away with you, McCarren.* My brain is still tumbling through the possibilities as we arrive at our destination.

The two bars in this hotel are accessed on the other side of a doorman. It's pretty exclusive. A stay here does not guarantee admittance to the bar. A nod passes between Mack and the doorman. And again between him and the bartender. He's planned ahead.

The Jade Bar is an intimate space, and people tend to keep to themselves. I wait until we're seated at our small table and order drinks.

He tips his head as the server walks away. "A Rose Bar Bellini? You've been here before."

"Yes, with Raif."

His eyes widen. "Oh. Didn't mean for this to make you sad."

"I'm fine. Tell me what you think about me seeing this through." I try to look chagrinned. "We've already extended our room stay by four days. The kids want to keep digging for information."

He lifts a shoulder. "Sounds like you're leaning toward getting more involved. I might be able to help narrow your options and make it safer."

"I'm all for safer. Shoot."

"From what I heard tonight, Kalashnikov doesn't know any more than you and I. He could have asked Kolya to keep an eye on us, but he didn't send him to stalk and intimidate you."

"My take on both counts."

"Which isn't to say Kalashnikov's not very interested in acquiring Angel Falls and won't steal it given the chance. It would disappear into the Russian jewelry community immediately. Much more lucrative for him than claiming the reward and/or charging you a *finder's fee*."

Brutal, but probably true, which feels like a punch in the sternum. "I know we discussed leaving this all up to the police, but there are too many leads for them to follow right now. Shortage of manpower probably leaves the theft of my necklace somewhere near the bottom of active investigations."

He gives a slow nod. "No one knows its status. Your necklace may have been stolen and replaced months ago, which doesn't give the police much reason to put a high priority on it. I think Kalashnikov's interested because it's showed up on his radar."

Our drinks arrive, and our server leaves.

Mack leans across our table. "In any case, I figured you weren't done yet. What's your next step now that Kalashnikov says he's calling off Kolya?"

I shake my head. "I don't think we can count on that. From what I've seen, he doesn't have the control over Kolya he thinks he has, or wants us to think he has. The kid's a wild card, and it looks like once he gets something in his head, something he wants to prove, it'll take a crowbar to dislodge. He decided me and mine are Kalashnikov's target, so we're his too."

He sits back and sips his bourbon. "You may be right. You've had more interactions with him than I have, and Detective Pavlycheva's rundown sheds an ugly light. That means you'll continue to be a big part of his focus. I don't like that."

He just complimented you again, Cara.

I smile to cover my embarrassment. "I don't like it either, but I intend to be a hard-to-find target while I'm working on this."

"The main reason we're here."

I look around the bar. "Here?"

"Kolya's persistence got me thinking about your hotel rooms. They're accessible by anyone with enough cash to bribe or intimidate the right employee. And there are lots of Russians on housekeeping staffs at New York hotels. McCarren Multinational keeps two small apartments for short-term occupation by international visitors or partners. Unfortunately, one has a guest for the near future, and the other is being remodeled."

I sigh. "Raif and I had a small, one-bedroom condo with a river view. Very secure and our place to recharge before his next assignment. I miss it."

Mack nods. "I'm hoping this will be almost as good. McCarren also has a permanent, two-bedroom suite here at the Gramercy. It's available, and since I have keys to all McCarren properties, you can move in right away. If you're bent on staying in New York, might as well make you as hard to find as possible."

I like the sound of his suggestion. "Our hotel has sub-level deliveries. I can have a limo service pick us up down there. We won't even go through the lobby. By the time whoever's watching the hotel realizes we've checked out, we'll be here."

"Good plan. You work the hotel angle, and I'll put a limo on hold until you're ready." He gets the attention of the server and sweeps a hand over our glasses, indicating another round.

As pleasant as this is, I'm reluctant. "Whoa. We already had a potent drink at Club Bear. No more. Alcohol puts me to sleep."

"Then we'll order appetizers. I want to talk. Tell me about Raif and Rippa. People important to you."

How can I argue with that?

****

I'm not a night owl, but atmosphere, good alcohol, great noshes, and interesting company conspire to keep me out way past my usual bedtime. I wake to a gentle nudge from Rippa the next morning.

"Ben and I are going downstairs to eat, then to the magazine stand on the corner."

Not all my neurons are at full function, so I mumble agreement.

Sometime later, I awake again to urgent whispering between Ben and Rippa in the sitting room. I can't tell the content, but the sound conveys distress. I roll to a sitting position, my head foggy from the previous night, and call, "What's up?"

They walk slowly into the room. Ben pinches off his words. "That Kolya guy threatened Rippa."

"What!"

Rippa sends him a look of betrayal, arms crossed. "It wasn't really a threat. He was just flirting."

I have skipped the slow part of becoming fully conscious and rocket to attention, the thump in my head as fierce as the pounding of my heart. "What *exactly* happened?"

Ben crosses his arms, mirroring Rippa. "Seriously? It was so a threat. That's why I tried to drag you away."

I scrub my face with my hands. "Rippa, please. And talk slowly."

"He walked up to me when I was looking at magazines. All he said was he hoped I was enjoying New York, and he'd like to see more of me."

"Yeah. Emphasis on *more*." Ben's words stumbled. "Like, you know…"

A focused look at Rippa reveals she's mortified. And scared. A pale constellation of freckles stands out against paler skin, and she's rubbing the side of her nose. Which tells me she's distressed and downplaying the encounter.

Cold fear in the form of a sharp cramp in my stomach overrides my shock. I did this. I thought if I said something directly to Kalashnikov, Kolya's stalking would cease. How stupid. I am way above my pay grade in this, and Kolya's single-mindedness is winning…unless Kalashnikov hasn't spoken to him yet. Or has and Kolya's ignored it.

Pacing is good. I need a few seconds to wrap my head around a decision without coming off as a total control freak. I stop and rub my hands up and down my face again. "Okay, we need a new plan. This guy is unstable, and we're not going to stay within his reach. Suggestions?"

Ben doesn't hesitate. "We fly to Atlanta today, then on to Benning to visit my dad a little early. He won't mind."

A solid plan of action. Danger presents itself; get out of Dodge. Ben also has no stake, no skin in the game. No emotional tie to a piece of jewelry. Which doesn't make him a coward. Just focused on problem solving.

No response from Rippa. Her gaze scrapes Ben, then she casts it downward.

When she doesn't speak, Ben heads for the door, confident in his plan. "I'm going to pack."

My niece's silence speaks volumes.

"You okay?" I ask.

Her face color is returning to normal. "Freaked me out a little, but I'll get over it." She looks at the closed door. "You know he meant for us to drop the whole thing and retreat. You didn't so no, and that doesn't make sense." Her gaze jerks to mine. "Unless you're thinking of sending *us* to Georgia, and you stay here."

Go with them, Cara.

Busted. Was I unconsciously agreeing with Ben and making that choice, thinking Rippa and Ben would be safe? "I could join you guys when I get a few things straightened out."

The stare that needs no words.

I fold my arms. "Do you have a better plan?"

Rippa pushes her palms toward the floor. "Does there have to be a *plan*? Right now? Ben freaked out, but if we take extra precautions like using McCarren security drivers and stuff like that, I think we, at least I, could stay too."

Ben's freaked-out response to Kolya's appearance and the hangover pounding at my temples have infected my decision-making skills. I close my eyes. "Sorry. Not good enough. I'm going to make reservations and notify your mother and Colonel Brown."

Rippa is angry with me, but it's a knee-jerk anger that includes taking a swipe at me. "Have fun telling Piper you're shipping me to spend extra time on a US military base."

Yeah. Good luck. I huff a breath. "Just get packed, okay?"

The man with thousands of armed personnel at his command will be easier than my sister, so I call Ben's dad first. A number of gatekeepers later, I'm speaking to Benjamin Brown Senior. "Hello, Colonel. This is Julianne McCarren. I hope it won't be too inconvenient, but I'd like to make another change in plans and send the kids down a couple of days early."

A short pause. "I've been to New York, so I doubt that you've run out of things to do."

An astute man. "In a nutshell, a piece of valuable jewelry, my wedding gift from my husband, has been stolen. In trying to recover it, I've been exposed to an unhealthy element. I don't want that to extend to the kids."

"I see. Since you haven't mentioned you'll be with

them, I assume you're going to stay and that you have help."

A nice way of asking if I'm out of my depth. "Yes, I am and I do. The police and a security specialist are working with me."

"Then good luck."

Another offer of good luck. I wish I had more than that at my disposal.

Colonel Brown pauses. "If you run into more problems with this 'unhealthy element,' I can put you in contact with some ex-military security operatives who don't mind not playing nice."

I put a smile in my voice. "Good to know. Thank you, Colonel. I'll send the trip information as soon as I get it."

Next is Piper. It's nine here, six at home. Piper's a very early riser so she can get in some meditation. To my surprise, the call is picked up before the first ring is complete.

"Can you make it short? I'm expecting a call."

"The kids are going to Benning a couple of days early. They'll be staying on post for four days instead of two. I've run into a situation here, and it's for the best."

Heavy sigh. "You know I don't like Rippa being exposed to all that military crap."

"She's seventeen, Piper. And extremely smart. Five days at Benning will not turn her into a camo-wearing, M16-toting skinhead."

A grudging tone enters her voice. "I'll call her before I leave."

Ah. A new "save-the-world" project. "Where to?"

"West Africa. Our group received funding to install

a small desalination plant on the southern coast. Now that it's finished, the government wants to take it over."

I love Piper, but she seems to think do-gooders are invincible. "A government that no doubt has the backing of the military. Please be careful."

"Always."

"We should be home in a week to ten days."

"Okay, text me. I have to pack."

And that's my sister. Easier than I thought because she's distracted.

I'm online, checking flights to Georgia, when Rippa clears her throat. I look up.

"I think Ben should go and I should stay." She rushes the words, then holds up her hand. "I've been working with you for almost two years and fully understand what's going on here. I know it's dangerous, and that's half the battle. I'll stay in the room and do all the online research you need. I won't leave the hotel, and if I have to, I'll wear my pink wig and sunglasses. I'll even give up my bowling shirts for regular T-shirts. Please."

I don't have any words except no, and that's too weak. I stare at this younger blonde who looks very much like I did a dozen short years ago. I fall back on the only excuse I have. "I promised your mother…"

Rippa puts her hands on her hips. "Two things. First, I'm seventeen, and that's legal age in New York. I checked. So I could get a hotel room anywhere in the city if I wanted. Second, if Piper was that worried, she'd be here instead of taking off on another rescue mission somewhere."

Good points, but this is not a matter of Rippa choosing a college close to home so we can stay in touch. This is a matter of me exposing her to a total psycho. For a necklace. My mind searches for a way out that will give me the edge. I huff a breath. "You heard that. Fair enough. How about letting Mack break the tie? New York is his turf, and he has a much better handle on security than we do. I promise not to push my stance."

I see the wheels turning and realize I'm no longer going to make all the big decisions for us. And that I intend to stand by my promise, no matter how much terror it causes me if Mack's decision doesn't go my way. I also have Colonel Brown's ex-military contacts as backup.

Rippa sucks in a gulp of air and expels it. "Okay."

Chapter Thirteen

Mack is in his office when I call. I give him the short version of the situation, and he agrees to come over. I have time to take a shower but hate how fresh he looks when he arrives. I haven't had a real hangover in years and feel like five miles of bad road. He's holding a greasy bag of fast food that looks at odds with his GQ suit.

A cool rinse in the shower didn't help much, and I peer at him with puffy eyes. "You didn't have to dress up."

He grins. "Department head meeting. I hate 'em. Besides, a McCarren with a security problem trumps all else. So here I am." He notices the half-packed suitcase on Rippa's bed. "Your problem with Kolya?"

I open the door to Ben's knock. He has his carryon in hand.

"What time are we leaving?"

"Yes" to Mack, then "schedule on hold" to Ben, who looks crestfallen.

"As I said on the phone, Rippa and Ben were approached by Kolya this morning near the hotel. Ben considers it a threat, but Rippa isn't so sure. I don't want to take any chances."

Mack takes in Ben's duffel. "Are we putting last night's plan into action?"

Well, three kinds of hell. Between my hangover

and focus on keeping Rippa safe, I've forgotten about the Gramercy Park Hotel option.

Rippa gives me a squinty eye. "What plan?"

"In a minute," I say. "Please tell Mack what happened."

Chin up, she tells about Kolya coming up to her and Ben. She glosses over the young Russian's comment.

I turn to Mack. "We can't be sure whether Kalashnikov already talked to Kolya, but if he did, I'm supposing the kid blew it off."

"What do you need from me?" Mack asks.

"Instead of sending the kids to visit Ben's dad at Fort Benning in a couple of days, I bumped it up to today. Rippa wants to stay here."

Mack looks confused. "Wouldn't take any chances where she's concerned, but how am I involved?"

"Jules doesn't think it's safe. She said you're the expert and we'd let you decide." From Rippa, with an edge of stubbornness. "I agreed."

I wasn't there to hear Kolya. Doesn't matter. Mack is the best I can do. "Sorry to ambush you, but I told Rippa since you were local and more aware of the dangers, you could explain better than me why her staying was a bad idea."

Even as I say it, it sounds lame. If I knew another girl her age, with her smarts and promise to be responsible, would I push this hard?

"In the hotel," Rippa amends. "I'd stay in the room and do online research."

"My vote's with Julianne."

I've almost forgotten Ben's in the room. We turn to see the very definition of a truculent teen—hard stare, arms crossed, shoulders pushed forward.

Rippa returns the stare, but her chin buckles for an instant, revealing her feelings toward the treason. "Thanks a lot."

"This trip was supposed to be a graduation present." Ben's gaze skips to a spot over my shoulder, then he ducks his head. "Sorry. I know that necklace is important."

"No need for apologies. You're right."

"Jules kept her promise on all the stuff she said we'd do, so stop being a whiner," Rippa shoots. "Things have changed, that's all."

Mack makes a slicing motion with his hand. "In the interest of getting everybody moving, what does each of you want? Julianne?"

"Honestly? I want to stay in New York to narrow down the leads or find my necklace, but that comes second to seeing the kids safe."

"Rippa?"

Chin high. "I want to stay too. I'm perfectly capable of staying within the boundaries I promised."

"Ben?"

Heavy sigh. "I guess what I want most is to spend time with my dad. And that Julianne and Rippa are safe."

"Done," Mack says to Ben. "You okay with their decisions, then?"

Ben nods, and Mack faces Rippa. "Your aunt's right. This is not a decision to be made to prove a point. Gang activity is vicious. Lives are not negotiable, and the only things they care about are profit and power. They're looking for the same thing we are, but they won't pull punches or cut breaks because you're an innocent tourist. Nobody who comes up against them is not afraid. Scared yet?"

Rippa doesn't hesitate. "Yes. I get it." She turns to me, her stance fractionally taller. "Leave out emotions and relations. Do you think I have enough common sense to make the right decision if something bad starts to happen?"

Trying to be fair with the love I have for my niece falls squarely on my pounding head. "No question. But that isn't the issue. If something bad started to happen, it would be common sense against weapons or brute force. You don't have either."

Her chin starts to fold again.

I turn to the two males. "Can we have a few minutes, guys?"

Mack tips his head toward Ben. "We'll be next door."

"You didn't even ask him to be the tiebreaker," Rippa accuses. "You just wanted him to scare me."

I wish I could hug her but keep my distance. "That wasn't my intention."

She doesn't look completely convinced, but her shoulders ease a little. "Maybe not."

"Until we're on safer ground, what compromise do you think we could both live with?"

A small nod. "To begin, I think two or three more days isn't unreasonable." She holds up an index finger. "Hotel chains aren't very safe. If we somehow sneak out of here and move to a different place, that would lessen the danger, right? We could even check in under Parkes instead of McCarren. There are a gazillion other places we could rent that would take Kolya a couple of days to find. By then I'd be on my way to Benning.

Besides," she says, waving a hand between us, "two Parkes women can certainly outsmart one wackadoodle Russian."

I feel a smile tilt the corners of my mouth. Is she sharp or what? As much as it rings my cautious bell, two or three days really isn't too much to ask. Especially since she's come up with an improvement on the plan already in play. "That's more or less what Mack and I came up with last night. You're in, but only under tight ground rules."

Raif jumps in. *The first being, don't hang out with bears.*

All negativity disappears as Rippa nods like a bobblehead. "When we get back home, we can continue discussing my helping out more on your cases."

Um, apparently in my hangover state, I missed agreeing to that. "Back to the ground rules. You, I, and Mack are leaving from the hotel's underground delivery level by limo. We're going to a luxury hotel in a gated community. It's high security, low profile, and big money where a Russian gang member would definitely stand out."

"Why would you hire a limo when the McCarren company car is...? Oh, I get it. Kolya or one of his buddies already knows what they look like."

A tap at the door. "You guys work things out?" Mack asks.

"Come in. Yes. Rippa will be staying the extra days. Under strict rules," I amend as I feel Rippa practically vibrating with excitement. "And why are you carrying fast food?"

Mack looks down as if remembering the sack. "Two greasy burgers and fries for your hangover."

My gorge starts to rise, and I feel as green as I probably look. "You're kidding."

"Best medicine for a hangover I know of. The fats help soak up any leftover alcohol in your system. And I feel responsible since I encouraged you to stay and talk."

I reach for the bag, trying for a smile. "I don't remember you forcing me. Hope this works. If not, I'm going to go all Veronique on you."

He hands it over, grinning. "Almost guaranteed. If it doesn't work, you won't have the energy. I win either way."

I've heard of this cure, Cara. He's trying to help.

"Am I still going today?" Ben asks quietly.

I look at the upset teen. "Yes. As soon as I can book the flight. Your dad's looking forward to it."

At the mention of his dad, Ben cheers but takes advantage of me feeling sorry for him. "Can I fly first class?"

An eye roll pinches at my hangover, so I settle for a slight nod. "If there is a seat available at this short notice, it's yours."

Fifteen minutes later he's booked on a flight to Savannah, with an hour layover, then on to Atlanta where the colonel will have a car waiting.

I glance around the semi-messy common room. "Can you get Ben safely to the airport while Rippa and I wrap up things here?"

Mack cuts a side glance at Ben. "Baseball hat and sunglasses?"

This elicits a grin from Ben.

"I'll call one of my guys to pick him up at the side entrance and escort him to his gate at the airport. Have him hang around until Ben's flight leaves. That okay?"

I try to give Ben a stern look. "Promise not to leave the airport in Savannah?"

He gives me a cheeky smirk. "Not even to fly to Atlanta?"

I step over and give him a hug. "Go with Mack and call or text us when you get to Benning."

Ben offers a two-finger salute. "See you in a couple days."

Rippa stands in the middle of the room as I turn from the door. "Thanks for working that out in my favor."

"Fair's fair. You had some good points, and I tend to be a little overprotective."

Rippa's shoulders relax. "Just a little?"

I nod, with a mouth full of hamburger.

Chapter Fourteen

Mack knocks a half hour later, a grin lighting his face. "I spoke to the concierge about your security issue. She agreed to check you out a half hour after you leave, and kept saying it was like when she arranged a secret escape for a boy band last year."

"Thanks. Did Ben get off okay?"

His grin is still in place. "Wasn't too hard to spot the teen gang member watching the side entrance. I pulled out my cellphone and took his picture. Over and over, from all angles. He started toward me, then changed his mind and walked away, looking over his shoulder. Ben saw the opportunity and slipped into the car. Clean getaway."

My optimism hikes. "Great distraction. I'll have to keep it in mind."

Rippa and I grab our bags, and Mack escorts us to the hotel delivery bay. The employees in this part of the sublevel give us curious stares. Especially when the white limo with darkened windows arrives.

Rippa is in a high state of excitement. "This is so cool," she declares, wearing the T-shirt she got at Fuji, sunglasses, and a baseball hat.

The limo driver is a very pretty young woman, with an amazing mass of curls. Her accent likely places her from Georgia, USA, rather than Georgia, previously of the USSR. A random association I make since

Russians are on my mind. Mack and I touched on the subject of our next steps last night, but I intend to wait until we're at the hotel and have some privacy before reviving it.

We arrive at the hotel, and Rippa scrunches her face at the tall façade. "Old."

Mack laughs. "Very. It went through a gut-job in 2003 and 2004. It's considered Boho-eclectic chic."

I shake my head. "Which means a little bit of everything."

Rippa leaves her sunglasses on as we pass the hotel reception desk and go straight to the elevator. We ride up a dozen floors and arrive at a quiet hallway. Mack lets us into the suite and hands me the single key.

The room is over the top. Heavy velvets, linens, and silks in jewel tones of green and red grace the furniture and bedding. The French slipper chairs look like real antiques and too dainty to sit on. Rippa bounces into the en-suite bathroom. "So retro."

Mack checks out the slipper chairs and opts instead for a deep-red velvet padded number. Since we left the Hilton, he's taken off his tie and suit jacket, looking more comfortable. "Where to? We haven't talked to Nadya or had a follow-up with Ian."

I'm more comfortable too. My headache has subsided, but I'm still parched. "And Veronique still has some explaining to do about borrowing Angel Falls without my permission."

Good luck. She's a chronic liar, Cara.

The lines fanning from his eyes deepen. "Does this have to do with poking your sister-in-law, or do you honestly think it'll help the investigation?"

I'm flattered but disconcerted that he's able to pick

up on my intentions so easily. "Both."

He holds out his hands, palms up. "Okay. Who first?"

"Ian. Thought it through last night and changed my mind about giving him more time. The connection, weird as it seems, makes sense. Bank vault escort, to fiancé, to fiancé's sister, to her boss with a key to my safety deposit box."

His poker face fades as his mouth turns down at the corners. "*Or* obsessed sister-in-law."

I puff out a breath. "I feel for Ian too, but he's high on my list, and I want to eliminate him first. Veronique's not going anywhere."

He nods. "He could be a flight risk."

I reach for my wallet. "He wrote his number and address on the back of his manager's card. What do you think about just showing up and surprising him?"

"That's one way. If he opens the door."

I wouldn't blame him if he didn't. When I lost Raif, I pushed everyone away, let alone strangers. I sigh. "He did give us permission to recontact him."

"Don't think that included an ambush, but it *will* give him less time to think up a good story."

Rippa leaves the bathroom. "Can I have the room with the most red?"

Outside a view of the upscale neighborhood calms me a little, but I still worry. "Sure. But keep the drapes drawn."

She cuts a gaze to the window, then back to the laptop that has magically appeared as an appendage to her hand. "Got it. Anything I need to research?"

"Find out what you can on Ian Ward. He's the bank escort who had access to the safety deposit vault and ties to Nadya."

Rippa sits at the pretty vintage desk and fires up her sleek machine. "Common last name. A middle name would help."

Mack pipes up. "Leslie. He lives on Greenwich in Tribeca."

I'm impressed, as I haven't shared the information on the card with him. "And you know this how?"

"I peeked when he wrote it down at the bank. The address he gave is very exclusive. One bedroom, one bath starts at four point five million. I emailed his Ms. Barrick to verify. She attached a copy of his employment application when she responded. His social and most of his personal information was blacked out, but he hadn't changed his beneficiary yet. Timur was his primary, his father, second."

Rippa gapes, stuck on the pricey address. "Four and a half million for one bedroom and one bathroom? Geez!"

My own eyebrows settle to a normal level. "See if you can solve the mystery of how a bank clerk can afford that."

"On it." Rippa rattles off her email address. "Mack, will you forward me that email?"

He pulls out his phone. "On its way."

Rippa scans a nearby tabletop. "Do they have room service here?"

Okay, whiplash change of subject. "No idea, but I'm sure they can come up with something." My turn to look around. I find the mini-fridge and grab two bottles of mineral water. "And make sure they leave it outside the door."

I receive a wrinkled nose and nod for my

cautionary warning. Which I ignore. "Want anything, Mack?"

"No, thanks." He eyes the water. "How's the stomach?"

I concentrate for a couple seconds. "Better. I'll have to remember greasy food for my next hangover."

He stands. "Glad to hear it. Ready to go?"

I walk to the windows and pull the drapes partially closed. Rippa cuts me a gaze full of pity, which I deserve since we're so high, but my love for her and keeping her safe over trusting anyone else rears its ugly head. I shoot her an apologetic look.

She favors me with an adult nod of understanding.

Mack calls his driver on the way down, and when we reach the street, she's waiting for us. We take Broadway through the East Village, a colorful, almost-aging hipster area trying to survive gentrification.

Ian's apartment is in a big, square brick building. We turn the corner onto Greenwich. There stands our quarry in a shouting match with another person on our list. Nadya. She is getting the worst of it. The driver pulls to the curb.

Mack and I open our windows. We don't have to get close to hear them.

"You killed him," Ian yells, his head straining forward. "Just as if you were driving the car. I hate you, and I hope you die too."

"Stop it," Nadya yells back, shoving his shoulder. "He's gone, and there's nothing we can do about it. We have to deal with what they know. They know it isn't only me, so you have to do this. I don't care how much you hate me."

Ian shakes his fist in her face. "You made the deal

that got my Timur killed, you cold-hearted bitch. I loved him. I would trade your useless life for his in an instant. If hanging you out to dry puts both of us in danger, I. Don't. Care."

Tears stream down Ian's face. Watching his anguish is heartbreaking. People who have never experienced losing someone they loved more than life have no clue how long it takes to stop the guilt of still being alive. And alone.

Nadya crosses her arms. "I am going to tell them everything. I want to come back here and have a good life. I can't do that looking behind me all the time. You're going to help so I can get my share. Otherwise you'll end up as dead as Timur."

She never sees it coming. The sound of Ian slapping her bounces off the glass and brick of the building. Mack shoves out his door, and I'm a close second.

He takes half the number of steps I need to reach them. "Ian, Nadya, that's enough."

Nadya whirls, her hand to her face. "Who the hell are you?" Her glare finds me next. "What are you doing here?"

Ian steps back and dabs his eyes with the sleeve of his shirt. "I'm not sorry."

Nadya's mouth works, her jaw knotted. "I don't understand why you are here, but this is private conversation." Her glance scales Mack from head to toe. "Are you police?"

"Macklin Pierce. Head of security for McCarren Multinational."

Nadya's face takes on coyness in spite of the red handprint on her cheek. "You work for Mitch

McCarren?"

"Not directly." He tips his head toward me. "Ms. McCarren and I are investigating the theft of her diamond necklace."

The handprint is even more pronounced as the blood drains from Nadya's face. "I know nothing about this."

Of course not.

"I understand you're returning to Russia soon," I say, as Nadya's coyness segues into slyness. Hasn't anyone ever told this girl about holding a poker face?

"Yes, I am. Timur was going to help me pay for the ticket, but all his money was in joint checking account with Ian. That is discussion we are having when you interrupt. Ian refuses to help me." She cuts him a sharp look, clicking her gold bracelets together.

The lie is so transparent I almost giggle.

"Liar!" From Ian. "Get out of my sight."

"We aren't done," she spits, then turns to leave.

I touch her arm. "As Mr. Pierce said, we're investigating the theft of my necklace. We'd like to interview you."

The clicking of her bracelets escalates. "And as I said, I know nothing about this."

Residual pain from my hangover and getting lied to at every turn has taken its toll. I'm done with this selfish girl. "The McCarren name has political ties that reach the state department. Reentry into the US could become complicated."

Threaten her with Veronique. Nadya's more afraid of her, Cara.

I hold up a hand as she starts to speak. "A complication Mitch would be unable to help you with.

I'd see to it."

My blackmail attempt works.

Nadya lifts a shoulder. "I will talk to you, but you are wasting your time. I don't even know this necklace." She steps close to Mack. "If you have pencil, I will write down my address for you."

"Already have it," Mack says with a half smile. "We'll be in touch."

Clearly annoyed her charms didn't work on a handsome man, Nadya turns and totters off on deadly heels.

Chapter Fifteen

Ian stands with shoulders rounded, still crying. I wonder if we'll get any worthwhile information, but Mack's earlier assertion that the young escort could be a flight risk is more credible in light of his expensive address. Nothing to stop him from hopping on a plane to anywhere.

I clamp my teeth. I've been where Ian is. Still am sometimes when a memory surfaces and makes Raif's death fresh again. I pull Mack to one side. "He's so overwhelmed I think it would be better if I interviewed him alone. Do you mind?"

For the second time in an hour, I get a look of adult understanding. He tips his head toward the limo. "I'll be in the car."

The weather is trying to be summer but can't live up to the name. It's warmish enough so I won't feel guilty that Mack and the driver are waiting outside, though. I offer Ian my arm, and we walk to his building entrance.

His apartment is small and decorated in expensive pieces of mid-century modern. I got a crash course in that style when Raif and I stayed with a friend of his in Copenhagen. Frederik was obsessed with it. I recognize an Eames chair, a low, boxy sofa that echoes Mies van der Rohe design, and an oval coffee table with very slender legs. A few dark, Russian iconic pieces painted on wood are hanging on one wall, reminiscent of the ones in Kalashnikov's office. They look genuine. My gaze travels to Ian. "You have some very nice furnishings."

Ian follows my line of sight. "Those are—were— for Timur." He waves a hand. "Excuse me."

The first-floor living room windows offer no view, so I wander around. Its mantel holds what looks like a shrine to Timur—a red-and-black checkered cap, two fat pillar candles, and a handsome brushed silver urn with Timur's name inscribed. It's almost too personal to look at, so I move to the middle of the room and wait for Ian.

He appears more composed when he comes back. "Can I get you some coffee or tea?"

"I'm fine," I say, having decided on the tack I will take with him. "Nadya could charge you with assault for what just happened."

He lifts a shoulder. "She won't."

My opening salvo to gain his confidence has failed. I don't want to reveal personal feelings to a near stranger, but I will. "Tell me about Timur."

Damp eyelashes threaten tears again, but he holds them in check. "Why?"

"Because I'd like to know about him and because memories are important."

He crosses the room and picks up a small framed picture, bringing it to show me. In it he is smiling broadly, arms around a handsome, dark-haired man who grins into the camera. If I squint, I can see the resemblance to Nadya.

"This is Timur. We met a half year ago at the birthday party of a friend, held in a club." He runs a finger across the glass. "He had the best smile. We loved our time together on the island."

"And when he died, you lost a piece of your soul."

He holds my gaze. "Yes."

He is so bereft; he radiates the pain of loss. Is my necklace worth prodding his grief?

Don't beat yourself up, Cara. The necklace is just a symbol.

It's more than that. I can remember standing in our hotel suite here in New York. Since I said yes to his proposal two days before, Raif had put the wheels in motion. We'd appeared in the city clerk's office first thing the day before with the required documents— mine overnighted from my sister—filled out the application, and the twenty-four-hour wait was over. Raif pulled this unbelievably stunning, blue-and-white diamond necklace out of a velvet bag and leaned close, slipping it around my neck. "This was a wedding gift from my father to my mother. Now it's mine to give to you."

I thought my friend Jilly, my maid of honor, would faint.

Ian clears his throat, interrupting my reverie. "Your husband?"

I nod, amazed that my feelings of sharp distress are less than since this whole mess started. Or maybe Ian's are stronger.

He puts a gentle hand on my forearm. "You should have your necklace. Your husband and my Timur are gone, but we have things to remember them by." He pulls a thin gold chain from under his shirt. A gold band and the letter T hang on it. He rubs his thumb across the ring. "It's not a diamond necklace, but it means the same."

I put my hand over his. "It does. Ian, is there a family member or friend who can stay with you? At least for a while?"

He looks exhausted. "My sister was here for a couple of days but had to leave. I have friends asking to come over."

"Good. Take them up on their offer. Do you have a few more minutes?"

He nods and perches on the edge of the couch.

I can only hope he'll be straight with me. "Thanks. Mr. Pierce and I can only think someone at the bank was paid to help steal the original, have a copy made, and put the copy in its place. Can you think of anyone who could have done that?"

He holds out his hands, palms up. "Bank personnel are notoriously underpaid. One of the two other escorts is expecting. She and her husband are desperate for a bigger place. The security guy for our floor has huge college debts and is still getting his degree. Ms. Barrick is a single mother whose little girl has some nasty disease whose only hope is a trip to Switzerland to be included in a possible cure under research, for an outrageous amount of money. Take your pick."

Almost sorry I asked. A rich girl getting all bent about the theft of her diamond necklace sounds pathetic compared to others' needs. I tip my head to indicate our surroundings. "Obviously, you don't need money."

"Annuity baby," he admits.

"How about circumstances other than a bribe, like somebody hacking the security system at the bank?"

He shakes his head. "The system is custom programmed by a guy who used to work at the DOD. It has all kinds of fail-safes." His eyes roll up and to the right. "The digital photo system broke recently. No one's picture was taken entering or leaving the vault for a half day. Only two people signed in that afternoon."

Not helping. And he's looking everywhere but directly at me. "Any other ideas?"

Dried-eyed anger resurfaces. "I heard you say you're going to interview Nadya. That's a step in the right direction."

"Because…?"

He closes his eyes and lowers his head. "Because she approached us about the necklace with some dramatic story about bloodthirsty Russian gangsters killing Timur and her if we didn't help. I believed her, but Timur got angry. He told her he would go to the police if she tried to steal your necklace."

I can't think of a single thing to say, but Ian raises his gaze. "I didn't help her, and Timur died. And your necklace was stolen. No way to prove any of this. Nadya's a greedy, sociopathic liar. Emphasis on greedy. She claims she's going home to Moscow, but that's not true. Her parents brought her and Timur up in an industrial city in central Russia called Yekaterinburg. Her father works in the public service division on the line that builds garbage trucks in Kalinin Machine Building Works. She never even saw Moscow until she was seventeen.

"Timur told me Nadya planned to go back, allow her parents to throw her a big celebration, accept the money they set aside to help her get settled there, then come back here. She plans to find a rich husband or lover who'll support her. Your brother-in-law proved to her the plan would work." He hangs his head. "Timur's death won't change anything."

Greedy bloodsucker. A new nickname for Nadya.

His cathartic monologue is good information that I can pass on to Detective Pavlycheva, but he's right about proving anything. "If you didn't help her, what does all this have to do with my stolen necklace?"

He brings his head back up, naked hatred on his face. "About five months ago, Nadya started going to Russian clubs. Hangouts for gang members. She told Timur she wasn't going to live in a dirty city and marry some man who came home smelling like oil with grease under his fingernails like their father. Timur reminded her of the sacrifices he had made to send them to the US for an education. She laughed and said that education had taught her living the wealthy life was what she was made for and that she was working on a plan to get that for herself."

"And you think Nadya is getting a head start on her rich life by stealing my necklace for the Russian gang leader?"

"Oversimplified, but yes, based on everything she tried to set in motion, I do think she's involved."

"That may be true, but it's a big leap from being a greedy woman to the mastermind who overcomes a custom-programmed bank security system."

He rubs two fingers up and down the center of his forehead. "Nadya uses people. You heard her say 'they' were a threat to us. Ask her who 'they' are. Or maybe she used her lover the professor to take the necklace and have a duplicate made. When she sets her mind on getting something, nobody and nothing is out of bounds. I think she stepped in it this time, though."

I hope Mitch wasn't this stupid, Cara.

That Nadya could have influenced Mitch to the point where he didn't just allow her access to the safety deposit box keys but may have helped her steal Angel Falls and have a duplicate made has never occurred to me. Before now.

"One more thing, if you don't mind."

Ian shakes his head.

"It sounds as if Timur was killed only a couple of days after Nadya demanded your help under threat from the Russian gang. Why would they kill the one leverage they had to make you do as they wanted? That doesn't make sense."

He clasps his hand over the ring and T hanging from his necklace. "When Nadya first demanded my help in taking your necklace, Timur and I laughed her off. Russian gangsters? Blackmail? She made it sound like a plot from a 'B' movie." He wipes his eyes with the back of his hand, and my heart hurts for him.

"What changed?"

"The first accident."

News to me. "First accident?"

He nods. "Timur was good at his job. Really good. He was one of his company's most requested messengers. The day after Nadya threatened us, Timur got *doored*. Bad."

"I don't know what that means."

"The messengers ride in between the cars in traffic, right?"

I'm beginning to get the picture. "Yes."

"They stay away from cars in the curb lanes. Somebody might swing a door outward, and the messenger, going at a pretty good clip, would run into it. So they keep to the center lanes as much as possible.

He was in the center lane, coming up on a land yacht, something big from the sixties, when the back door swung open. Clocked him good. He hit his head and shoulder, knocking him out. The car left the scene." His voice turns hoarse. "Timur wrote it off as the cost of the job, but it scared the hell out of me. I was convinced he was in danger, but he wouldn't let me contact Nadya. Two days later, he was gone."

I stroke his upper arm. "Thank you. Please let me know if you want to talk. I'm staying at a hotel in Manhattan for a while. If we run into any roadblocks you might be able to help with, may I contact you again?"

Ian nods, and as much as I would like to stay, I give him a tight hug and leave.

Mack is standing outside the car when I return. He studies me for a moment. "You okay? You look like you had a rough time in there."

I huff a breath. Rippa, too, can always tell when my emotions ride close to the surface. "Not at my best when I'm talking about the death of a loved one. Did better than I thought I would, though."

He gives me a look of sympathy. "That's good. Anything new?"

I take in the car. "Can we walk for a block or two?"

He leans into the car window, speaks to the driver, then turns to me. "Of course."

The weather and my emotional state combine to make my skin clammy. I slide my hands down the front of my navy cotton crops and answer Mack's question. "Couple things that may or may not pertain. In addition to laying it on thick about Nadya being the guilty party, he reminded me of her reference to 'they' being dangerous if not getting their way. As for Timur's death that Ian claims wasn't an accident, he says a few days prior, Timur got 'doored' by a land yacht."

He sucks air through his teeth. "Ouch. Like riding full speed into a wall." He tilts his head. "The accident report on Timur's death had one witness. An older man who said Timur was hit by Detroit Iron."

My grandfather loved his late sixties Pontiac. He showed me the model once, and the thought of getting hit and dragged by a behemoth like that makes my stomach lurch. "Ian didn't say so, but it'd make sense to use the same heavy car both times."

Mack's cellphone rings. He glances at the readout. "Overseas. I need a minute."

I forget he's the head of a multinational security team and not at my beck and call. I nod.

He takes a literal minute while I look around at this microcosm of lower Manhattan. He finishes his call. "It's really tough what Ian's going through, but unless Nadya or someone else who had access to your box also had the bank's vault master key, they had to have help."

"True, but if Ian had a role in the theft, it's totally subsumed by his grief and hatred of Nadya right now."

"Then we come back at him another time?"

"Yeah. One more time ought to do it." I brighten. "But first, Veronique and Mitch."

He grins. "Both of them in the same room?"

"The only way. I'm going to play to her fear of bad publicity making her a pariah in her social circle and his fear of losing his position because of relations with a student. I'm tired of waiting."

He pulls back. "Why didn't we start with that?"

You are too softhearted, Cara.

Heavy sigh from me. "Because they're family and even though we're not close..."

"Their loss. But I get it."

I punch Mitch's number into my phone. "Thanks. By the way, are there still cellphone transmission holes on the West Side Highway?"

Mack's eyebrows take wing as he nods.

Mitch picks up on the second ring. "You still in New York?"

Abrupt, but not unfriendly. "Yes. I'd like to meet with you and Veronique at your townhouse this evening to talk about the progress Mack and I are having in locating my necklace."

"Oh. I might be able to spare some time, but I think Veronique's busy. She's very social. Can't you just tell me over the phone?"

"Seven o'clock. Tell Veronique that unless she wants her social invites to dry up, she needs to be there."

A pause. "I don't understand the hostility, Julianne."

"Think of it as finishing the conversation we started several days ago. This time, I'd like real answers."

"I was under the impression..."

I keep talking as I slowly pull the phone away from my mouth. "Hitting the West Side Highway, Mitch. Losing reception. See you at seven." *Click.*

Mack's shoulders shake as he tries to hide his laugh. "I know this is serious, but that was awesome."

"Glad you think so. I'll tell you how it turns out."

He stops laughing. "You're kicking me to the curb? Why?"

"Because as shallow as they both seem, if there's a backlash, and I know Veronique is capable of creating one, I don't want you involved. Let's keep it at that."

"I appreciate the thought. But aren't you going to hold them in place with blackmail of sorts?"

"Yes, but I'm a McCarren, and as much as Veronique hates it, I own the same amount of stock as they do. Using her position to screw with you would be her prize for not being able to get to me."

He pulls my hand to his mouth and kisses it. "You're cute when you get all vengeful."

Warmth spreads toward my toes, and on its way, my stomach growls. "How about lunch? My treat."

"So far, you've bragged about New York Italian and deli. I know you've had Chinese. Want to try seafood?"

I start to salivate. "Lobster?"

"I know just the place. Ed's."

He keeps looking for ways to impress you, Cara.

****

I give Mack some more salient points to my discussion with Ian as we walk to the car and get in. It's a half hour drive, but greasy burger and fries notwithstanding, I'm more than ready to eat when we arrive.

I am halfway out of the car when Mack reaches into the pocket on the back of the front passenger seat and pulls out a manila folder.

"What's that?" I ask as he rounds the front fender.

He taps the cover. "Susan Pavlycheva had this sent to my office. It's the copy of the accident report she promised."

The lunch crush is over, so we're seated and served

right away. My stomach demands attention first, so I comply. After we finish, Mack flips open the folder.

"Have you read it?" I ask.

"Yeah. Pretty spare on details. The witness didn't see the actual impact, but he did get the plate number and description of the car."

I cringe at the word impact. "Have the owner and witness been contacted?"

He skims the page. "A Mrs. Greenspan is the owner. And no. She was out of town when they tried, but that was right after Timur was killed. The witness, a Mr. Perryman, was interviewed at the scene, but hasn't been since the 'accidental death' determination was questioned. It's been changed to 'undetermined.' "

He hands me the report, and I open it to the scaled drawing. Even with the dry details and spare representations of people and the vehicle involved, it forms a cold knot in my stomach, overriding the pleasant fullness.

"You okay?" Mack asks.

I huff out a breath and shiver. "Makes me sad and angry at the same time. Timur, by Ian's account anyway, was a hardworking, honest man, looking forward to a happy life. Nothing left but a colorless report and an inscribed silver urn containing his ashes."

He reaches to pat my hand and close the report. "Sounds like you care as much about finding Timur's killer as finding your necklace."

I relax. "Maybe that's more important." I glance at my watch. "It's only one. Can we get to both interviews before I go back to the hotel?"

The waitperson slides a small hot fudge sundae in front of me. I rub my hands together, and Mack laughs.

"I'll verify with Bret that it's okay and make the calls while you check in with Rippa."

Chapter Sixteen

In front of the restaurant, I'm ready for a nap after the fabulous lobster roll. I can't hide my yawn from Mack.

He smiles. "You sure you're up to taking on a couple of senior citizen households?"

"Yes, smart ass. Just not used to the night life. If this was a hike up one of the tougher trails on Mt. Rainier, betcha I'd come out ahead."

He holds up his hands in surrender. "No contest."

He pulls out his cellphone, and I pull out mine. I learn Rippa had a continental breakfast and is deep in her research. Ben's flight to Savannah hasn't landed yet, but she's keeping tabs on the time. Can I bring some dark chocolate back? I text *Good* on all counts.

Mack is waiting for me to hang up. "News and interesting news. Bret says we're okay on the interviews. Mrs. Greenspan will be available when we get there. Mr. Perryman's also agreed to a second interview this afternoon."

"What's the interesting news?"

"Voicemail from the concierge at your former hotel. A half hour ago a teenage boy brought in a bouquet of flowers claiming they had to be delivered in person. He was very upset to learn you'd checked out."

A skitter of cold rides my arms, leaving goose bumps in its wake. "Guess we made the right decision in moving, although the hotel wouldn't have given out my room number anyway."

He nods. "The Gramercy is even more discreet. None of the household staff knows you except for the surname Parkes."

We get into the car for the trip to an older Manhattan neighborhood.

"Works for me. Are the apartment buildings for the Greenspan and Perryman residences close together?"

"Good guess. Similar neighborhoods about six blocks apart. We'll try Mrs. Greenspan first. Be there in about twenty minutes."

I wake with a start when the driver turns the car off.

"She tried not to hit any potholes," Mack says. "Luckily, your snoring kept her alert."

A chuckle erupts inside my head. *Told you you snored, Cara.*

I turn toward my door and surreptitiously check my chin for drool. "Very funny."

****

The outside of the building that houses Frieda Greenspan's apartment is brick and old but well-maintained. Iron fire escapes scale the sides. We arrive with only a couple of minutes to spare.

Inside, the vintage cage elevator gasps and squeaks as if ready to expire. I step onto the metal floor and clutch one of the cast-iron side bars casually, hoping Mack doesn't notice.

He stares straight ahead. "Death defying."

I don't bother turning around. "We are taking the stairs down."

"Octogenarians use this every day."

"Shut. Up."

We disembark onto a time-tunnel hallway with a patch of weak light at the end. It is provided by a window that probably has a painted-in-place frame. No air-conditioning cools the space, and the color of the dust-embedded carpet is barely discernable by the low-wattage sconces.

As we get closer to apartment 312, a wizened female face appears at a crack in the doorway of 311. She steps out to meet us. "I'm Rose Nieman, Frieda's neighbor and friend. Today, I'm the lookout. We're single, so we have a pact. Our own neighborhood watch." She grins, displaying perfect porcelain. "She also said I could sit in on the interrogation."

Rose's eagerness to catch any conversation train to push back the boredom of her days pings a sad thought that's been nagging at me since Rippa started her senior year. *Will this be me in fifty years?*

Mack smiles at Rose Nieman. "Of course. But it's hardly an interrogation. Besides, I forgot my harsh light and billy club."

"Now you're just kidding, cutie. Hope you didn't forget some ID."

I exchange a glance with Mack. He maintains a sober expression. Outfoxed by a security-conscious oldster, we both produce identification. Although I at least wonder what she would do if we were intent on doing harm.

Rose inspects our photos and nods.

Mrs. Greenspan's door opens to Mack's light knock, and she lets the three of us in, accepting a head bob from Rose. Possibly a pre-arranged acceptance of our genuineness. The room smells like chocolate baked goods and jasmine tea. Our hostess steers us to comfortable chairs. A Bundt cake and teapot occupy the table in the small living room. Frieda Greenspan is clearly taking the opportunity to entertain.

Where Rose Nieman is small and slight with rigid posture, Frieda is fleshy and has a dowager hump. Her fingers rub against her palms. "Where are my manners? Let me get you two a slice of cake and some tea before it cools."

Mack looks solemn. "A shame to cut such a beautiful cake. However, you talked me into it."

Our hostess beams.

The hot fudge sundae of a half hour ago haunts me, and I send hope into the ether that she will cut me a small piece. "Very kind of you. May I help serve?"

Rose Nieman hops up like a small bird and reaches for the teapot. "I got this."

Mack spreads a real cloth napkin Mrs. Greenspan has provided across his lap. "Thank you for seeing us."

Our hostess passes slices of cake around, and my luck has run out as I look on the size provided. I let out a lobster-tinged breath. "Could I possibly have this cut in half? My niece, back at the hotel, is a big fan of chocolate, and I'd love to take some of this wonderful cake back to her."

Mrs. Greenspan titters and blushes. "Oh, that's not necessary. I'll wrap up a piece to take with you."

Not my day for overcoming overindulgence. Mack's eyes sparkle, and he makes a *mmph* sound around his bite of cake.

Mrs. Greenspan brings in the wrapped slice, then sits. "The policeman on the phone said my car's been impounded because it was stolen and used in a crime."

Mack puts down his plate and nods. "Yes, ma'am. It was used in a hit and run of a bicycle messenger."

Both women suck in breaths.

"Poor Bernard," his widow says. "He would be so upset to learn his car was used that way."

Mack refers to the paperwork. "There are scratches on the ignition and wires hanging down from the dashboard that indicate it was hotwired, but just in case, do you leave an ignition key anywhere on the car? Say in a magnetic key box in a wheel well or undercarriage?"

Frieda looks surprised. "No. Bernard trusted the garage and the security system there. Nothing like this has ever happened."

Yeah. It's not like a nearly fifty-year-old car is high on the list of "most likely to be stolen."

Mack scans the document before looking at Frieda. "When did you leave for Florida?"

Frieda names a date two days before Timur was doored.

Rose interjects. "She insists on keeping the insurance and tabs up to date. But she never drives it."

Mack scribbles a note. "I'm afraid the car is being held as evidence."

Frieda shakes her head. "I don't care about that." Her voice trails off, and she pulls a handkerchief out of her pocket to dab at her eyes. "Maybe it's a sign I should sell it."

Rose reaches to pat her friend's hand. "We'll talk."

Frieda twists the hanky. "I just thought of something. Since my car was used to commit the crime, will I be charged like a criminal?"

Mack pretends to consider the fix Frieda is in until

I elbow him in the ribs. "No, Mrs. Greenspan. Your car was used without your knowledge or participation. I imagine you will only have to go down and make a statement."

Rose pats Frieda on the knee. "I'll go with you. In case you need a witness to say you were really out of town."

I tap the edge of the flower-decked cake plate with my fork. Both women turn to the sound. "This is the best chocolate cake I've had in ages, Mrs. Greenspan. What's your secret?"

Frieda blushes. "Adding boiling water to the ingredients at the last minute."

"Oh. I've never heard of that. Thank you for sharing."

Mack clears his throat, addressing Frieda. "There was a black cigarette butt between the front seats. Can you account for that? I mean if you don't drive, would you have loaned your car to a smoker?"

"Absolutely not," Mrs. Greenspan says. "Neither Bernard nor I ever smoked. It must belong to the thief. Can't you get—what's it called where you test spit or something and match it up with a criminal?"

"There's a DNA test in process, but we wanted to make sure the cigarette butt wasn't yours or someone you know."

Eyes shining with interest, Rose tries for nonchalance. "So who have you got under surveillance?"

Mack dons his serious frown. "There are a few people who match the eye witness description loosely. No one definitive. And I'm afraid that's all I can say on the subject."

Rose winks. "Will you come back and let us know when you catch him, cutie?"

Mack winks back. "With charming company such as yourselves? Of course."

****

We bid good-bye to our octogenarian friends and repeat our harrowing elevator ride to the ground floor. I pry my fingers from the bars. "Guess we can strike Frieda off as a danger to the community."

Mack glances in the direction of Frieda Greenspan's apartment. "Figured as much. You still up for visiting another senior citizen?"

"I can't imagine it'll take long to verify Mr. Perryman's account. Sure."

As we step outside, the air in front of Mrs. Greenspan's building closes in like hot, wet wool. The area around Seattle can't boast much summer weather, and even though gray skies are the norm, when the sun does shine, it's not nearly this humid.

Our driver pulls to the curb, and we get into the air-conditioned vehicle. I turn to Mack. "How long before we get the results of the DNA test on the cigarette butt?"

He curls his lips inward for a couple of seconds. "Still in line. It could be weeks. Or months."

My patience, usually an attribute, has worn thin. "Do you think we could get it released to a private testing facility? As long as the chain of custody is intact? I'll pay for the test."

"I don't know how you'd do that without a judge's order. Unless…"

"Unless what?"

He shakes his head. "Unless the judge is convinced

the hit and run was premeditated. Janean Barclay texted me while we were inside. She can meet us at The Gramercy day after tomorrow, in the morning. If her documentation is compelling enough, we might be able to swing it. Especially if, when we turn it over to Bret or Susan, they can convince Homicide to volunteer an officer or CSI to be the legal link in the chain of custody."

The driver turns to us. "Here we are. When do you want me to pick you up?"

Mack glances at his watch. "Quarter of an hour."

The hallway in this building is similar to the one where Rose and Frieda live. Thick, commercial carpeting in a dark wine pattern so as not to show too much dirt, and low wattage bulbs provide the tired ambiance.

Mr. Perryman answers the door in dapper pants and blazer. His wife, or the woman I assume is his wife, hovers behind him holding a squirming little dog. He introduces Mrs. Perryman, and we go to the living room.

Mack holds out his hand. "Thank you for agreeing to a second interview."

Mr. Perryman shakes it. "Welcome."

"Would you like some coffee and coffee cake?" asks Mrs. Perryman, setting the dog on the floor. It makes a beeline for my shoes and sniffs the edges.

Why does everyone want to feed us? "Thank you for asking, but I'm sorry to say we have a tight schedule."

"Of course," Mrs. Perryman says. "Please sit down."

We do, on a very comfortable chintz-covered sofa.

Mack opens the manila folder. "Mr. Perryman. Can you please repeat what you told the officer who interviewed you at the scene?"

"Well, we were facing the wrong direction, so we didn't see the young man get hit. We heard a terrible crunch of metal against metal and turned around."

I hold my hand out. "Excuse me. There's nothing in the report about a second witness."

Blank looks occupy the faces of both seniors. Mr. Perryman is the first to respond. "What gave you that idea?"

"Um, you referred to *we.*"

Mrs. Perryman laughs. "Oh. My husband was walking our shih tzu, Mitzi."

On hearing her name, the little dog trots over to Mrs. Perryman.

Mack runs his finger down the paper he's holding. "That's not mentioned in the report. Thanks for the clarification."

"Anyway, we turn around, and there are pieces of bicycle flying over the hood of this car and landing near us in the road. It was an early seventies Oldsmobile Cutlass. Brown on brown."

I look at Mr. Perryman's thick glasses. "That's pretty specific. Are you sure?"

He smiles. "Owned one myself. Blue on blue. We used to take trips to the Catskills every summer in it."

Mack makes a note. "Good enough for me." He raises his gaze to the older man. "Did you hear an attempt at braking?"

"None. I don't have a cellphone, but I pushed the button on my alert bracelet and had them call in the emergency. Poor kid must have been hit at full speed.

They said later he was dragged a block. There were lots of police and ambulance cars, but he had been killed instantly. Did the driver of the car get away?"

"The car was abandoned," Mack says.

"Oh, that's too bad."

Mack nods. "Yes. Is there anything else you can tell us? Perhaps you saw other neighbors in the area?"

The older man thinks for a minute and nods slowly. "They're not there now, but when the accident happened, there were detour stands closing off the intersection a block and a half west. Mitzi and I were walking east. When the racket started and we turned around, I caught a glimpse of a young man as he turned and ran north down the alley the bicyclist must have come from."

Mack scans the paperwork he has, then again quickly. "That isn't in the original report."

Mr. Perryman rubs his hands together. "I didn't think it was important at the time. Everything was pretty chaotic."

"I'm glad you've remembered now."

I lean forward. This could be important. "Can you describe him?"

"No. Maybe a teenager. And that's based on the way he ran. Like one of our grandkids. Anyway, my eyesight is not so good."

Mack finishes scribbling. "Thanks again." He flips a page. "The report states you got a vague impression of the driver. How vague?"

Mr. Perryman shakes his head. "The headrests on that model car are smallish, but the driver also wore a hood. Sorry."

"No," Mack says. "This is good information."

I tap my foot and yawn.

Mrs. Perryman stands. "I think these nice people need to get going, Arthur."

He pops up like a piece of toast. Hope I have that much spring in my hips and knees when I'm his age.

"Oh, sure. Hope I was helpful."

"Very," says Mack. "I'll forward this to the accident reconstructionist and the police. They might want a follow-up interview."

Mrs. Perryman looks delighted at the thought of more company. "I'll just slip this cake into the freezer."

Mr. Perryman and Mitzi usher us to the door.

We walk outside where our car waits and get in.

I settle back. "Believing more and more in Ian's theory. It looks like Timur was set up both times." My hands shake, and I clasp them together.

Mack puts his hand over mine. "We're closing in. One less psycho on the streets of New York."

****

Rippa is eating ice cream and watching some weird dystopian movie when I get back to the room.

"You look drained," she says, pausing the action. "And not in a good way."

I laugh. "How does someone look drained in a good way?"

"Want some ice cream?"

"No, thanks."

"Why is your aura all streaky?"

I laugh again. "When did you turn into your mother?"

"Feel better?"

"Marginally." I huff out a breath. "It looks like Timur Vasilyev was murdered. Before you ask. Yes, we think it was Kolya or he was at least behind it."

She nods. "One percent of the world's population are psychopaths."

"That's a creepy statistic. You think that's where Kolya falls?"

"Cunning, manipulative, high estimation of himself, big risk taker. Sound like him?"

I sit on the edge of the bed. "Google?"

She grins. "Interesting stuff."

"For all that, you didn't mention homicidal."

"Bigger percentage of murderers in prisons fit the psychopath profile. Also Google."

I tip my head. "Mack thinks we're getting close to catching him."

She crosses her eyes. "Good, because I'm getting cabin fever."

"Sorry. I can stick around through dinner, then I'm off to confront Mitch and Veronique."

Rippa frowns. "You and Mack?"

"Nope. Me alone. Don't want you or him to have to face the fallout when one or both of the New York McCarrens explodes."

Her lower lip protrudes for an instant. "Are you going to use the driver, and am I going to get a blow by blow?"

"Absolutely, on both counts."

Chapter Seventeen

My driver, the younger man from the first day, slides the car to the curb in front of Mitch and Veronique's upper eastside brownstone a few minutes before seven. "What time would you like to be picked up?"

A half hour should do it. Unless I get tossed out unceremoniously before then. "Seven thirty, please."

I climb the steps. The last time I went through this beautifully-carved door was for Raif's funeral reception. A tug of sadness weighs on my chest for an instant. Not a happy day for me. Truth be told, I hardly remember the event. Just a swirl of soberly dressed McCarren family and friends. Most of whom I barely knew.

I was with you even then, Cara. I'm sorry I caused you such pain.

I sigh and tap the knocker. Olga, the resident housekeeper, answers almost immediately. Her gold tooth winks at me—a smile, which is unusual for her. Next, she examines my outfit. Apparently, my short-sleeved cotton tunic sweater, linen slacks, and tan flats work for her. She opens the door wide.

True New York brownstones are now valued at ten to fifteen million if restored properly. This one is absolutely beautiful. Though the structures are narrow, the ceilings are tall, and the detailing on the molding, plasterwork, and woodwork is stunning. Olga keeps it immaculate.

She ushers me into Mitch's inner sanctum. The library. I've only been in here one other time, with Raif. The difference between my brother-in-law's small office at the university and this designer's dream is startling. Floor-to-ceiling books, some accessed by a cherrywood library ladder, attest to his collection. His fondness for antiquarian books extends to rare volumes in temperature-controlled display cases.

He stands from behind his desk and comes toward me, arms outstretched. "Glad you decided to stop by before you returned home. It's too long between visits."

I hope my unsmiling expression conveys this is not a social call. I glance around. "Are we waiting for Veronique?"

Mitch hugs me and steps back, eyes showing a deer-in-the-headlights look. "She'll be here soon. I told a small white lie. Said you'd be here at seven fifteen. I wanted to find out what your purpose in coming was, first. And..." He looks at the closed door for the second time in the last minute and lowers his voice. "And let you know there are a couple of things I'd rather she wasn't privy to. Might stir up some bad feelings."

I hold back a smile. Knowing it's not in his character to protect a wife with Veronique's strong personality, I *am* interested to know the kind of secret Mitch is willing to lie to keep from her. "I'm at the point where bad feelings don't matter, Mitch. I told you on the phone I wanted to finish the conversation we started, but this time I want real answers." I look at the beautiful Art Nouveau clock on his mantel. "Since we're on a time constraint, go ahead."

With one more glance behind me, he pulls a safety deposit box key out of his pocket.

My heart trips into high gear. Is he about to confess something? "What's this about?"

He rubs his other hand across his jaw. "Remember when I told you the third safety deposit box key on my ring was to a box in my name only and I would rather Veronique not find that out?"

"Yes."

"Here's the thing. You know Veronique controls our finances?"

I'm wondering about Nadya's expensive gold bangles and the fact that most of her living expenses are not paid by her. "More or less."

"About five years ago, my uncle, on my mother's side, passed away. My mother abhors my wife and saw to it that Veronique never learned about my inheritance. She didn't want Veronique to 'get her hands on it.' "

That explains money spent with no accounting to Veronique. A fact I don't really care about. My patience thins, and I inhale deeply, taking in the rich scent of old leather. "Why are you telling me this?"

"Because it all ties together. My personal box is a sort of war chest. Cash, precious metals, bearer bonds, all things that can be liquidated quickly. Mother and I have been adding to it and occasionally sending some to an account in her name in the Caymans."

I rub at a developing frown line. "For pity's sake, Mitch. Why didn't you just have your mother keep the money? She's surely got a safe. Or put it in a safety deposit box in her name?"

He cuts his gaze to somewhere over my left shoulder. "She wanted the access key right under

Veronique's nose. Mother thought that would be funny."

Save me from the machinations of these absurd people. "If the box is in your name only, Veronique wouldn't have access. And again, what does this have to do with my necklace?"

"Because I let my secret slip to Nadya, one day in the throes of, um, intimacy. Since then, she's extracted favors, little gifts, and promises. In return for not telling Veronique."

I think I finally see where this is going. "Clear this up for me, Mitch. How, exactly, did Nadya find out about my necklace?"

He spread his palm on his chest. "I didn't *tell* her about it. She found out by accident one day. Overheard Veronique and me arguing about it."

"Then I'll bet one of the promises she extracted has to do with her part in my necklace's disappearance, doesn't it?"

He ducks his head. "I couldn't help it. She said a Russian gangster was going to kill her if she didn't help steal it."

Of all the weak-willed men. And he can't even look me in the eyes while telling me what he's done. "So you sacrificed my wedding gift to keep a liar and blackmailer silent. Then you had a duplicate made."

Mitch's head jerks, and he shakes it. "No. *I* didn't have that done. And I promise you, Julianne, I didn't walk into that bank the other day with it in my pocket."

The sound of which convinces me he didn't make the switch at the bank. I figured that. But he knows something about the duplicate and isn't telling me. His adamancy rings real, though, and his confession is a start. "Did it not occur to you to just give Nadya money, the value of the necklace, instead of letting her steal it? Or at the very least calling her bluff?"

He blinks. "Where would I get that kind of money?"

Lord give me strength to keep from slapping this selfish man. He's sitting in a room with books worth many hundreds of thousands, and who knows how much money is in his safety deposit box and the Caymans, yet he chooses to let my necklace be stolen instead.

I unclench my jaw. "You're going to tell this to the detectives in charge of my case. Nadya is already a material witness and known associate in the investigation."

I think you are showing admirable restraint, Cara.

His eyes go wide, and he shakes his head again. "I can't do that. My whole secret will be exposed."

As with Nadya, I am done with Mitch. "Do you like being a university professor? In your case it seems to come with young blonde perks."

His eyebrows furrow. "That's a very crass way of asking, but I do like my position. Very much. Why? What does that have to do with our topic?"

"Because I understand many university professors sign contracts. With morals clauses."

This takes a few seconds to sink in, but before he can respond, Veronique sweeps into the room, five minutes early. She displays her couture alphabet labels of choice.

Mitch sucks in a breath.

"What is this nonsense, I must be here to talk to you about necklace? I have told you I did not steal it," she says. "I can give you five minutes."

"Hello to you too, Veronique. Yes. I want to talk about my necklace. I don't believe you stole it. I do, however, believe you're involved in having the duplicate made."

"That is ridiculous. You are ridiculous. I should have ignored your demand and left for my important dinner."

"Really? You're going to stick with that?" I take the picture showing her wearing Angel Falls from my purse, unfold it, and hand it to her. Mitch looks over her shoulder.

"This is fake," she says, handing it back. "Made by computer."

I flick a meaningful glance at Mitch, and his shoulders slump.

"We have to tell her, Veronique."

His wife whirls on him. "Shut up, you stupid man."

I call a bluff of my own. "Does the name Ansel Fuhrman ring any bells, Veronique?"

Her mask of righteous indignation slips for an instant as her eyes widen and her face pales. "Yes, of course. He is upscale jeweler. I am one of his best customers and have purchased many beautiful pieces from him."

"Then you'll want to be aware he's under investigation for copying Angel Falls."

"What is that to me?"

How does that work for her? The *you have to believe me because I said so*? "He had to get the original from somewhere, and I'm guessing it was from you."

"No" from Veronique and "yes" from Mitch at the

160

same time.

I focus on Mitch. "Since your wife seems bent on lying, I'd like to hear your version."

Veronique grabs his arm, but Mitch shakes free. "A half a year ago, Veronique came to my office with a ludicrous demand. She wanted to donate $20,000 to a charity that supports some endangered pocket of algae halfway around the world. Just so she could have her name on a list of big donors at the fundraiser luncheon. I refused and we argued."

Enter Nadya's eavesdropping. "I thought Veronique *oversaw* your finances."

The idiom, *if looks could kill*, comes to mind in the nasty glare Veronique sends her husband.

"There are limits," he says, sending the glare back. "She offered a compromise. A copy of Angel Falls. She's been lobbying for one for years since I've only let her wear the original twice." His head tips toward the picture in my hand. "Needless to say, she got her way."

Poor Mitch. Having to choose between his wife and his mistress, he chooses to throw his wife, and subsequently me, under the bus. However, Veronique is not done.

"Necklace is McCarren family heirloom. Temporary loan was no big deal."

I don't give up easily, but it's becoming clear I will not be penetrating Veronique's thicker-than-Russian-tundra skull to get through her belief that what's mine is also hers.

"I define a loan as when both parties are aware of it. And since your 'temporary loan' more than likely led to the theft of Angel Falls, you're lucky I don't press charges and have you both arrested as accessories."

"Thank you," Mitch says. And I know he means for also not telling about his and Nadya's roles.

"And Veronique. When I recover my stolen property, it will be returning home with me. If I hear you are wearing the copy and claiming it's the real item, I promise to make such a stink in the society columns and any of your charity organizations committees who will listen, you will never come back from it. Is that understood?"

"They will not listen to you. You are nothing in my circle."

I decide to fire my most lethal salvo. "They might. If I let them know you don't come from exiled Russian nobility as you claim. Your parents were potato farmers."

All color drains from Mitch's face. His wife will know this came from him or his mother. Too bad.

Veronique's look is beyond hatred, but she is such a sad cliché all I feel is pity.

She will never change, Cara.

Even with the outright liberties Mitch has taken with my property, I understand his situation and choose not to interfere in his plans. Maybe all this sneaking around and subterfuge will get him the freedom he wants, but I'm far from convinced.

As I head for the library door, I turn. "On second thought, as my reward for not having you prosecuted, I'm going to send the replica on tour. Mr. Barone has said that's acceptable."

Veronique starts to sputter. "You cannot do that without my permission. The replica belongs to me."

Mitch shakes his head. "Give it up, Veronique. You lost."

I muster a questioning look. "Hunh. So permission is required before taking something that belongs to someone else and using it for your own purposes. Guess that wasn't clear to me."

Mitch physically restrains Veronique as I make one last statement.

"One of the officers handling my case will be by to get statements from both of you."

Veronique's head doesn't actually explode, but it's fun watching it try.

I close the door quietly, hearing her voice rise in pitch. "Stupid man. Why didn't you stop her?" Then in an icy tone. "Jeweler has plenty of blue diamonds. Confession will cost you bracelet to match necklace when it is returned to me."

I freeze and my stomach clinches. Fuhrman has plenty of blue diamonds?

Olga is standing some ways down the hall, ready to escort me out. I catch a half smile and realize she's been listening.

I smile back. "You can file that away to use later."

Her smile blooms.

Outside, I stand on the bottom step and count the interview a success. I learned how Nadya found out about the necklace, when it was put in my box, who created the duplicate, and that he has more blue diamonds.

My feeling of euphoria is overshadowed by the fact that I burned bridges with the only two McCarrens left that I could call family.

Not a huge loss, Cara.

But a loss, nevertheless.

Chapter Eighteen

Being a few days short of summer solstice, at seven fifteen, it's still light out. My meeting with Mitch and Veronique took less time than I thought, so I call the driver. He was expecting me to take the full half hour and is running a personal errand. No big deal. I can't zip back into Mitch and Veronique's, so I scan the area for suspicious teens, and finding none, I walk a half block over to Central Park and sit on a bench. My only company heat, humidity, and disinterested passersby.

The necklace has become secondary to my situation with Rippa. She's mentioned several times, not too subtly, that she wants to stay involved in my cases, but I can't in good conscience encourage her to skip college to sit in cars and stalk con artists. I—or should I say we—need to think of a happy medium.

I could encourage her to take a few elective courses in police or forensic sciences or criminology. However, I'm not even sure those are offered at the UW. Maybe agree that if she gets that bachelor of science in industrial design she's been talking about for years, she and I can work together. And she can have that as a backup. I'll bite the bullet and broach the subject later.

And what about Mack? What do I want to happen there? He's a great guy. Sweet and smart and sexy as all get out. And definitely willing. But I won't consider being a New York woman, and his whole life and history are on the East Coast.

Get close as you want, Cara. I want you to have love again.

I can't answer him, but I want Raif to know I am making headway in that area. I'm not in love with Mack, but I could easily make love to him.

The warm evening has triggered that same thought in couples waiting to take a carriage ride through the park. Raif insisted we do that on one of his business trips here. The January weather gave damp and depressing a bad name, but we didn't care.

The horses were treated well, though. According to the hotel brochures, laws regarding extreme hot and cold temperatures and water and feeding schedules stayed enforced. On the day Raif chose, only a couple of carriages remained available, but it turned into one of the most fun times we had in New York. We pretended to be tourists and let the garrulous driver talk about the sites while we snuggled under a blanket and drank hot chocolate.

We do have a lot of memories, Cara.

I refocus on the blue diamonds Veronique mentioned after I left the library. If Fuhrman has enough to make a bracelet, could some of them be from my necklace? I'll do some shopping tomorrow morning and buy an expensive scarf and upscale shoes. Borrow a little of Veronique's penchant for designer labels to dress up and pretend my boyfriend, if I can talk Mack into it, and I are shopping for blue diamonds.

I stand and walk toward the park exit. My driver should arrive at Mitch and Veronique's in a few minutes. At the exit, grouped in a knot of black leather, are Kolya and four other gang members. I think there are four anyway. His presence freaks me out to the extent that it blurs other realities. He breaks away and walks through my personal space, stopping uncomfortably close. I can smell cigarettes on his breath and a musky male odor from wearing leather in the heat.

His look is not one of intimidation or posturing this time. He's pissed. "You have caused big problems for me, Ms. Rich Bitch. Stop interfering in my business and the business of my boss."

More people will come this way. Stall, Cara.

And remember McCarren's first rule. Don't poke the bear. In this case, the Russian bear.

Thinking my luxury hotel on high-priced property wouldn't be found, I've been too lax. Mostly because my work as an insurance fraud investigator involves on the computer and behind a camera activity. Not up front and personal confrontations. And this is the result. Maybe the hotel hasn't, but it would be easy enough to have boys staked out at my brother-in-law's house, McCarren Multinational offices, and of course, the precinct station that houses the detectives who investigate crimes in the area the bank is located.

I gaze into Kolya's flat, angry stare, afraid to look away. It's dinnertime, and the park, though not deserted, has only a few people on this path. A couple of hard knocks to the head and I go down. Then a number of kicks to my ribs and kidneys with his heavy boots and I'd be in serious trouble. I breathe out, stow this hopefully irrational and scary scenario, and lean back. "I don't understand. The sole purpose of my investigations has been to recover my necklace. I have nothing to do with any other cases the police are pursuing."

Kolya is not buying it. "What other cases are you *not involved in*? You've been seen going in and out of the police station. They're sharing information with you, and I want to know what it is."

I dare a sideways glance at the boys he's brought with him and realize that's what they are, boys, in their mid-teens maybe. They're loitering near one of the hundred-plus-year-old brick pillars that form this entrance, pretending at not paying attention to us. Window dressing, watching out for Kolya. In any case, I give silent thanks Rippa is not with me.

Kolya is bat-crap crazy, and his menacing may turn physical unless I can diffuse it. I take a half step back and hope he doesn't notice I am in a self-defense stance. Not that he would care. He's all about brute force, but I will not go down without trying. My insides are jelly.

"As I said, the only information I've been given has to do with the theft of my property. I don't know anything privileged. Why you think so is not my problem."

A muscle jumps in his jaw. My response clearly does not deter his intent, but I'm saved from further verbal volleying by one of New York's mounted park enforcement patrol. Kolya is so focused on me he doesn't hear the horse approach at first, but a loud whistle from within the group at the gate gets his attention.

His window of opportunity closes as I wave at the officer and smile. "Good evening and thanks for your service."

The officer is young and looks in really good shape. He smiles back and touches two fingers to his helmet. "Where're you from?"

"Seattle area," I say shading my eyes.

"Hawks fan?"

"Absolutely." I nod. "You a Bills fan?"

"Nope. Live in New Jersey. Jets all the way."

His banter is secondary to scoping out Kolya and the group at the gate. He activates the mic at his collar and calls in his position, then pointedly stares at Kolya.

The angry teen is not finished. His body language radiates a willingness to going off on me, park patrol guy or not. After an uncomfortable thirty seconds, Kolya leans in. "We are not finished, Ms. Rich Bitch."

We are if I have anything to do with it. Until he's in jail and on the hook for murder, my wandering unescorted is at an end. Luckily, I see the driver has returned to the front of Mitch and Veronique's residence. I wave my thanks to the officer and head down the half block to get in.

Although the teens are still gathered by the park gate when I leave, I'm on high alert. Kolya's rage as his plans unravel is focusing on me, and no one in this world stands between us. If he had his way, I would leave charred at the edges, thanks to his trusty lighter.

I use my bubbling-over adrenaline to take measured, careful steps instead of giving in to the fight or flight my body wants. When I get in the car, I ask the driver to watch for tails. He looks at me in the rearview and nods, then takes an indirect route to Gramercy Park.

****

Adrenaline shakes aside, I'm calm enough when I

reach the hotel to consider if I'm going to share my encounter with Rippa. For about a minute. Of course, I am. Not in the interest of scaring her, which it will, but a lesson learned for both of us about being hunted, the flip side of how we usually operate.

Rippa is not alone. She and Mack are sitting at the small table. And it smells really good in here.

I put my purse down. "What's going on?"

Rippa makes herself understood around a bite she is still chewing. "Mack brought some warm pineapple rum cake. OMG. His mother made it, and it is to die for. Oh, and Ben called. He's safe and sound with his dad at Benning."

Mack grins. "Rippa and I are discussing her research. She's really good at mining information online. Asking her if she'd like to intern with McCarren Security." He sees my face. "Um, when she's ready or even interested, you know."

Rippa could star in a toothpaste commercial. She is over the moon.

My brain doesn't want me to be happy about the offer, but my mouth says, "Wow. That's amazing. Something to think about."

Rippa's smile fades a little. "How did the interview with Mitch and Veronique go?"

"I learned a few things we already suspected. Veronique used my necklace to have Fuhrman make a duplicate. Apparently, he has lots of blue diamonds. We need to look into that. Also, Nadya had access to my box, and it looks like she was blackmailing Mitch about his personal box."

Mack lays down his fork. "The box he mentioned during our talk?"

"Yep." I try to keep the wry twist out of my voice. "Mitch and his mother are building a war chest to get away from Veronique."

Rippa squeals with laughter. "Then he better have his mom pick out his next wife."

I give a half nod and so does Mack.

His eyebrows draw together. "Anything else?"

"Yeah." I move my gaze to the window. "I keep second guessing myself in favor of, I don't know, thinking I can handle anything that comes up. Stupid and no more. I walked a half block over to Central Park to brood about burning bridges with Raif's last two relatives, and Kolya showed. Very pissed."

Rippa stops eating too. "But that's like a big, public place with tons of people around, right?"

Mack leans forward. "I don't think that concerned him much, did it?"

"No. He apparently had gang members watching the precinct we're dealing with and Mitch and Veronique's townhouse. He kept demanding to know what we were doing at the cop house." I shrugged. "Told him the only reason I went there was to discuss my missing necklace. Didn't even dent his anger."

Rippa stands. "Are you okay? Did he hurt you?"

I shake my head. "Luckily, a sizeable Park Patrol officer on horseback made it clear he didn't like the looks of Kolya and the others."

Mack's voice holds a tinge of anger. "That kid's a deep crazy kind of psycho and losing it. His goal as a gang enforcer for Kalashnikov was probably never achievable, but he doesn't see it that way. He sees it's gone and is focusing the blame on you." He gives me a careful onceover. "I know you're smarter than him and can take care of yourself in most situations, but no more wandering off without me or a driver in sight. Okay?"

He's right, Cara. Please do as he says.

I know Mack's not bullying me. He's doing his job. I nod repeatedly like an idiot and head for the table. I'm not in Kansas anymore, Toto, and am apparently a slow learner. "Pineapple rum cake is perfect."

Mack's cell rings. "Macklin Pierce." He listens for a minute, then smiles. "Good news, Bret, thanks. We'll come down to the station first thing in the morning. Nine, okay?"

I wait a long minute to hear the news before he hangs up. "Detective Hagen?"

"Yep. Break in your case. I told him we could come in and get the scoop first thing tomorrow. You good with that?"

My heart thumps heavy and loud. "Did they find it?"

"Not yet. They've arrested someone with ties to Kalashnikov. A guy who wants to trade information for a reduced drug charge and possible deportation. Some of what he's giving up has to do with your necklace."

I want so badly to have this done I start to shake with disappointment.

He takes a step toward me. "Hey, that's supposed to be good news."

I lean into him and push out a deep breath. "Last couple of days have been a roller-coaster ride."

He puts his arms around me. "This okay?"

I feel his warmth and embrace the offered comfort. It's been too long. "Preferred, actually."

Mack kisses the top of my head.

Rippa grins and scrunches her nose at us.

Chapter Nineteen

We arrive at the station a quarter hour early. I'm anxious to hear what this informant has to say. We're shown to Susan's empty desk.

"I've been thinking," Mack says. "This connection doesn't sound like Kalashnikov. I believed what he said about steering clear of the drug trade."

I shift a shoulder. "Maybe that's what he wants everyone to think. My necklace is a pretty specific piece for this guy to know about."

Susan walks up. She's dressed in a tan jacket over jeans. More casual than the suit she wore the other day. "They're bringing him in now. He gave just enough information for the ADA to be interested in a deal. If they give him a pass on the drug bust, he says go ahead and deport him. It'll be safer."

Bret steps to the end of the hallway and waves us over. "The ADA will join us in the viewing room. Susan's sitting in while the lead detective in the drug unit finishes the interview."

We enter a small room on the other side of a two-way mirror. Just like in the movies. Mack and I do a double take. The prisoner handcuffed to the table is the large man who stood guard in Kalashnikov's office during our meeting. I come up with his name. "Viktor Avakian."

Bret and the ADA give us questioning looks. Bret

leans forward to push an intercom button just as Susan enters the interrogation room. "Pause for a minute, Detective Pavlycheva. We have new information."

Susan excuses herself and leaves the room to join us.

Bret hikes his thumb at us. "They recognize Avakian."

Detective Pavlycheva lifts an eyebrow. "From where?"

"Remember the club card Kolya gave me? I told you about it when we first met."

"You used the card to meet with Kalashnikov?" Susan tips her head. "That might have been a very stupid thing to do."

I make sure my reply carries a sardonic edge. "They didn't say we could bring our friends, the police."

This elicits a smile. "And?"

"And this guy escorted us to Kalashnikov's office. We were introduced, and he stayed in the room during our discussion about my necklace."

Susan pegs me with a look. "You understand this man telling us he was in the room when your stolen necklace was discussed could be the same instance as your meeting?"

"Yes, but I'm hoping there was more than one time my necklace was discussed in his presence."

She gives me a "could be," shrug. "Anything else?"

I glance through the window at a disinterested Avakian. "Kalashnikov made it clear during our meeting he's a Russian *businessman*. He deplores the attention drugs and violence bring and is squeaky clean in his real estate dealings."

I get an appreciative appraisal, then Susan hooks her thumb toward the glass. "Smarter than drugs if you're a criminal. We think the 'safety' Avakian is talking about in his request for deportation is a chance for him to get under the radar of MS-13. Nasty competition."

"One more thing," I say. "After we met with Kalashnikov, we peeked through the blinds into the small room at the back of the building. We saw teenage boys with headphones on sitting in front of desk computers. Didn't match the setting of the rest of the occupants."

She pulls a cellphone from her pocket, thumbs through her list, and presses a name. The call is answered after two rings. "Detective Tomlinson. This is Detective Susan Pavlycheva. We have an associate of Pyotr Kalashnikov's in interview. We're starting with a drug interview wrap up. If you have an interest specific to the cybercrime's unit, we'll give you a crack at him." She listens for a beat, then hangs up.

Turning to Mack and me, she huffs a breath. "Are we done now? It would have been nice to know all this before we set this up."

I give as good as I get. "Didn't know it was Avakian before we clapped eyes on him."

The ADA mumbles, "Gonna need to expand our charges."

****

Viktor gives a sidelong glance at the two-way mirror after Susan returns to the room. He now looks resigned.

"Before we start," Viktor says, interrupting. "I

want record to show I am Armenian, not Russian."

"Big distinction," says the drug unit detective.

Susan sends him a glare. "It is if you're Armenian."

The detective rolls his eyes and focuses on the perpetrator. "Viktor Avakian, you understand your rights as they have been explained to you? And have you also waived the right to an attorney?"

"Yes. I understand and give up right to attorney. They are bloodsucking fools."

The ADA beside us snorts.

"Moving forward, then. You're being charged with distribution and resale of powder and crack cocaine. We're in this second interview to gather information you have on the involvement of Pyotr Kalashnikov in drug trafficking and other illegal enterprises."

The big man yawns. "Kalashnikov has not involvement in drugs. That is *my* organization. All men you caught reported to me and are proud Armenians. When I am given deal and sent back to Armenia, I take with me."

Susan shakes her head. "It's too soon to talk about a deal. For you or any of your men. In your first interview you said Kalashnikov had information on the stolen diamond necklace, Angel Falls. We need more specifics on that. Throw in the information you have on his possible cyber theft, and we may put a deal on the table."

Avakian's lips thin.

Susan continues. "Only if the information leads to the takedown of Kalashnikov and a conviction."

The ADA mumbles, half to himself. "That's right. Don't make any rash promises."

Viktor rubs his buzz cut with his free hand. "Okay. I tell you what I know about necklace."

I chew my lower lip. Could be something, could be nothing. Air in, air out.

This will be good news, Cara. I feel it.

Strange. Since he inhabited my head, Raif has never said he felt anything.

Viktor starts to speak, so I refocus.

"Greedy blonde girl who thinks she is better than anyone asks to see Kalashnikov. She has been bragging about diamond necklace, and he is very interested."

Greedy? Superior? How could Viktor develop that impression of me after five minutes in Kalashnikov's office?

"She is drunk, as usual," he continues. "And noisy. Always clanking jewelry, like cow with bell in field." A smirk tugs the corner of his mouth. "She is also stupid as cow but convinces Kalashnikov she can get her hands on priceless blue diamond necklace."

Susan interrupts. "What's the drunk blonde girl's name?"

"Nadya Vasilyeva. She is lover or assistant or both to man with key to bank where diamond necklace is kept."

Oh. *That* blonde. I'm insulted even though Viktor's remarks aren't about me. I smile, though. Raif is right. And Mack and I are right. Kalashnikov's fishing expedition with us wasn't entirely necessary. He was already dealing with Nadya.

"Kalashnikov has the necklace?" asks Susan.

Viktor shakes his head. "No. He tells girl to get necklace and he will see that diamonds are sold through Russian jewelers. He will split profits with her. Girl is so stupid drunk she believes him." He holds his hand palm out and rolls his eyes. "Kalashnikov does not share."

Viktor rubs his head again. "Then girl's brother is killed. She does not come to club like before. Kalashnikov wants to see her, so I find her and bring to him. She screams her brother's death is his fault. Now she can't get access to necklace because her brother's *boyfriend* is disappeared. Kalashnikov gets mad too. Tells her to find out where, exactly, necklace is. He will take care of rest."

The big Armenian doesn't say Kalashnikov threatened to kill her if she didn't come through. A little exaggeration on Nadya's part.

"I'm curious about Nadya's screaming," Susan says. "In your opinion, was she expressing sadness or regret over her brother's death? Or was she pissed about missing the opportunity to get her hands on the necklace?"

Viktor laughs sardonically. "She is cold, greedy bitch. What do you think?"

Susan nods. "How long ago was this last conversation?"

The big man shrugs. "Maybe ten days, two weeks."

The Russian gang leader's original plan didn't work or only partially worked. The necklace is still out there. Whole. Or at least it sounds like it is. Mack and I need to talk to Nadya again. Before the police pick her up. If I come armed with this information, she won't be able to squirm out of answering our questions.

Susan taps her notebook. "You're being helpful. We'll follow up on this information, and if it pans out, we'll put in a good word with the ADA."

Viktor slides his gaze toward the two-way glass. Skeptical chases hopeful across his face. "I tell you one more thing. Kalashnikov is paranoid. He has building swept for listening devices all the time."

Detective Pavlycheva stands and tips her head forward. "Good start, Viktor. Now, do you remember the blonde woman who owns the necklace?"

For an Armenian drug boss, Viktor Avakian has a number of cunning expressions. A wary slyness now occupies his face. "She came with security man."

"Did you or Kalashnikov send Russian *or Armenian* men after them last week?"

Viktor's mouth twists. "Will answer complicate deal?"

Susan's lips close, and crinkles show at the corners of her eyes, suppressing amusement at his question. "Complicate? Depends on if Ms. McCarren and Mr. Pierce want to press charges."

The big man mulls this over. "If they do not press charges, I will tell big secret in stealing by computer."

"Fair enough. I'll do my best." Susan turns to the drug unit detective. "Thanks for letting us interrupt. After you finish, Tomlinson from cybercrimes would like to talk to Viktor."

The interviewing detective taps the paperwork in front of him. "Am I wasting my time finishing this? We're just going over Kalashnikov's known associates."

Susan cuts a glance at the two-way. "Sorry. The ADA needs it." She leaves the interrogation room and joins us. "Looks like Viktor's a major catch. Drugs, theft, and cybercrime details. He has a shot at deportation if his information leads to jail time for

Kalashnikov." She turns to the ADA. "Right?"

The man is scribbling notes. "I hate to say it, but if it turns out this guy's only direct involvement is drugs, we can talk."

Mack shakes his head. "What I don't get is how anxious he is to go back to an Armenian prison."

"Yeah," says the ADA. "Some of the worst in the world. The conditions break every international law for the humane treatment of prisoners. We prosecuted a mutilator last year and set him up for deportation. He begged to stay in the US prison system."

Bret's gaze takes in a now-sullen Armenian. "No doubt our friend Viktor knows that. He's also aware that severe overcrowding puts drugs at the bottom of the list for incarceration there. Unless murder or worse are on the table too. If he does go back, he's probably just facing a stiff probation."

I am marveling at the machinations of the criminal class when I hear, "Kolya Vladimirhoff?" through the interview room speaker.

At the mention of the dangerous teen's name, my attention sharpens. I suck in a breath, and Mack turns toward the small speaker. We step to the window.

Viktor is shaking his head. "He is stupid Russian boy. Always bragging about low-class father who died in prison. Boy is not important but still brutal and cunning."

The detective interrupts. "I take it Vladimirhoff isn't part of your crew either."

Viktor shakes his head and looks disgusted. "He listens to nobody and tells everybody Kalashnikov will make him important inner-circle enforcer."

The interviewing detective frowns. "What makes

this kid think he's moving up?"

The Armenian lifts a shoulder. "Kolya starts rumor in club he has taken care of problem for Kalashnikov. Permanent. All are now afraid to cross this crazy psycho." He smirks. "Even, I think, Kalashnikov."

Great. His own head bully thinks the gang leader might be afraid of Kolya. If he is, we'll have to deal with the crazy psycho ourselves, because I don't think he's done with us. My next thought is how relieved I am that Rippa will be eight hundred miles away.

Susan turns to us. "You're thinking the problem he took care of was the hit and run of the Vasilyeva boy?"

I really do. "It's a strong theory. His fiancé believes he was murdered because he threatened to involve the authorities if his sister Nadya went through with her scheme to steal the necklace. There's a hole in the theory, though. If Kolya isn't part of Kalashnikov's inner circle and Viktor, the guy closest to the boss, thinks Kolya is a 'stupid Russian boy,' how the heck is the teenager getting his information?"

"Nadya is apparently loose-lipped when she drinks," Susan says, tapping her cheek.

"But she wasn't in the room when Mack and I met with Kalashnikov."

"Might be worth a chat with one of the kids who hangs around Vladimirhoff." Susan huffs. "Sounds as if he likes to brag."

Mack shakes his head. "I'm not so sure. The kids under his control are terrified of him. You wouldn't get much, if anything."

Susan hangs her head. "You're probably right."

Mack moves his gaze to the viewing window. "Speaking of Kolya and connections, I have an accident reconstruction specialist going over the evidence. She's sharing the results with us tomorrow morning."

Bret closes the folder he's holding. "We'd be interested if she's found a new twist on the original analysis. Another murder added to Homicide's caseload would be bad, but this might give PD a head start in solving it, *and* the theft of the necklace."

"I'd be surprised if Nadya has it," I put in. "Mack and I went to Ian Ward's address yesterday. He wasn't returning my phone calls, and we wanted to schedule one last interview."

Bret rubs his eyes. "Remind me again who that is."

"He's the safety deposit vault escort and was Timur's fiancé."

"Right, right," Bret replies. "I went through the accident report after our first meeting, and it has several statements from Ward claiming the hit and run was murder. He was so emotionally strung out he wasn't taken too seriously. Could be he was right. We'll ask him to come in."

Susan holds me with a questioning stare. "Why do you think Miss Vasilyeva doesn't have your necklace? She could have faked that meltdown in front of Kalashnikov to keep the diamonds for herself."

I shake my head. "She's self-absorbed but not that good an actress. When we got to Ian's yesterday, we found them outside arguing. She demanded his help or he would 'end up as dead as Timur.' "

Susan's mouth turns down at the corners. "Trying to intimidate him out of desperation."

"Yep, but before we could find out more, Nadya claimed it was a private conversation about money Timur had promised her and Ian was withholding."

"You didn't buy it," Bret says.

"Not only did I not buy it, I threatened her with State Department interference when she tried to return to the US."

"You can do that?" Bret asked. "Wait. Where's she going?"

I cut my gaze to Mack. "I sort of bullied her with the McCarren name and its influence. She's going home to Russia for a short stay, then returning to the US." Mack grins, but I feel justified, whether Nadya believed me or not.

Susan pulls her shoulders back. "You're taking a chance your necklace isn't going with her."

"I don't think so. She wasn't just angry yesterday. She was scared. The thing is Nadya doesn't know about this." I wave my hand to include the interview room. "She's more than likely avoiding Club Bear and the gang members associated with it because she doesn't have what Kalashnikov wants."

Mack chuckles. "If Viktor's information leads to what they think it will, Kalashnikov will be way too busy covering his ass to worry about Nadya and the possibility of getting his hands on your necklace."

I turn to Bret. "I'm not ruling out her involvement. She had the key from my brother-in-law, access through Ian, and the connection to the jeweler."

Susan and Bret raise eyebrows in unison. "Your brother-in-law and a jeweler?" Bret asks.

"I was coming to that. I found out last night Nadya blackmailed my brother-in-law for the key, in return for not telling his wife about his secret divorce funds stash at the same bank."

Susan's mouth forms a moue. "Busy girl. Who's

the jeweler involved?"

"My sister-in-law's jeweler, Ansel Fuhrman. She denied it, but when I threw out his name, she was forced, by her husband, to admit she 'borrowed' Angel Falls and had the duplicate made. She claimed not to know how it got in my box. I told them to expect to be interviewed about the case."

Susan finishes scribbling. "You do good work. Remind me to get your in-laws' contact information. And if that's true, why do you think Nadya is mixed up with Fuhrman?"

I'm just warming up, but I think it's all coming together. "It's a theory, but all the bank-issued keys to my box are accounted for. I think she used Mitch or Veronique's name to have a duplicate key made."

"Okaaay," Bret says. "Any other breaking news on our case?"

"Can't guilt me on trying to recover my property," I quip. "In addition, I need a favor."

Susan makes a wry face. "What?"

"Could you hold off on picking up Nadya for, say, an hour?"

Susan shakes her head, avoiding my gaze. "Sorry. Her being named by Viktor makes Nadya a person of interest. Both as a known associate of Kalashnikov's and as someone with information on the theft of your necklace. As much as Bret and I appreciate what you and Mack have accomplished, we can't take the chance you might spook her."

Well, damn. We blew it. We should have grabbed her for an interview outside of Mitch's office or yesterday at Ian's. I sure don't want to be left out of the loop now. I heave a sigh. "What can we do?"

"Give me details of your interactions or observations of her."

I close my eyes, trying to bring up details. "You already know about the gang member on Facebook asking if she was part of Kalashnikov's crew. We also found out her grocery bills, rent, and high-end department store charge accounts are paid for by someone else. Could be my brother-in-law, we don't know.

"Her parents were planning a big celebration—first college graduate and all. But that was before Timur's death. They offered to set her up on her own. According to Ian, Nadya's going to take their money and return to the US."

Susan expels a huff of breath in disgust. "Nice."

Bret scribbles a note. "I'll check on her flight departure. Let you know."

I continue to tick off a list on my fingers. "She's also asked my brother-in-law not to reveal her trips to the bank on his behalf. He's already interviewing for her replacement, so she might be on shaky ground there.

"In her confrontation with Ian yesterday, he accused her of 'making the deal that got Timur killed.' He said he wished she had died instead. She responded that if he didn't help, she would tell *them* everything and he would end up as dead as Timur. That's when we walked up."

Bret whistles. "Miss Vasilyeva seems to be up to her ears in this." He crooks an eyebrow. "Were you planning on sharing with us?"

"Of course. We learned about her plans to take the money in Russia and the threatening confrontation just yesterday afternoon. We told Nadya we wanted to interview her too. She reluctantly agreed."

Susan is nodding. "Wait. We can use that. People involved in something illegal, especially if they're in a panic, are more likely to open up to civilians accompanied by a cop. *If* they're convinced the interview is harmless. This might work."

I hope my tone conveys skepticism. "Unless they're the kind of people who, when they open their mouth, a lie falls out."

"She starts lying, and I bring her in here to finish," Susan responds.

This sounds good. Not as disappointing as not being involved at all. "Can we leave now? Nadya could skip off to one of the dozens of airport motels and hide out until her flight leaves."

Detective Pavlycheva tilts her head. "You think that would occur to her?"

"I don't think *she* thinks she has many options. No family here, Mitch is moving on, and she hasn't had time to learn the Viktor factor."

Mack agrees. "She's also not the type to have girlfriends she can count on."

Susan and I laugh. "Astute observation," I say.

"Can you wrap up the notes on the interview?" Susan asks Bret. "Sounds like we should get going."

Bret is scribbling madly. "Go. I got this."

Chapter Twenty

From the looks of her apartment building, Nadya's doing a lot better than her contemporaries. Most twenty-two-year-olds just graduating from a prestigious university live near campus in older complexes or fringe neighborhoods. Not so our Nadya. Her address is in a well-kept-up area with clean streets. She even has a doorman.

Mack is busy at a screen on his cell as Susan pulls into a "deliveries only" slot four car lengths from the front and slips a card in her window.

"This should hold off parking enforcement for a few minutes. They're brutal in this neighborhood."

Mack holds up his cell. "They need one dedicated to this building alone. Units here run six thousand a month. Three for a studio."

Susan cuts a glance in our direction. "She must give great administrative support."

I'm sure Mitch would agree. I give an unladylike snort. "Something like that."

Mack holds up his cellphone. "Let's make sure she's in."

"Or if she'll be out soon," says Susan.

Mack calls and identifies himself, then asks for some of Nadya's time, which she grants.

Susan makes a quick call to Bret, then checks her watch. "I give her five minutes."

He leans against the car. "Generous. Here she comes."

Sure enough, Nadya breezes through the front door in about two minutes, a large tote slung over her shoulder. She ignores the three of us standing four cars back and steps to the curb to hold out her arm for a cab.

Mack is the first to speak when we reach her. "Hello, Nadya."

She turns so fast she nearly loses her balance owing to her five-inch heels. Mack has to grab her elbow to keep her from toppling over. I say on the lam perps should have appropriate footwear.

Seeing Mack is not a threat, Nadya looks past me and assesses Susan. "Who are you?"

Susan reaches under her suit jacket and unclips her badge from her belt. "Detective Pavlycheva. Ms. McCarren's stolen necklace is my case."

Dismay, in the form of tiny lines between heavily penciled brows, is clear on our prey's face. She turns her pout on Mack. "You didn't say you were bringing police. That is naughty of you."

Mack smiles. "You said you were available for an interview, and here you are, hailing a cab. That is naughty of you. So we're even."

Ms. Vasilyeva is clearly not used to men who can think on their feet. She twists a strand of hair. "I was going to make coffee for you but realized I am out. I am going to store for more."

I smile with what I hope is encouragement. "Very nice of you, but we'll pass. May we all go back to your place for that interview?"

Nadya shifts her tote on her hip and, looking around, shrugs. "Sure."

We troop toward the bored doorman, but I slow as I see an interesting figure now leaning against her building, near the corner. Kolya. He must have spies watching Nadya's building too.

Something between a gasp and a whimper escapes from Nadya, and she makes a beeline for the door.

I put a hand on Mack's arm. "I don't trust her not to skip out a side or back door. I'm going to have a chat with the doorman."

Mack stops and faces me, putting his hand over mine. "Good idea. You've gone pale. You okay?"

I take a shaky breath. "Nothing a bunch of distance between me and Kolya won't fix. He still maxes my creep meter."

Susan stops too, looking at Kolya. She calls Bret and requests a squad with warrant-print capabilities, asking him to send one for Kolya. She walks over to the teen. "Kolya Vladimirhoff, I'm Detective Pavlycheva. I'd like to speak to you regarding your association with Pyotr Kalashnikov."

Kolya cuts me a malevolent glance, then looks her up and down and smirks, not bothering to hide his disinterest in her title or request.

I take a deep breath and walk to the doorman, a youngish guy in a gray uniform clearly intended for someone with shoulders. "Hi. Do you know Nadya Vasilyeva?"

He pulls his attention from the threesome near the building corner and points to the elevator at the end of the small lobby. "Yeah. She ran as fast as those shoes would go. You want her apartment number?"

Helpful guy. We could be a team of murderers.

"I have it, thanks. Is there any other way for her to

leave the building?"

He ponders this and nods. "Yeah. Down some stairs by the elevator, then through a short hallway near the laundry room and out the back exit."

"Could you give a shout if you see that happening? We'll only be a few more minutes."

Doorman grins and bobs his head. My guess is he gets short shrift from Nadya and would like to see her taken down a peg or two.

I thank him and walk to stand slightly behind Mack. His feet-wide-apart stance near the teen clearly conveys his lack of tolerance for any sudden moves. In his effort to appear threatening, Kolya has made a strategic mistake and hemmed himself in. His posture remains defiant, though, as he pulls out a cigarette and lights up.

Susan waves at the smoke his first drag expels. "Bad for your health." She tips her head toward the building behind them. "You're a long way from Brighton Beach. Mind telling me your interest in this neighborhood?"

Kolya blows a smoke ring. "I am looking for new apartment."

"You planning on coming into money?"

He lifts a shoulder. "I have rich relatives in Russia."

Susan laughs. "No, you don't. You're here to intimidate Nadya Vasilyeva and get your hands on the missing necklace to impress Kalashnikov."

His motives exposed, Kolya turns to me. "Are you enjoying new hotel?"

He *almost* gets to me. *Almost*. My gut reaction is fear. He knows where I am and can hurt Rippa or me whenever he chooses. Then I remember the major hole that's being blown in an organization that probably won't survive the week. I dredge up a smile. "You have bad information or have confused me with someone else. I'm not in a hotel. But thanks for asking."

Kolya's confidence wanes for just an instant as his gaze takes in the street. He shrugs, then drops and crushes his cigarette as a squad car pulls up.

How does he look so unconcerned, so at ease with circumstances not in his favor? Or control?

Two officers approach and hand Susan a warrant. She scans it, then tells Kolya he's being taken in for an ongoing investigation. He is searched for weapons, relieved of a knife and his lighter, cuffed, and loaded into the back of the cruiser. He looks straight ahead as they pull away.

Susan grins and dusts her hands. "Wow. I've only seen his mugshot. He's quite the package up close. His idea of a Russian gangster is from about 1980. And the hair and fake accent are awful. Still, he's pretty nervy for someone his age."

She's pretty cool herself. Even though Kolya was made physically impotent by Mack's and her presence, he was still able to freak me out a little.

Mack watches the car pull away. "He knows you don't have anything to hold him and he'll walk."

"Nothing yet," Susan says as we make our way toward the building entrance. "We have enough with Viktor's allegations to hopefully keep him for forty-eight hours. If Mr. Ward is right, and we concentrate on the hit and run, we may have Vladimirhoff for good. That would make my day."

We arrive at Nadya's door, and I knock. Dead

silence.

Susan knocks louder. "Ms. Vasilyeva, it's Detective Pavlycheva. We need to talk."

The door opens a crack, chain on. Nadya's pale face appears. "Is he gone?"

"If you mean Kolya Vladimirhoff, yes. He's been taken into custody."

Nadya takes off the chain and opens the door, her eyes wary. "He is going to jail?"

"I can't talk about an open investigation where Mr. Vladimirhoff is concerned. I'm here about Mrs. McCarren's missing diamond necklace. May we come in?"

Nadya accedes and waves us in. Susan sits near the door, although the chances are slim that Nadya will make a break for it in her imitation Jimmy Choos.

Our hostess sits in a dainty pose on the edge of a small, brightly upholstered chair. A mild smell of cabbage, a Russian soup staple, wafts from the kitchen.

I watch as expressions shift across Nadya's face and wonder how she'll play this. So far, her repertoire consists of flirting, coyness, and the unchecked anger we saw in her confrontation with Ian. Her shoulders slump, and the winner is—sadness.

Huh? Sad that she didn't make it out of town before being caught? This should be interesting.

Her gaze focuses on me, and it is not a happy one. "I have already told you I know nothing of your necklace. Now you are getting me all mixed up with police when I have to take Timur's ashes back to Russia. I cannot miss my flight."

"That's the purpose of your trip? To take your brother's ashes to your parents?" asks Susan.

Quivering lips and a nod confirm Nadya's pain. "Yes."

Susan stands. "I'm taking her in. Maybe she'll stop lying in an interrogation room."

Nadya springs up like a jack-in-the-box. "What are you saying?"

Susan holds up her cellphone. "I'm saying that's a lie. My partner's text says your flight was booked weeks before the death of your brother." She looks around the apartment. "Where's the urn holding his ashes?"

Apparently, our girl Nadya can call for tears on demand. She wrings her hands and takes a shuddering breath. "Ian stole from funeral home. He will not return to me."

Susan takes this in stride. "Then how did you plan to get them back to Russia?"

Out comes the quivering lip. "I will beg on knees with Ian. My parents will be overcome with grief if he does not allow me to take my brother home."

Susan flaps her hand indicating that Nadya should sit down. "What's the name of the funeral home?"

Nadya sits again and hesitantly names the same funeral home that handled Raif's remains. This instantly conjures up the events after Raif's accident. When his parents died suddenly in a plane crash, Raif had contracted with a service that handled the transport of remains to anywhere in the world. If it hadn't been for their representative and Fletcher, I would have been lost. A kaleidoscope of flashbacks play. Damn. This trip has triggered way too many unhappy memories.

You've come further than this, Cara.

Raif's right. I push out a breath and concentrate on

the little storyteller in front of us.

"Impressive," Susan says. "For a bicycle messenger. Who paid for it?"

I glance at Nadya and wonder at people who lie without hesitation and with so much guile. It's a little unnerving. Especially since I believe she's involved up to her heavily mascaraed eyelashes in the theft of my necklace.

"I am poor foreign student," she begins, head bent. "My parents are poor, also." She peeks to see how this is going over. "And old-fashioned. So when accident happens, I tell them local Russian church is paying. They would be very upset to know about Timur's *relationship*."

The part about the relationship might actually be true. I jump in. "Ian paid for everything, didn't he?"

Nadya squirms as if telling the truth is painful. "Yes, but our parents want Timur's ashes, and Ian won't give to me. Have you talked to him about this? Plus, he attacked and hit me. You saw this. He should be arrested."

The girl does an excellent job of redirecting. She should take this act to Vegas.

Susan moves her hand to take in Nadya's apartment. "Seems like you're used to others paying for what you think you need. If Mr. Ward paid for everything and he was your brother's fiancé, I assume the funeral home has the paperwork releasing the ashes to him. Now let's get back to the reason we're here, your association with Pyotr Kalashnikov as it relates to Mrs. McCarren's necklace."

A single tear blights Nadya's pretty cheek. She angles her head to make sure it's seen by Mack and sighs. "Is very sad story. Timur and Ian force me to…"

Susan stands again. "This isn't working for me. We have a witness who puts you in Kalashnikov's office brokering a deal to steal the necklace. I want your version in writing and on record. I'm taking you in."

Nadya's eyes go wide. "Who is this witness? All these men who work at club are cowards and liars. They will say anything to protect owner."

Susan tips her hand, palm up, in a "stand up" motion. "We'll discuss how you know that in interview."

Our hostess stands reluctantly, shoulders curled inward. "I can make call to get help?"

I take way too much joy in responding. "If you're thinking about contacting Mitch, I wouldn't. His generosity has probably dried up."

She turns the only honest expression I've seen from her, an unbelieving wide-eyed stare of fear. This is new and not good information for her. "Why do you say this?"

"Because, thanks to you, he's implicated in the theft. And I'm willing to bet the law believes a wealthy American tenured professor over a visiting student from Russia."

Maybe so, but Mitch will still not learn from this, Cara.

A sad but very accurate assessment of Raif's half brother.

The switching of gears is almost audible as Nadya straightens. "I am victim. You will see I tell true story."

That'll be refreshing.

"Done with the drama." From Susan. "Since my car is full, I'll have Bret send a unit with a warrant to pick her up as a material witness." She eyes Mack and me. "I suppose you two are interested in whatever airy-fairy tales Ms. Vasilyeva wants us to buy."

"I'm in," I say. "If only for the entertainment value."

Mack grins. "Ditto."

Chapter Twenty-One

Susan, Mack, and I are waiting when Nadya arrives. Not having been here before, she sees a roomful of detectives, a large number of whom are male. Her appearance does not have the effect she probably intends. Our girl is either ignored or receives glances of disdain. Halfway across, her strut loses its mojo. Possibly not realizing heavily made-up blondes in tight clothes and pouty expressions are seen as another type of interviewee. Her outlook brightens, however, when Bret comes out to meet us. Her coy smile sends a strong signal his way.

Bret gets the play and greets Nadya warmly. "Miss Vasilyeva. Thank you so much for coming to help with our investigation."

Nadya preens at her conquest. "I will help you see I am victim."

Not to mention her dead brother and his fiancé, who I suspect she intends to sacrifice without a qualm. It'll be interesting to see how she handles the questions generated by her meeting with Kalashnikov and confrontation with Ian. They can also throw in Mitch's allegations. Her Russian goose is truly cooked.

I turn to Susan as Nadya is being led to the interview room. "She can tie everything together, but it will be difficult convincing her it's in her own best interest to do so."

Susan nods. "I'm going to let her dig a deep hole, then offer her a ladder. That usually works with her type. All she'll see is the ladder as the way to save herself."

Bret's solicitous demeanor toward Nadya is followed by a wink in our direction.

"He's a natural at making persons of interest comfortable," Susan says, a wry twist on her lips. "I call it girlie-man mode."

"Bet he appreciates that," says Mack.

"Not really. But it works like Novocain followed by an extraction."

I rub my jaw. "Even on sociopathic liars like Nadya?"

"A liar, yes," she allows. "But probably not a diagnosable sociopath. All her energy is focused on saving her own skin with a little narcissism thrown in. She's a tad shy of being a cult leader or politician."

That may be true, but under that makeup, tight clothes, and fake tears, the fact remains Nadya set the scheme in motion to steal my necklace out of pure greed. She's also indirectly responsible for the death of her brother. Another fact that doesn't seem to faze her.

I tip my head toward the now-familiar hallway. "Same viewing room?"

"Yep. If Ms. Vasilyeva lies about something and we don't call her on it, but you know different, tap on the glass, and I'll come out." She holds up an index finger. "If you have a verifiable source."

She escorts us to the viewing room, leaving us at the door. "I'm going to pull my notes and join the fun in a minute."

Inside, I hear Bret offer Nadya a beverage. Mack

smiles at the cozy tableau. "Nadya looks pretty happy for somebody in as much trouble as she is."

I follow the direction he's looking, annoyed this girl is deriving pleasure from her situation. "Of course. She's in her element. Alone with a good-looking man who's interested in her."

Mack turns to me. "You think Bret's good-looking?"

Raif's laughter echoes in my head as Mack swings a deadpan gaze back to the glass.

I blink, momentarily speechless. What's this about? "Um, yeah, I guess."

The interview room has become a new happy place for Nadya. Bret sits relaxed, one hip on the table's edge. She's smiling up at him like he's the center of her world. Is this how she acted toward Mitch? Maybe, but Bret isn't buying it. He's just really good at what he does.

Susan enters the room, and Nadya frowns, casting an imploring look toward Bret. He gives her an encouraging nod and pats her hand.

"Detective Hagen has advised you of your rights?" Susan asks, sitting across from Nadya and opening a folder.

Nadya nods, doe-eyed.

"Please speak up," Bret reminds. "This is being recorded."

A little-girl voice accompanies the innocent look. "Yes."

Bret smiles. "Tell us what you know about the theft of Mrs. McCarren's necklace. From the beginning."

My insides are all jittery. I don't know why any of us thinks Nadya will revert from her natural tendency and tell the truth just because she's in a police interview room. Hope springs eternal.

Nadya hugs herself and whispers, "First I will tell you I am in fear for my life."

And hope goes out with the tide.

Bret's eyes go wide in surprise. "We'll certainly keep that in mind, but in order to protect you, we need to know everyone involved."

She lifts a shoulder. "Yes. About three months ago, I am bringing Professor McCarren's lunch to him when I hear his wife—" Nadya wrinkles her nose, making a distasteful face. "—yelling at him. She wants money, as usual. For some silly cause she has joined with other bored wives."

Bret frowns. "Not seeing how that's associated with the necklace."

"I will explain. Mitch...Professor McCarren asks all his assistants to call him by first name, you see. Anyway, he is tired of paying his money for stray-dog causes his wife likes, and he tells her no."

"That must have angered her," Susan puts in.

Mitch's former assistant tips her head at Susan as if she finally understands.

"She is not nice person," Nadya pronounces, flipping her hair. "And she is not aging well."

This elicits a soft snort from Mack, and I can't hide my smile. I'm glad Veronique and Mitch aren't here to listen to this. Especially Veronique, the queen of meltdowns. At twenty-two, Nadya's small world consists of looking pretty and wearing pretty things. It's always about her. She likely hasn't considered a future that involves the upkeep required for women approaching forty.

"Let's stick to the facts," Bret says.

Nadya turns surprised eyes on him, her arched eyebrows high. "That *is* fact."

Mack and I laugh outright, and the muscles in Susan's jaw bunch.

Bret's effort not to crack up is monumental. He barely succeeds. "Okaaay. Back to what you heard and how it ties into the McCarren necklace."

"When he says she can't have money and means it, she says, 'All right, but I get McCarren diamond necklace to take to jeweler for copy.' " Nadya rolls her eyes upward. "What is his name?" She nods. "Yes, Fuhrman."

This is going better than I thought, and I force myself to relax a little. However, we aren't to the real pointing-fingers part yet. That's coming, and Ms. Vasilyeva will make sure someone else gets all the attention.

Nadya lowers her gaze to the tabletop. "When I hear about diamond necklace, I am, of course, interested." She cuts another pleading look at Bret through her lashes. "But only to see, not take. I am honest person."

I'd use the term larceny-minded over interested, but that's just me.

Bret nods when Nadya says she's an honest person, and her shoulders lower. He smiles. "What happened then?"

Our Nadya grips her hands together on top of the table. Blood-red nails curved against her pale skin. "I am poor student from poor family. I have never seen a real diamond necklace. When Mitch's wife leaves, I tell him I overheard about beautiful necklace and ask him if

I could see it."

I can only imagine the persuasive measures she used to convince my dear brother-in-law. And his besotted response.

Not exactly the same story Mitch told, Cara.

Nope, it isn't.

From Susan. "What did Professor McCarren say to your request? Be as clear as you can."

"He is upset I have heard his wife yelling at him. Not for first time, but I don't tell him that. He said it was not good idea. Maybe when necklace comes back from jeweler, maybe not. Depends on whether his wife is the one to take back to bank." She ducks her head. "I decide to wait until he is not so upset."

"So you did nothing then," says Bret.

"No, but necklace is on my mind. I keep secret until night I go with friends to Club Bear to celebrate graduation. I have a bit too much to drink and talk silly about diamond necklace." She shrugs. "Next thing I know, I am being dragged by Viktor into Mr. Kalashnikov's office."

Semantics, I guess. Viktor said she was the one who asked to see Kalashnikov.

Susan interrupts. "Viktor who?"

This turns out to be a hard question for Nadya. A worry line appears on her forehead. "Just Viktor. He is big bully who does whatever Mr. Kalashnikov wants."

"Go ahead."

"I am embarrassed to say I don't remember all he said, but he wanted to know about diamond necklace. Mostly, could I get my hands on it?"

Bret taps the table lightly. "What? Steal it?"

"Yes."

"What did you think about that?"

Her fingers twist together. "I am scared and feel stupid for talking."

Wow. Another honest emotion shown by Nadya. Fear will do that. In her case, though, fear barely outweighs greed. Which is going to cost her.

Susan stands and puts her hands flat on the table, her laser gaze on Nadya. "Back up."

Nadya spreads her fingers across the top of her chest. "Me?"

"Yes, you, sunshine. Back up to the part where you weren't interested in stealing the necklace. We know for a fact…"

"Susan, can I have a word?" asks Bret.

Detective Pavlycheva continues to stare at Nadya. "What?"

"I think Ms. Vasilyeva has more to tell us about Kalashnikov's involvement."

"Miss," Nadya says, the correction aimed at Bret. "I am Miss. Single and not married."

He nods. Duly noted.

Susan manages to convey, in a single look, disappointment but that she still holds cards and can play them at any time.

Nadya inches closer to her only friend. He pats her shoulder.

"Impressive," Mack whispers, and I have to agree. Susan and Bret have this pincer action down. They need to convince her they're focusing on Kalashnikov.

Bret leans toward his interviewee. "Back to your encounter with Kalashnikov. How did that end? Did you agree to anything?"

Nadya builds on her lies. "I am so afraid, I agree to

anything. Especially when he threaten Timur's life."

Susan is nodding in acceptance. "In exchange for your brother's safety, not money, you agreed to help steal Mrs. McCarren's necklace."

The young Russian makes a play for sympathy without answering Susan's question. "They kill Timur anyway."

"Who killed him?" asks Bret.

She lifts a shoulder. "Kalashnikov say he did not give order to kill my brother. Police say is accident. Maybe that's true, but I don't think so."

"You don't think what is so?" asks Susan. "That Kalashnikov didn't give the order or your brother's death was accidental?"

Nadya's darkly penciled brows are about to take wing. She looks to Bret for support. "If I say truth and he finds out, he will kill me. I tell this to Ian, but he doesn't care. He slap me, as I say before, and tell me he wishes I am dead instead of Timur."

No empathy is forthcoming from Bret on this point and no offer to bring in Ian for assault.

Cynic that I am, though, I wonder if Nadya has been directly threatened or assumes what will happen if she talks. It *is* interesting that she doesn't think Kalashnikov gave the order.

For a fleeting moment, I'm sorry for her loss. I really don't know her or how she felt when Timur died. Maybe they weren't close, or maybe she was raised with a practical, instead of emotional, view of death. And maybe my reaction is tainted due to losing Raif.

I feel sorry for her, Cara.

Leave it to Raif. He sees someone unable to express a broken heart. I see someone who looks at the people in her life as rungs on a ladder. Who can she step on to raise herself up?

Mack gives me a quick, sideways hug. "What are you thinking?"

I sigh. "That maybe I shouldn't judge Nadya's reaction to Timur's death based on the feelings I had when Raif died. I don't know the first thing about the dynamics of her relationship with her brother."

He gives me another squeeze. "I think you're cutting her too much slack."

He's right. I got sucked into her poor me's. I cut my gaze to him and smile, making a conscious effort not to lean too close. I refocus on Nadya. She's moved past her illusionary grief and is again concentrating on Bret.

Susan snaps her fingers in Nadya's face, making the young Russian jump. "You didn't take the necklace, but you agreed to help steal it, and now it's missing. Fill in some of the blanks."

Nadya gulps air. "I sometimes take papers to Mitch's safety deposit box. The one he shares with his wife. I use his key ring." She plays with her gold bangles. "The day after I am forced to tell Kalashnikov about necklace, I talk to Mitch again about seeing real diamonds. He says no, but I can see replica. His wife has brought back from jeweler and put in their box."

Bret holds his hand up. "That wouldn't do you any good. Kalashnikov would find out when he took it to a jeweler to have it broken down."

Nadya avoids eye contact, and her next words are almost a whisper. "I can get real necklace with key ring. I know which key goes to which box."

Susan shakes her head. "Wait a minute. Professor

McCarren gave the bank authorization to allow you access to his sister-in-law's safety deposit box? Why would he do that?"

Nadya's charms might do the trick, but I say nothing.

"Mitch doesn't know. He is thinking I am going to see replica, so he let me use key ring." Nadya's gaze hardens. Just a little. "I may have told Ian, who has master key at bank, there is threat to Timur, so he must let me look at real necklace. Besides, Mrs. McCarren from other side of country almost never wears. She doesn't even care she has beautiful expensive diamonds. If I take to save brother's life, no one will know."

I'm conflicted over her assertions. On the one hand, it's Nadya being herself, lying and making excuses. On the other hand, her observation that she, and maybe others, see me as indifferent to Angel Falls pulls me up short. A quiver of regret slides into my stomach.

We both know that's not the way it is, Cara.

"Oh," says Susan. "Then it's okay."

Nadya, for once, clues in to the detective's tone. "Is not the same. It was to save Timur."

Susan smirks. Nadya has played that scenario one too many times.

Bret chimes in. "Ethically and legally, it's exactly the same, Ms.—excuse me, Miss—Vasilyeva."

Nadya looks hurt by his disloyalty.

Susan extends her ladder. "That brings us back to access at the bank. Give us the exact details there, and we'll see if we can help you."

Mack shakes his head. "She bargained with her

brother's life to get her hands on the necklace for Kalashnikov. Damn."

Chapter Twenty-Two

I'm not so sure. "Or. Think about it. Viktor never said Kalashnikov threatened Nadya. He said their deal centered around her stealing the necklace, him fencing it, and cutting her in on the take. What if we leave Kalashnikov out of the equation altogether? Ian is still afraid to refuse. And now that Timur's gone, Nadya has no way of holding Ian's feet to the fire."

Nadya's bracelet clanking intensifies as we turn back to the interview. "Timur always like boys. He thinks he is in love with Ian and they will get married."

Susan shakes her head. "What does this have to do with bank vault access?"

Bret flips through a manila folder of case notes. "Whoa. This the same guy who's the bank vault escort? The one we haven't been able to interview because he's on personal leave and nobody seems to know his whereabouts?"

"Bingo," Mack says. "Connection."

Susan leans toward Nadya. "We got some information on him from Julianne and Mack. He's the same guy who's been claiming your brother was murdered. That puts you in the middle of the action, sunshine. Finish your story."

Nadya sighs and squirms, but I can see the wheels turning. "I don't know who is Julianne and Mack, but Timur and Ian meet about six months ago at club where only boys go. Ian sees my name when I come in to put papers in Mitch's box one day. He is all excited to meet Timur's sister, but I do not care for him."

"Except to use him in your scheme."

Nadya tips her chin up. "I don't have choice."

"You always have a choice," Susan replies. "Where's Mrs. McCarren's necklace?"

Nadya's face hardens to match her eyes. "I didn't steal. I get copies of keys to both boxes, but Timur gets angry and doesn't believe me when I tell him of threat. So he refuses to make stupid Ian let me get into box with real necklace. Then Timur has serious accident in traffic. He is still not convinced like Ian. Ian wants Timur safe and agrees to take necklace. I give him copies of keys, but then Timur is killed, and Ian blames me. He takes necklace ahead of schedule. On day when vault camera is broken."

Wow, the timing on this is amazing.

Susan doesn't care about Nadya's feelings or difficulties. "Ian Ward has the real necklace? You're positive? Have you seen it?"

Nadya returns the favor. "Of course not. I beg, I threaten, but he wants to see me punished. He says he is sorry about necklace but he cannot live without Timur and doesn't care what happens to either of us until killer is caught. Stupid, crazy man. I am ready to tell Kalashnikov Ian has necklace and take my chance to get away when you come to my apartment. You see for yourself he has sent Kolya to scare me."

"Or Kolya has taken it upon himself," I mutter.

Bret interrupts. "It's illegal to have safety deposit box keys duplicated. Who did that for you?"

Nadya hugs herself and slumps in her chair,

shaking her head. "I watch television shows of police. I won't tell you now. I also know of other crazy person who might steal necklace. I want to make deal."

I turn to Mack and raise my eyebrows. *Just like Viktor. Is deal-making something certain foreigners learn before coming to the US?*

He lifts a shoulder. "I figured she knew less than you and me. You think she's been holding back?"

From what I've seen and heard of Nadya, that doesn't seem likely. "No. I think she realizes a little too late she's given up everything of value and is trying to bargain with information she doesn't know the police already have."

Susan looks ready to speak but turns toward a knock on the door. "Yes?"

Another detective opens the door and steps inside. He hands her something small and a piece of paper. She scans the paper, and her head swivels to the two-way glass, then to her partner. "Let's leave Ms. Vasilyeva alone with her thoughts for a while. We have some paperwork to review."

I know Susan and Bret have other cases, but I hope whatever information she just received has to do with mine.

Bret looks surprised his partner is interrupting the interview at this point, but stands.

"Will you be back?" Nadya asks. Her unblinking plea made in a small voice.

He pushes a pen and tablet toward her, smiling. "Yes. But in order for me to help you, you need to write down what you've told us so far. Okay?"

Susan opens the door to the viewing room and sticks her head in. "Can I talk to you guys? In our office?"

The room she indicates would be claustrophobic for one person, and now there are four of us. I sit in a chair beside one of the facing desks, but my knees have to slide in sideways. Mack, at a half a foot taller than me, is forced into a contortionist's pose.

Susan places a metal disc about the size of a dime in front of us. "Somebody wanted to hear what was going on in Kalashnikov's office. Our guys scrubbed it trying to find a direct connection to his computer ransom operation. This was slipped between the corner pieces of one of the old paintings. Don't know if it's associated with your case, but it's very interesting. Any idea who would have the receiver?"

I pick it up. "State of the art. I know next to nothing about Kalashnikov's associates. And speaking from experience, I'm assuming Viktor was present for his meetings. Unless he wanted some insurance in case his Russian boss found out about his drug dealings." I shrug. "Since he knew Kalashnikov had his office swept once a month, it'd be risky. Are you going to look at anybody who knew about his paranoia and had access to his office?"

Susan nods. "That's the question. Who would take the chance, and why?"

She lays a small, slightly bent piece of metal with a rounded top encased in plastic next to the bug. "Whoever it was didn't stop there. Our team also found this on the roof. The building's been reinforced since Superstorm Sandy, and sandbags are stored up there. That part of Brighton Beach took on a lot of water. Somebody drilled a hole that was intended for the corner of Kalashnikov's office. This little beauty would slide into it and transmit. We're guessing it failed. Kalashnikov's ceiling has no hole, and apparently the genius who drilled it didn't bring a long enough bit. It was under a sandbag."

"Could it be more than one person or persons tapping in?" I ask. "You'd think the little transmitter in the picture frame would do it. Why put in a second one? Is the smaller one broken?"

Bret throws me a look and sucks air through his teeth. "Our first assumption would be that the attempt on the roof was a backup. Thanks for giving us another theory to work on."

"My pleasure." I grin.

"Could Kolya be behind this?" Mack asks.

I tinker with the bent device. "He'd be my first guess too, but these don't look like they would be anywhere near his skillset."

Bret picks up the round one. "Vladimirhoff hangs around enough to know there were computer guys involved in hacking and hijacking. Intimidation and threats are certainly in his skillset."

"I'd love to uncover something solid on him," Susan interjects. "He's an arrogant little bastard."

"Speaking of Kolya, isn't he still being held?" I ask.

Bret shakes his head. "Maybe for another couple of hours. Although Viktor mentioned him, it wasn't in association with any actual crime he had details on. We could have held several of the other teens longer, but none of Kalashnikov's wannabe crew had any serious records. Add the appearance of an overzealous public defender who claimed we were profiling based on looks, and they'll all be released. Viktor's information on the real location of the computer theft center garnered a goldmine, though. Club Bear and that little restaurant have been shut down since they were financed by the hacking operation. Plus, there's no one left in charge with Kalashnikov and Viktor out of the picture."

Mack turns his attention to Bret. "When did you pick up Kalashnikov?"

"We haven't yet. He's got a small army of lawyers who keep pushing paperwork at the ADA's office. Matter of time."

My legs are falling asleep from the knees down. I try to shift, but without success. "Has anyone checked into the janitorial service?"

Susan holds up the paper. "First thing they did after finding the bugs. They aren't independent contractors. Kalashnikov owns the company. Seven Russian women who clean the restaurant, the club, and his office."

I sigh. "He really is paranoid."

Mack grins. "Lots of paranoid people are very successful. Besides, is it paranoia if someone really *is* listening?"

"Six degrees of separation," I murmur.

"Pardon?" Bret asks.

"Nothing that convoluted. Just wondering if any of the cleaning women are related to any of the teens who hang out with Kolya. They look like ants about to be stepped on by a size thirteen when he's nearby. He couldn't have been all the places the kids and I went without having more than one informant watching us."

Susan taps the paper. "We'll run a surname and address comparison on the two groups, although some of them may no longer live at home. If something comes up, we'll let you know."

"Thanks for keeping us up to date. Maybe something in all this will lead to the recovery of my necklace."

"We'll also continue our active attempt to locate and bring in Ian Ward," Bret says. "Nadya's a practiced liar, but her attempt to lay the blame on someone else could actually have a grain of truth. I'll finish the interview and see if there's anything more she has to say that could help. What are you two doing next?"

I lift a shoulder. "Overheard my sister-in-law say Fuhrman has lots of blue diamonds. Mack and I are going shopping to see if he's a viable source in case my necklace has been broken up. If what Nadya said is true, however, it might be a fool's errand. If Ian Ward does have it, and I'm not saying that's not possible, I won't see it again until Timur's killer is caught."

Bret, who is sitting to my right, leans forward a little. "If we continue using you two as a resource, and it's out there, you can count on it, but be careful."

Chapter Twenty-Three

The rain that washed the windows of the city's skyscrapers overnight morphs into the morning's humidity. I take a deep breath on the bottom step of the cop house. "Bret's right. I think we're getting somewhere."

Mack nods while checking his cellphone messages. He pulls his lips in and out. "Looks like I've been caught ducking one too many meetings."

"Chased you down?"

"Yeah. Papers to sign, reports to read, and an employee evaluation I've been dodging." He snaps his fingers. "Speaking of reports. I heard back from Interpol and my other foreign connections. Not a whisper about your necklace or a new cache of blue diamonds on the international market."

Not surprised, but I still get a jolt of disappointment. "Thanks. As I said. I think Ian's the key. And if that's the case, I'm hoping it's still in one piece."

The car pulls up, and we get in.

"Listen. It's unfair of me to ask you to take that run at Fuhrman with me. I can always do it myself since I've been sucking away a lot of your time. First, though, I have to shop for some designer accessories so Fuhrman buys my story. Can I have the use of the driver and car?"

More lip maneuvers as Mack thinks. "Give me three hours, then I'll meet you in front of Fuhrman's. In the meantime, give Rippa a get-out-of-jail-free card. Maybe shop a little, have lunch. Shop some more."

Really nice of Mack to think of Rippa. "Good idea. For someone who lobbied hard to stay here, there's a lot of heavy sighing when I'm in our room."

Mack laughs. "Where does she go when housekeeping comes in to clean?"

"She stays in the bathroom when they're doing the rest of the suite and vice versa."

"Uh, then she's really ready to get out."

I mock shudder. "What do we do for security? I don't think there's much danger of Kolya finding us on Fifth Avenue, but I didn't count on him finding me in Central Park either. Is that female driver we used to get to the Gramercy available?"

Mack smiles. "Better. McCarren has a new security driver. Tangee Pike. A multi-talented young woman, Tangee was offered a position on the White House Security Staff but came to us instead. She has all kinds of martial arts certs and could probably be talked into shopping and eating."

Multi-talented indeed. "Sounds like a good fit."

"I'll arrange for her to pick you up when we get to my office."

****

Rippa is ready. She Googled "the best burger in New York," and here we are. I feel bad when she sits, face turned to the sun, while we're waiting to be served. Not going to tell her that.

"Your choice to stay."

She glances at the young woman sitting at the tiny

table behind us. "I like Tangee, but she's really quiet."

"Guess chatting is a distraction."

"Hard to tell. Looks like she's reading, but those are the darkest sunglasses I've ever seen, so she's probably really scoping out what's going on around us."

"Um, don't think we're supposed to be aware of her."

She turns her gaze back to me. "Right."

We're finally served, and the burgers are as big as my head. "Can't finish this."

Rippa pulls out her cellphone and snaps a picture. "I can. And Ben is so going to hear about it."

The next ten minutes are spent trying to make inroads through my meal.

She eyes my plate. "Ask for a doggie bag. I'll have the rest for breakfast."

"Okay. Get any more scoop on Ian Ward?"

She shakes her head. "His parents are traveling— apparently that's what they do every summer. An occasional splash in the social columns or mags, but almost no social media presence."

"Didn't expect much. I get the feeling there isn't a lot of emotional support from Ian's family."

"That's sad. I would be totally freaked."

In the totally freaked zone myself when Raif died, but Rippa is well aware. I slap my hands on the table, bent on changing the subject. "Wanna hear the expanded version about my take-no-prisoners quarter of an hour at Mitch and Veronique's?"

She throws back her head, laughing. "Of course."

"It's a little more complicated than we figured." I hold up fingers, ticking off each item. "Mitch was being blackmailed by Nadya, who overheard about the necklace by eavesdropping on him and Veronique. Veronique was demanding she get a copy of Angel Falls because Mitch wouldn't let her subsidize endangered algae. Nadya got the use of Mitch's key by telling him she would be murdered by Russian gangsters if she didn't bring them the necklace."

Her laughter escalates to near hysterical, and she flaps her hands at me. "I'm sorry. That is so Agatha Christie. Do they actually know where your necklace is? Or how Russian gangsters found out about it in the first place?"

Gotta admit it continues to sound like a bad movie plot. I fold my arms and try to look aggrieved by tilting my chin. "I'm getting closer. Supposedly, Nadya brought the Russians in, and she's claiming Ian Ward has it. He took it so she would be thrown, so to speak, to the Russian wolves. And no, she can't prove it because she hasn't seen it."

She wipes her eyes. "Do you believe her?"

I think for a second. "I believe she's scared. And desperate to stop what she set in motion. The accusation against Ian Ward is plausible. He'd like to see her pay a terrible price for the death of the man he loved."

"So where does that leave us?"

"Mack and I are trying an end run. Ian's theory that Timur's death was murder."

"Can I see the evidence that it might have been murder?"

"Um, Mack turned the accident details over to the reconstructionist McCarren uses as a consultant. We're meeting with her in the morning."

"Oh." Rippa swirls the last few sips of her cola.

"Speaking of the next day or two."

I think I know what's coming. Made my decision and I'm okay with it.

"Can you and Mack meet her in our room? I know you told me I'd be bored, but I am soooo bored." Famous eye roll.

My conscience pricks. "Okay. That way we all get to find out the real breakdown of what happened to Timur. But afterward, you're still stuck in the room. Kolya is back out there, and he's crazy and pissed. A bad combination for us. My brain tells me if I loosen the bonds, it's like giving you permission to run in the streets with scissors."

She huffs out a breath. "You've been running in the streets with scissors ever since uncle Raif died."

She's right, Cara.

****

The afternoon sun cuts through the skyscraper canyon to leave a swath across Fuhrman's shiny black awnings. The scripted name graces an immaculate storefront with sparkling windows.

We're smack in the middle of Manhattan's jewelry district. According to their website, Fuhrman's is a "five-star establishment that caters to a discerning clientele desiring custom diamond pieces with stones of the highest quality."

Mack is right on time. He's wearing navy-blue slacks and a cream-colored shirt, open at the collar. I'm wearing a newly purchased Hermès scarf and designer shoes that have more shine and logos than comfort.

He looks at me and grins. "Is this the effect New York has on you?"

"Funny man. We're going in as a couple looking

for blue diamonds to have a custom piece made. I'll do most of the talking. You are my preppie arm candy."

We step up to the shiny brass and glass door and press the buzzer.

The pretty blonde saleswoman looks us over none-too-subtly, then buzzes us in.

"May we see Mr. Fuhrman?" I ask.

"Do you have an appointment?"

I fidget with my scarf. "No. My name is Emily Parkes. We're in the city for the day, and he was mentioned by a friend as someone with exquisite taste in diamonds. I'm sure he'll see me."

"Everyone who works here is trained on quality gems," she responds. "I can help you."

I borrow Veronique's persona. "But *you* aren't the one recommended by my friend."

The arrow hits its mark. The shop assistant gives me a look of disparagement, poorly disguised behind a smile before she turns to walk to a door at the back of the shop.

"Wow," Mack whispers. "Can I hire you the next time I need to buy a car?"

I lean over the glass case and pretend to primp in the reflection in case the security cameras are being monitored in the back. "Sure."

The saleswoman returns, followed by a tall, sallow-skinned man dressed in a very continental style. His suit jacket is one of the most perfect fits I've ever seen, and having attended a number of McCarren functions, I've seen quite a few.

I hold out my hand. "Mr. Fuhrman? My name is Emily Parkes. This is my friend Macklin Pierce." I nod toward Mack. "Of course you've heard of Pierce Island off the coast of Maine."

Mack affects a pained expression. "Emmie. I thought we weren't going to mention the *island*."

I ignore Mack, and the fact that Fuhrman's expression of surprise indicates he has never heard of the Pierces, or the Parkes for that matter. "My friend Veronique McCarren highly recommended you. She has this beautiful blue diamond necklace, and I would love to have one specially designed for myself." I pin him with a knowing stare. "With a few more diamonds than hers."

Fuhrman acknowledges my wish but does not mention that Veronique's necklace is crafted in moissanite. Diamonds, at roughly seventy-five percent higher in price than the top-end created moissanite, would be a much bigger score for him.

His body language, leaning slightly forward, head tilted toward us, indicates interest, but he gives a slight chin dip. "Let me see what I can do. Please come to my private showing room."

We trail after him to a small, elegantly appointed room and are seated. He excuses himself, and a minute later we hear agitated, muffled conversation. Fuhrman returns with a jewelry tray, followed by the sales associate with a silver coffee service. She is not happy in this role and doesn't speak when she leaves. Fuhrman uncovers the display tray with an impressive selection. Like a shoe salesman, he has brought white as well as other colored diamonds, plus drawings of custom styles.

I choose a particularly gaudy one. "Something like that one. In blue diamonds."

Fuhrman is scratching notes on a pad of paper.

"How soon would you want your necklace?"

"Oh, as soon as possible."

"And is there a price limitation?"

"No, silly. Of course not."

He lifts his gaze to mine with an expression that can only mean I have been escalated to a new place in his pantheon of best friends.

I point at the tray. "But I would like to look at a few of them through a loupe."

The jeweler seems surprised and hesitates for just an instant, then lays a loupe and jeweler tweezers on a black velvet pad in front of me. I take a deep breath and pick a blue diamond at random to inspect. There is no number lasered on it. I chose another one with the same result. The stones in Angel Falls all have laser numbers as ID.

I point at the one I'm holding. "How come there aren't lasered numbers for identification? All my other pieces have them."

Fuhrman shifts slightly. "I see you know your diamonds. These are part of an estate piece that has been broken up. When the piece was made, laser identification was not the norm."

Mack picks up my hand and is playing with my fingers. "Isn't that how stolen diamonds are laundered?"

I'm sure his act of affection is part of the image I asked him to play, but it's so distracting I have to clamp down the urge to jerk my hand away.

I loved playing with your fingers, Cara.

Fuhrman laughs politely. "Any diamonds used in a new piece will be ID'd."

I nod. "I almost forgot. My friend Maisie Wilton

has a really pretty necklace, and I love the back and sides, but not the very front." I point to the style I've chosen. "Could you duplicate the parts I like from a picture and make the front match this?"

He frowns in thought. "There would have to be a number of very explicit pictures, along with the sizes and placement of the stones."

"How about if Maisie loaned me the piece for a few days? You could see those areas in person."

"Emmie?" Mack says. "Why would you borrow from her? She would spread nasty rumors all over about you copying her jewelry."

"Oh, pooh. That would only last until I wore my new piece. Everyone would forget about hers."

Mack gives a deep sigh. "You know best."

"Yes," I chirp and point to the tray, addressing Fuhrman. "Are these natural or treated?"

He folds his lips inward for a second. "My dear. Ninety-nine percent of gem-quality precious stones are heat or chemically treated."

"That would make the ones I want one-percenters like me, wouldn't it?"

Fuhrman's eyes sparkle at my inferred income bracket. "There are, of course, international sources I can tap into."

I nod. "Do you have any more blue diamonds? These aren't exactly the color I was thinking about. I'd like more in the teal blue range."

Fuhrman has no doubt had lots of experience with picky clients and smiles benignly. "I'll make inquiries as to precisely what you are looking for. If you can come back in say, a week, we can finalize everything."

"I'm looking forward to it." I glance around. "As

long as we have some privacy, I need a teeny favor."

Fuhrman shrinks back. "Favor?"

I nod. "Daddy insists I use the family safety deposit box for my things, but he won't let me have an extra key since I've already lost two. He's so mean." I add a pout. "Anyway, Veronique says you're brilliant at making things. So I want a duplicate of my safety deposit box key in case I lose another one. Okay?"

Fuhrman stiffens. A huge custom order and breaking the law, his choices. "My dear," he starts. "That is highly illegal."

"That's what Daddy says, but I don't care. Who's to know? I certainly won't tell anyone." I glance at Mack. "Neither will Mackie."

I pull my hand from Mack's and root around in my capacious bag to produce a key to an empty box I rented at another bank, earlier this morning.

Fuhrman slumps and hesitantly reaches for the key, greed winning. "You understand the consequences to *both* of us, my dear, if discovered."

Mack interrupts. "Emmie, sweetie. Let me help. Store your key in my box. It will safe from your silly little forgetful brain."

I shrug and give my boyfriend-on-loan a peck on the cheek. "Okay."

Fuhrman blows out a breath with relief when I hand the key to Mack. I've accomplished the two things I came for. With Mack as my witness, I have found out the jeweler doesn't have my blue diamonds. At least he hasn't brought any out. Secondly, he was reluctant but willing to make an illegal safety deposit box key. I pop out of my chair and pull a calling card with Emily Parkes on it. I have several with a fake number printed on them. "Call me when you have my diamonds."

Mack and Fuhrman stand, following as I head back into the store, but nearly running into me as I stop abruptly.

"Oh, look at these shiny diamonds. They must be very expensive."

Fuhrman steps behind the counter. "These aren't diamonds, my dear. The stones are moissanite."

I try to look suspicious. "They're fake? You sell fake diamonds?"

"They're not sold as diamonds, my dear. But since they closely resemble them, we make pieces that can be worn in public without fear of having the real jewelry stolen."

"For example," I say, not making eye contact, "Veronique's blue diamond necklace?"

The jeweler doesn't respond.

Mack takes my elbow and leads me outside.

On the one hand, I'm glad I didn't find any of my diamonds, and my stomach stops churning. On the other hand, if Ian doesn't have it…

With or without it, you are amazing, Cara.

Mack takes me aside, chuckling. "Emmie," he wheedles, "I think you tricked that poor shopkeeper."

This cheers me right up. "Greed wins again." I mock curtsy. "Dropping Veronique's name smoothed the way, but we could have been jewel thieves. He had all those unmarked diamonds and took us right back and brought out the good stuff. He didn't even ask for ID. I could see a real struggle when I asked for a duplicate key, though. He must ride a fine line between avoiding breaking the law and making his clients happy."

Mack calls our driver. "A limo pulling up will reinforce our status as big spenders in case that cranky assistant is watching."

As soon as he hangs up, a cop-car siren sounds, and he looks at the caller ID. "Speaking of the law, it's Bret." He answers, "Hello."

I can tell it's unexpected information from Mack's perplexed frown.

"Okay. Thanks. I'll tell Julianne. 'Bye."

"What's up?"

"Nadya made bail. Then disappeared."

"Bail? How did they end up charging her? And what does he mean disappeared?"

"Guess the McCarren name is a New York institution you don't mess with. The DA asked for the max—conspiracy to commit grand larceny in the first degree."

I rub my fingers up my forehead. "The penalty for that, if she's convicted, must be unthinkable. And she's a huge flight risk. Didn't they take that into consideration when they granted bail?"

Our car arrives, and we get in. Mack continues. "Her court-appointed attorney brought up her squeaky-clean record and agreed to a warrant to search her place for her passport and/or the necklace. Turns out she was packing her passport in that huge purse of hers. It was turned over to the DA's office. When they went to serve the warrant, she wasn't there and had not been there since her release."

"Who paid her bail? Kalashnikov has bigger problems than trying to track down my necklace by springing Nadya."

"Bret went to the bail bondsman to check. It's only

two blocks from the courthouse. The bond was paid by a nicely dressed, good-looking guy. In cash. The description matches your brother-in-law."

If Mitch thinks Veronique doesn't know, he's a fool, Cara.

It strikes me that this is the second time since I've been in New York I've heard Mitch described as good-looking. Not true. He's very average. His features are too big, and if it wasn't for the beautiful gray eyes he and Raif were both blessed with, he could be described as ordinary. As someone who studies faces, looking for people trying to hide theirs, I have come to theorize that wealth adds overly pleasant features to those without them. But that's just me.

"Guess I shouldn't be surprised. Nadya's sneaky. She made it her business to get as much on Mitch as she could, and now she's using it. There goes my theory that he wouldn't help her. I'm sure she called him as soon as allowed. He must really want his secret stash kept from Veronique if he's paid Nadya's bail and maybe even helped her hide. That would be a possible aiding and abetting charge, wouldn't it?"

Mack barely raises an eyebrow at my assertion.

I sigh. Mitch is protecting Nadya while trying to distance himself from his wife. Don't blame him. I just wish his *help* wasn't falling smack in the middle of the recovery of Angel Falls.

Chapter Twenty-Four

The driver is moving slowly in traffic.

Mack leans back in the seat. "Bret called me earlier with the lowdown on the Kalashnikov interview. Short. Wanna hear?"

"They finally got past all the paperwork his lawyers were filing?"

He nods. "Guess he thought he might as well get it over with since the judge froze his assets. Flight risk and all. Bret thinks he had money squirreled away somewhere because he came in with bookend lawyers dressed in very expensive suits. He agreed to answer some questions in the presence of his lawyers. 'Because I am a loyal American and believe in justice system.' "

"You mean because he believes in *using* the justice system."

Mack taps his temple. "That too. First, he denied any connection to Viktor's drug operation. And from what Viktor said, that's probably true. Although it's hard to believe some of his people ran a completely separate enterprise and he didn't know about it. Made him look a little foolish, but better foolish than in prison for something you didn't do."

"Did he know his office was being bugged?"

"According to Bret, that came as quite a shock. His lawyers immediately advised any accusations stemming from illegal listening devices was inadmissible.

Kalashnikov turned pale and asked for water."

"So far, it sounds like he's going to slide on jail time."

"Maybe. The computer ransom case looks pretty solid and is still building. He was also asked if he ordered the hit and run of Timur."

I rub at a frown line on my forehead and look out the car window. At this point, I think it's all Kolya, all the time.

Mack continues. "His first assertion was that he had no idea who Timur was. Bret says he didn't look like he was lying either—that he looked genuinely surprised at the name. Even though Nadya has the same surname. Kalashnikov went on to say the accusation was ridiculous. Why would he be involved? He refused, under strong advisement, to answer any further questions on the subject.

"Same could be said about the stalking of you and the kids. He claimed that was ridiculous, and although he had spoken to the owner of a certain necklace, it was in the hopes of helping her. It is part of his business plan to ingratiate himself with owners of businesses with which he might someday form a partnership."

I choke on a laugh. "Yes, I went to a Russian nightclub hoping to get help from its shady owner in return for recommending him as a legitimate business partner for McCarren Multinational."

Mack smiles. "When asked for the source of his income, he said from his restaurant, Club Bear, and different real estate deals. The condos mentioned on Nadya's Facebook page being one of his partnered investments. Unfortunately, a quick financial audit of Kalashnikov's books revealed your name isn't on any of his paperwork."

"Well I *am* a silent partner."

"That's what he said. 'It is a common business practice.' "

"Sounds like he was prepared to defend himself at every turn. Any other questions he refused to answer?"

"Bret says not many. He was way more cooperative than his attorney liked, who told him several times not to answer, but he did anyway, claiming each time he was a proud American."

Mack's cellphone goes off, and he excuses himself to lean forward and give the driver an instruction, then gets comfortable again.

I think, on some level, Kalashnikov does consider himself a genuine, law-abiding businessman. His illegal enterprises the same as "everyone cheats on their taxes, right?" Either that, or keep denying everything, even in the face of incontrovertible facts.

"Did they ask for his passport?"

"Here's the funny thing—they did, and he produced one that had expired. Apparently, he hasn't traveled to Mother Russia in fifteen years, has no family there, and considers America his adoptive country. No more recent passports on file. At least in his name."

"Wow. So the prosecutor stating he was a flight risk didn't have any basis."

"Pretty much. When asked about the computer-for-ransom operation, Kalashnikov claimed the computers setup in a building he owns were for classes to teach kids at risk how to use computers so they can get off the street and into productive society. 'This is what I was told. I know nothing of this so-called stealing. I cannot track what goes on in all of my buildings.' They did find coursework in one of the rooms, but the guess is it was a stepping-stone to the real core business. Just as easy as teaching them legal stuff.

"Bret says Kalashnikov's attorneys restated their client cannot be held legally responsible for activities in his buildings. When he was told the real location was raided, he turned pale but said he had no knowledge of the place. Sure enough when they tracked who legally owned that building, it went into a Gordian knot that may or may not eventually lead to him or one of his partnerships. You gotta admit that part is genius."

It sounds like the "honest businessman" is winning. "What about bail?"

"Yeah, it was big. He got the money from somewhere, went straight to his home on Long Island, and began working like crazy—on the phone all day. He seems to be using a burner cell. Not sure, since they couldn't get a warrant to bug his house or calls. No idea whether he's working to get himself out of trouble, keep his territory and real estate, or track down and deal with the people he thinks are involved in his takedown."

I mock shudder. "That option is unsettling. Did he ask about Victor's status?"

Mack smiles. "Nope. Probably coached not to since a lot of the information they had against him came from his head bully. And he's too busy saving his butt to have any more interest in your necklace. That they're aware of."

I yawn and check my watch. "Sorry. It's not the company. Just need a break. Going back to the hotel and veg out. Maybe watch a movie and go to bed early."

He grins and gives me a quick hug. "That was my plan. I'll drop you off and do a little more catching up at the office."

Guilt takes residence. I get to take it easy for the rest of the day, and Mack, who's been at my beck and call for over a week, has to work late to keep up. "Sorry you're stuck doing that. I'll find a way to make it up to you."

Not the best thing to say, as he grins and his eyebrow hitches. "I'll remember that."

We ride the rest of the way in silence. As I reach for the car door handle, he says, "Janean Barclay and I'll see you at around nine tomorrow morning. Oh, and if you decide you need to go somewhere, remember your security driver is on twenty-four-hour call."

I thank him and get on my cell. I order one of those giant burgers to be delivered to his office for dinner with the message: *Found a way to make it up to you.*

Chapter Twenty-Five

Sleep abandons me about four thirty a.m. I make hotel-room coffee and stand at the window for a few minutes. It promises to be sunny, so the early morning light and lack of traffic noise make it a calming time of day. The Gramercy Park Hotel is beautiful and in a pretty setting, but I miss the slope of lawn at our house on Lake Sammamish and the shimmer of sun, infrequent though it is, on the water. It's my happy place, and I'm ready to return.

I'm proud of you for sticking this out, Cara.

Raif and I traveled. A lot. We both were in love with the countryside, so Raif attended to business, and I toured city museums. Then we both spent one more day in the city we were visiting before taking off for the country.

I grab my laptop, take a page from Ben and Rippa's book, and stalk Nadya's online personality. I open her Facebook page. Unfortunately, there haven't been entries for the past couple of days. Her previous history shows multiple entries almost every day.

I pull down her list of friends. The page is still wide open. No filters. I recognize a few of the girls that were in the hall outside Mitch's office waiting for a pre-interview. Kolya and several other Russian boys make sure their pictures include their gang tattoos. One is an especially round-faced teen named Mikhail Nikolaev. I remember catching a glimpse of him at Club Bear and thinking how young he was. He was also in the cluster of teens in Central Park. Here he seems a little out of place as the camera captures no visible tats, but one ear is pierced.

I have better luck when I go on Twitter and open #Clubbear. I scroll through dozens of rants about Viktor and Kalashnikov and the closedown of the club. Subsequent posts denounce Viktor as the rat who gave up Kalashnikov and his computer ransom hackers.

I'm still working at my laptop two hours later when Rippa pokes her head around the doorway. "Any coffee left?"

"Sorry. You need to make a new pot." I glance at my computer's clock. "Room service doesn't start delivering until seven."

She starts a new pot, then retrieves her tablet. "Since Kolya seems to be the star of the show, let's focus on what we think we know so far."

I huff out a breath. "I think he's part of this at pretty much all levels except for actually being in the bank and the possession of my necklace. If he can be tied to the listening devices in Kalashnikov's office, we know he was aware of the necklace and Nadya's connection. If his intent was to get the necklace for Kalashnikov, he might have killed Timur to show Nadya he meant business. And she was willing to do anything, thinking Kalashnikov was behind the threats and using Kolya to carry them out. Why not? That's what we thought."

She continues tapping away. "All supposition, but it makes sense."

"After Timur's death, Kolya had no control over

Ian because Ian no longer cared what happened to him, let alone Nadya. I don't think Kolya counted on that."

"If Timur's death is the linchpin, maybe Janean Barclay can get us closer to the truth this morning. Especially with the new possibility that the person who hit him had someone as lookout."

I'm leaving my breakfast tray in the hall for pick up when my cellphone rings. It's Susan.

"Hey. I thought you and Mack would be interested in an interview we're conducting this afternoon since you were the one to suggest a connection between the cleaning women and gang members. We hit on one. Her name's Lila Ivanicha. She's the aunt of a kid named Mikhail Nikolaev and very anxious to come in. Says her sister's in long-term care and Mikhail has no dad on the scene. She's been caring for her nephew, and now he's missing. She admits to planting the mic in the picture frame under the threat from Kolya that Mikhail or his family would be hurt. She desperately wants to help us and get her nephew back safe."

I immediately feel sorry for the woman. "Are you going to charge her for planting the mic? Especially since she did it under duress, in defense of her family?"

"Still up in the air since the place that was being bugged is property we're investigating. Kalashnikov and his sleazy lawyers may want to press charges as a part of his defense—poor businessman just trying to do business in this wonderful country the best he knows how and all of these people are against me wanting to take over my business and frame me. Tsk, tsk, tsk.

"Anyway, we're starting at one thirty this afternoon since the woman in question works nights. The interview doesn't even fall under our unit, but I got the word out about Kolya, and we offered to take it when she came in. This whole case is turning into something bigger than a piece of beautiful jewelry being stolen and copied. Or copied then stolen, it seems."

"Coincidentally, Mikhail Nikolaev is a Facebook friend of Nadya's."

"Which begs the question of how innocent he is. Maybe sending in his aunt to paint a picture and see how well it goes over while he hides out."

"Scary how your mind works, Susan. We'll come in with the information the accident reconstructionist has put together and an additional interview with the accident witness we think you'll find interesting."

"Fun. See you then. By the way, Bret called your brother-in-law to find out if he knew where Nadya landed after he paid her bail. He didn't deny paying her bail but said he had no idea where she went. If he hid her and his wife found out, his home would be colder than Russian tundra. Bret believed him."

I nod, the phone not transmitting the visual. "Me too."

I decide to notify Mack of the interview. He picks up on the second ring. "I know you're probably on your way, but I wanted you to know Susan is interviewing a Russian cleaning woman coming in to the station house this afternoon at one thirty. She's the aunt of one of the kids Kolya intimidates. Can you make it?"

I hear a smile in his voice. "Although I've been neglecting my in-basket in favor of a certain blonde McCarren who has caused me no end of problems, it's back to normal."

I'm really glad he's helping you, Cara.

****

Mack arrives at the same time as Janean Barclay and the coffee and pastries ordered from room service. Rippa has been thrumming with excitement and appointed herself hostess for the meeting.

Janean is a petite Asian woman with shining black hair in a ponytail and beautiful, flawless skin. Mack introduces us, and after shaking hands, she looks around. "Very nice. And private. I've been looking for a place to take my husband on our anniversary."

She glances at the laden dining/work table. "I'm sorry, but the documentation and digital recreation displays on my laptop will require more room." She grins. "Can we move the food? However, I would love a cup of coffee."

We move the pastries to the coffee table and sit at the larger one. Janean hands us each a folder.

"Janean is a Crash Data Services, or CDS, specialist," Mack says. "She brings the next level of investigation to what exactly happens at an accident scene before and after. If, as in Timur's death, it's been ruled undetermined, whether accidental or intentional, she can make a clear determination."

"I apologize for the delay in your evaluation," Janean says. "You might have heard there was a six-car pileup on the Sunrise Highway last week caused by a roadside grass fire that distracted the drivers." She grins. "Believe it or not, no one took the blame for the accident, and two of the cars left before police and assistance arrived. Only one of the two had a rear plate. The driver in the front car swears she was doing the speed limit and didn't tap her brakes to 'gawk' at the fire." She touches the folder in front of her. "Luckily, in that case, as well as yours, I had a couple of helpers."

The same blank look that occupies Rippa's face is probably on mine. Mack's expression of one eyebrow raised only shows interest. What could Timur's hit and run have in common with a six-car pileup?

Janean smiles. "New York City occupants are among the most photographed in the world. Almost as much as London, but not nearly as much as Hong Kong."

"Security and traffic cameras," Rippa exclaims.

"That's right," Janean says. "Best one-eyed witnesses around. Can't change their minds on descriptions from one witness to the next. And they make my job easier. When they're working."

She opens the folder in front of her, and we do the same with ours.

"The first picture is the area in the street where there was trace contact evidence. Tire marks were all identified as braking. Some were acceleration. The investigator at the scene was evaluating his first fatality and might have made a judgment call that the driver tried to stop from hitting a messenger who popped out of the alley. That was the extent of the investigation."

A flood of sadness washes through me. "Ian was right all along. Timur was murdered."

"Tape proves vehicular homicide," Janean says, opening her laptop and loading a video. "This was filmed from the front of a construction site about a block and a half down. Evidence shows the driver knew for sure the cyclist would be at that place and time. It's pretty precise. The video isn't clear or close enough to give detail of the driver, but the action is definite."

She turns to Rippa. "It's graphic if you'd rather not

see it."

Staking out rip-off fraudsters is a lot different than watching someone being murdered. I'm not even sure *I* want to view it. But Rippa gives a jerky nod and leans back a little as Janean clicks it into motion.

The camera in front of the construction site swings slowly east, then west, where a large, two-toned brown car accelerates as Timur flies out of the alley. The car bears down on him, but he has no time to react before he's hit and dragged under. The rest is out of our view.

"Why didn't the police investigator use the cameras?" Rippa asks.

"Good question. I haven't talked to him, but think maybe he trusted his first instincts, then on to the next case. It looked easy peasy, but there's quite a learning curve."

My gaze is frozen on the screen, and my whole body is stiff. A beautiful, loving man high on sunshine and speed has a moment of recognition of what's about to happen. Then impact. The parallel between Timur's last moments and Raif's skiing accident rocks me. Three years ago, or even two, I would've had a mini freak-out at the very least, but I pull out or push through it. Whatever the term, I cope and realize Janean is speaking again.

"...put together a digital recreation from another viewpoint," she says, breaking the silence. "It includes the additional information the witness gave Mack and Julianne yesterday." She taps an icon on her screen, and a representation of the incident viewed from above fades in. A green icon in the shape of a bicycle moves down the alley. Another icon, this time red, in the shape of a car, moves down the street. A red icon in the shape of a man stands at the corner of the alley, and another two icons shaded red are on the sidewalk across the street moving away.

When the bicycle gets to the intersection and the man standing there turns green, the car turns green and speeds up, and the bicycle is hit. It turns red and is dragged to the next alley. While this is happening, the witness turns green, and the man at the corner of the first alley turns red and moves rapidly back through it.

Mack huffs a breath. "Tough to watch, I hope Ian never sees it."

Janean tips her head. "Who's Ian?"

Colored icons notwithstanding, the video is gruesome. "The victim's fiancé. He's the one who's been pushing to have it reclassified as murder."

"Based on the first incident Mack told me about, the fiancé's right. This might have been attempt number two. With the same vehicle."

Rippa leans forward. "Get me up to speed. What happened the first time?"

"Timur got doored. That's what it's called when a cyclist is weaving through traffic and someone opens a car door and they run into it. The injuries can be serious."

Janean pushes a key. "Caught by a security camera in front of a jewelry store near the incident."

We watch a grainy video capture a fast-moving Timur and the same car, now identified as the Greenspans' Oldsmobile, move into the lane on his left, and the back door swings open just as Timur is passing. He hits it hard. The back door slams, and the car drives into traffic without stopping, leaving Timur injured and dazed in the middle lane of traffic.

Mack, Rippa, and I offer a collective gasp.

Janean's gaze takes in the three of us. "Notice anything unusual?"

Rippa raises her hand, and we all laugh. "It was the back door. How come?"

Janean nods. "Gives the messenger, who is very nimble, a half second's less chance to react and avoid. It was well planned. Anything else?"

Rippa looks at Mack and me, then adds, "The car that caused it had no rear plate."

"Good observation." From Janean. "Speaking of which, if the driver immediately behind that incident hadn't been observant, Timur might have been hit and killed that day." She taps her folder. "I've documented all this in writing. Copies in each folder."

A huff of breath slips out as I slump in my chair. "I think we've underestimated Kolya. We, at least I, thought he had more cunning than brains. He told me he was smart, but I figured, with the persona he portrayed, it was just bragging. The kid has very lofty goals for himself, and we may have helped him along."

Mack frowns. "How so?"

"We started connecting the dots, which led police to increased surveillance of Kalashnikov's operations. Viktor was caught, and his offer to make a deportation deal started the dismantling. Which leaves Kalashnikov's territory open for takeover. If Kalashnikov gets jail time or probation and Kolya can threaten and intimidate enough of the people left standing, he has a shot."

Rippa whistles. "We need to get to whoever helped Kolya set up Timur."

I totally agree. "Could have a lead on that. Susan

invited us to an interview of a cleaning lady who came forward with information about her nephew. A gang wannabe who's supposedly been 'recruited' by Kolya under threats."

Janean stands and smiles. "If there's nothing else, I'm meeting a friend for an early brunch."

I stand too and lean across the table to shake. "Sorry. You've given us so much good information we jumped right into speculating."

"Not an issue. Glad I could help."

"If necessary, are you available to testify in court?" I ask.

"Of course. It looks like you're on your way to building a solid case." She turns to Mack. "Invoice to McCarren Multinational, care of you, as usual?"

"Right."

Janean closes her laptop and folder. "Nice meeting you all," she says and leaves.

Mack turns to us, one corner of his mouth tilted up. "I have to keep my copy for my paperwork. Can you turn one of your copies over to Susan and Bret? They'll review it, then get the Homicide unit involved." He stands. "I'll meet you two at the station house."

"Mine," Rippa says as soon as the door closes behind Mack.

"Your copy?"

She rubs her hands together. "Sure. Also my shot at interviewing. Easy peasy. Go to the place Timur used to work and find out how he was scheduled to be there and stuff."

My heart pounds, and I am on the verge of arguing for me or Mack to do it when she holds up a hand. "We already talked about my involvement. Baby steps."

I cheat and use the only arrow in my quiver. "Kolya…"

The name of evil does not faze her. "Has anyone seen him since he was released? Has he been lurking around here?"

I heave a sigh, not wanting to upset the delicate balance of our truce. "What's your plan?"

She squeaks and holds out her hand, ticking off the fingers. "Full disguise, I'm a student doing a video documentary on the death of a bicycle messenger. Looking for details from beginning to end. Some of the service requests probably come via email, so maybe I can get copies."

"What about an appointment?"

"What?"

"You're going in to interview a businessperson regarding a crime. A professional would ask for an appointment instead of just appearing on their doorstep." I point at my head and grin. "Especially if you plan on going all Lady Gaga."

She pumps her fist and pulls up her cellphone. "Lesson learned. Sooo glad you got my back."

Sooo glad she is still listening to me.

A short time later, with some truly creative begging, Rippa has secured ten minutes of the manager's time. "Putting on my wig and I'll be ready."

"I'll call Tangee. Make some notes and questions. We can leave in a half hour."

The light dies in her eyes. "I can handle this alone. You could work on finding Nadya."

I shake my head. "Sorry, Rip. My call. I needed Mack as backup, but you'll have to do with Tangee and me. I'll stay in the car while you work your magic. Not negotiable."

She presses her lips together, then lifts a shoulder. "Okay."

Rippa on the loose. New York will not be the same.

Chapter Twenty-Six

I don't think a trip to the bicycle messenger service requires a disguise, but Rippa is so sure it does I stay quiet. She looks all sparkly in her pink wig, hot pink T, and white denim shorts. Too hot for her jeans and her legs are Pacific Northwest fish-belly white, but she can carry it off. Her huge sunglasses cover the top half of her small face and complete the veil of deceit.

"Ready to rock and roll," she says, grabbing her cellphone. "Gonna tape the interview."

The hotel staff cast discreet glances as we pass through the lobby, but are too judicious to make any comment. Our car and driver are waiting outside the Gramercy Park gate. By her look of surprise at my niece's appearance, the driver has also had some training in diplomacy. We make good time and arrive two minutes before Rippa's appointment. Tangee slides into a slot marked *messenger service customer parking only, fifteen-minute limit.*

"Good luck," I say, but Rippa is already halfway out the door.

"Thanks!"

I have a good view of the office entrance and the alley exit. It's a busy day, and messengers are scurrying in and out, carrying bags and tubes and document cases. As I observe this, it surprises me that in this digital age, there is still a demand for actual hardcopy documents.

Rippa comes out in about ten minutes, a big smile on her face. As she leaves, she runs into a boy heading for the same door. He has a wild haircut and is wearing a black jacket. She points at him behind his back and holds her cellphone in the air as she turns and speaks to him.

The boy takes a step back in what can only be described as awe at her attention. She pats him on the shoulder and videos while she talks to him. His stance relaxes—who is this guy?

My concentration is such that I don't see someone approach the car from the back, at an angle. Tangee has been standing beside it and takes a step toward him. It's Kolya.

My heart-pounding fear instantly transfers to Rippa. I can't think she's seen him, and she's still out there. Tangee orders Kolya to stay where he is. He has no business coming any nearer.

Kolya squints at the back window, then holds out a cigarette. "Looking for a light."

Tangee's stance is solid. Feet apart, arms loose. "Can't help you. No smokers here."

Kolya gives me a grin, along with a stare from his flat, lifeless eyes. He lifts his hand, cocks his thumb, and mock shoots me. This is not a "hey, nice to see you, funny us meeting like this," gesture. It is clearly a threat.

I want to yell or do something equally useless, but I can only think that Mack told me if anything started to go down, do not split the driver's attention between me and whatever he or she is handling. Makes them way less effective. So I just sit here, my hands pressed to my thighs.

Tangee is taking care of Rippa too. She gives Kolya a no-nonsense "Move away. Back the way you came."

Rippa'll be okay, Cara.

Kolya doesn't leave immediately. He shrugs and scans the area, probably looking for potential witnesses. Then he winks at Tangee and backs up a few steps, his head turned toward Rippa and the boy, who are finishing their talk.

Tangee does a great job containing the situation while I'm staring at Rippa and willing her to look in this direction. But she's too busy playing her part.

Finally, the boy goes into the office, and she walks back to the car, giving us a thumbs up, seemingly unaware of who is standing farther back.

As soon as Rippa gets in, Tangee hops in, auto-locks the doors, and studies her side mirror as she starts the car. "Buckle up. Are you ready to leave?"

My heart starts up at the same time. "More than ready. Let's go. And thanks."

Tangee nods as she pulls out. "It helped that Mr. Pierce gave me some pictures of guys to look out for."

She turns onto a busy street, watching the traffic all around us.

I lean forward as far as my seatbelt allows. "Is he following?"

Tangee shakes her head. "Not so far. That junker he got into was pretty distinctive."

Rippa twists to look behind us. "What the heck is going on?"

I am pissed. "I could ask you the same thing. What was that all about? Standing there gabbing with a boy without even watching to see what's going on around you."

Rippa folds her arms in defense. "Didn't you recognize him?"

My nails are digging into my palms. "No. Who was it?"

"One of Nadya's Facebook friends. That Mikhail guy."

I'm not done being mad. "Yes, well, while you were having fun taping him, Kolya popped up."

Her pale face gets a shade paler. "Oh. I felt so lucky to run into Mikhail it didn't occur to me that Kolya might be with him."

I try to relax. "Hope you found out something we can use. I was scared witless."

She nods, her gaze toward the floor. "I think so. I told him I was a student at NYU, working a special project for the summer. 'Dangerous jobs in the city.' He thought that was cool." She raises her gaze to meet mine. "He looked down the street a couple of times. I should have known he wasn't alone."

"Second lesson of the day. Always be aware of who and what's around you."

I give her a clumsy side hug, and she uncrosses her arms.

She does get brownie points for one thing. "Guess he didn't recognize you."

Rippa tips her sunglasses forward to the end of her nose, giving me a pitying look over the top. "*Please*. I told you a disguise would come in handy."

"Okay, okay. Did he tell you why he was there?"

"Nope, and I didn't ask. I figured someone in the gang was involved and backtracking to maybe find out how interested the police are."

"You didn't tell him what you were there for, did you?"

This time her eyes roll. "I screwed up a little, but what do you take me for, a complete newb?"

Fine, I overreached. "Anything else?"

She nods again. "I told him he was interesting and asked if he wanted to have coffee tomorrow. I thought maybe I could tell Susan and Bret and they could pick him up. He liked the offer but shook his head and said he had other stuff to do."

I tap my knee. "Mack and I are meeting with Susan at one thirty this afternoon to watch an interview of a woman named Lila Ivanicha. She's Mikhail's aunt and has admitted to placing the listening devices in Kalashnikov's office. I'm hoping she incriminates Kolya so we can start tying the bits and pieces of this thing together."

"Can I go too?"

"Yes."

Chapter Twenty-Seven

Mack is waiting for us outside the station, but I still scan the area for teenage lookouts. We know where to go once inside, but Rippa goggles in fascination. "This looks like a set from a cop show filmed in New York." She cranes her neck and wrinkles her nose at the stale cigarette smell. "Smells like it should smell too."

We step to the desk and ask for Detective Pavlycheva, and in a few minutes, Susan comes downstairs. I introduce Rippa as my niece and partner-in-training.

Susan offers her hand. "Nice to meet you. Your aunt is a good choice as an investigative role model."

Rippa grins. "I think so."

I'm genuinely pleased at Susan's remark. "Thanks."

On our way up the stairs, I hand Susan the file copy given to me by Janean. "Hard proof the hit and run that killed Timur was premeditated. There's a disc with security camera footage and overhead re-creation that gives specific placements of the car, lookout, witness, and victim. Do you think you can get the cigarette butt out of police custody and into a private testing facility? I'll pay for the test. We can receive results within two days if it's dropped off today."

Susan's eyebrows hike. "You've been busy. Again. Wish our department had money for the same resources." She waves the folder. "Bret or I will push to get this in front of an ADA after the interview."

"I appreciate it."

She shakes her head. "Are you kidding? If we had the help you and Mack have provided on this, we'd be closing cases left and right." She glances back down the stairs. "Although if asked, neither Bret nor I have any knowledge of your investigation results. Which reminds me. I got a text saying you ran into Mikhail this morning. How and where?"

I nod at Rippa. "Your story."

She looks a little nervous but eases out a breath as we reach the second floor. "I wanted to work on my interviewing skills, so when we found out Timur's death wasn't an accident, we went to the messenger's office to see if there was a pattern for the setup. You know, like how did they know he would be coming out of the alley rather than straight down the street kind of thing."

Susan tips her head to pay close attention. "Smart."

"Anyway, I went in pretending I was a student photojournalist doing a story on the messenger hit and run for a summer class credit." Rippa shrugs. "They were really busy and didn't give me much more than the time of day. So I guess you'll have to check out their records yourself."

"Do you have a theory?" From Susan.

Rippa jumps right back in before Mack or I have a chance to respond. "I—we—think this was his third or fourth run to the same address. Could be they had someone dressed nice stand outside an office near the construction site. Then they watched and timed the other deliveries. Timur had figured out the shortest route, and since messengers get paid per delivery…they could've also thrown in a big tip. But they definitely counted on him coming out of that alley."

"Nice. And Mikhail?"

"He was heading into the office when I came out. I recognized him from Nadya's Facebook page and made a big deal out of approaching him and being impressed. Asking if he was a real gang member and that was why he was wearing black leather in the heat."

"Weren't you taking a chance that he was one of the gang sent to relay your whereabouts back to Kalashnikov or Kolya?"

"Nope. I was wearing a disguise." She pulls up her cellphone camera and slides her finger to a picture of her in her shiny pink wig and large sunglasses.

Mack peeks over her shoulder and grins.

Susan shakes her head, laughing.

"Her idea," I say. "I was sitting in a car with tinted windows across the street. He didn't see me."

"Did this Mikhail kid say why he was there?"

"Nope. Whole conversation took under two minutes. I left you an email including my video interview of him."

Susan rubs a finger up her temple. "Missed opportunity, I haven't seen it yet."

Rippa throws me a look, her mouth set. "Tell her the rest, Jules."

"The driver of the car that brought Mikhail was Kolya."

"What? Are you sure?"

"Yes. He looked frustrated, then cocked his thumb, pointed his finger, and mock shot me. Only backing off at our security driver's strong suggestion.

"Since Rippa was in disguise, Kolya must have glimpsed me through the back. Without our driver, Tangee, it would have been bad. Now he also knows Rippa in disguise and out. Plus, he saw her interest in Mikhail. He needs to be tracked down and fast."

Susan blows out a big breath. "Unfortunately, Mikhail is under Kolya's control and according to his aunt, is too terrified to say anything against him. And his aunt only knew about him by name. This is the first time Kolya's been seen since his release. Seeing you interested in one of his young charglings would piss off someone with Kolya's mindset." She checks her watch. "We've got a few minutes, so I'll fill you in on some additional information I got briefed on by the detective who took Ms. Ivanicha's preliminary interview."

Mack glances down the hall to the viewing room. "Good. I haven't heard any of this, except Julianne feels sorry for her."

"Only because I'm under threat by Kolya too. It's not a fun place to be."

Susan nods. "Mikhail's aunt is very verbal. And angry. She admitted to putting the listening device in when we hinted we were processing the fingerprints found on it. When she got through venting about Kalashnikov's cheapness and management style, we asked if she had a son who was a gang member.

"She said no, then started crying. It's her nephew. Her sister's son who's only fifteen and has no father at home. Her sister's in a state facility with terminal lung cancer. The aunt holds two jobs to keep food and shelter going but has little control over her nephew. She's agreed to talk to us but also wants us to talk to the kid."

Mack's eyebrows draw together. "About what?"

"The dangers of his gang lifestyle. She was told if he won't listen to family, he certainly won't listen to police, but she insists."

The image of the round-faced teen appears in my mind's eye. "That's a tough one. I don't think Mikhail has much wiggle room under Kolya's thumb. If he tries to back out now, he could be in real danger."

Rippa is nodding. "He's only fifteen. Worth a try helping him."

Compassion from a brilliant seventeen-year-old who realizes her home life and upbringing are partially responsible for the radical differences in their circumstances.

Susan doesn't look one hundred percent convinced Mikhail is as innocent as represented. "Let's see what she has to say that can help."

We enter the viewing room for the third time. A well-groomed woman of about forty sits at the table, hands clasped in front of her. She looks nervous but determined, pushing out deep breaths.

Susan enters. "Ms. Ivanicha. I appreciate your coming in to talk to us again."

The woman nods and opens her hands in supplication. "I know I am in trouble, but I am anxious to help Mikhail. He is very sweet boy but mixed up." She looks at her inexpensive wristwatch. "I wait tables at dinner, but I still want time to go and look for Mikhail if I am not arrested."

Rippa is staring intently through the glass.

The situation is hard to hear. Ms. Ivanicha's nephew wanted to belong. According to Susan, that's how gangs bring them in. *We're your family now. We got your back, so you owe us.* Works nearly every time. At least until the gang member is dead, in prison, or whacked out on drugs. Very few walk away successfully. Especially with vicious threats coming from someone like Kolya.

Susan is not immune either. This woman holds down two minimum-wage jobs, has a sister who is dying, and is trying to raise her nephew. As opposed to Nadya, who uses anyone she can via her body or blackmail. Instead of standing, hands flat on the table in an aggressive posture, Susan sits across from this interviewee, calmly making notes. "Please tell me why you and your nephew are involved in the situation with the listening device. And be specific."

Ms. Ivanicha interlaces her fingers. "Can I ask first if Mikhail is found? Have you locked him up? I would prefer that to having him with that Kolya boy."

Susan shakes her head, not divulging that Mikhail's been seen, since it would upset the aunt and break the flow of the interview. "I'm sorry. We've been looking for Mikhail but haven't found him yet. Our cruisers in Brighton Beach have copies of the picture you provided."

The aunt sinks into herself, worry deepening the creases around her mouth. "I have no husband or children, and my sister has just Mikhail. Not much of family life for the boy and he is so young to be on the streets with vicious gang."

Susan nods. "You said he was being blackmailed. What makes you say that?"

"I will start at beginning," Ms. Ivanicha says. "About six months ago, Mikhail comes to me very upset. The gang leader of the teens who hang around that club for young people at night has told him he wants favor. I can hardly listen because Mikhail has black eye. 'Where did you get that?' I ask. I want to take away the pain from his eye, but he brushes that off. 'I'm okay,' he says. 'The other guys usually look out for me. But you have to help with this.' "

Susan's voice is encouraging. "Can you be clear about the name of the gang leader you're talking about?"

Ms. Ivanicha tips her head. "I only know he is called Kolya. I do not know his surname."

"Okay. Go ahead."

"I tell Mikhail I will not help anyone who I think hurts younger boys and makes them do nasty jobs which are not legal.

"Mikhail beg me. He says, 'Kolya knows where we live and where mother is in hospital. He says it will be easy to pull plugs on her or hit you with car. Lots of hurtful things could happen when we are not looking if he doesn't get his way.' "

Rippa's freckles emphasize her paleness. "Did you hear that about hitting her with a car? We need to stop him."

Nice scenario, but delusional. I tip my head toward Susan. "Not up to us. He'll get his. Karma's a bitch, and being female, we should be happy our gender will take care of him."

Rippa snorts. "Good one. But just in case, I call shotgun."

Mack takes a wide step to the side. "Do *not* mess with Parkes women."

Ms. Ivanicha continues. "My heart is beating very fast now. And I think what can I do that this boy Kolya wants so bad he threatens young boy and two women, one who is very sick. I think he is evil young man and for a minute, wish in my heart that something will happen to him so I will not have to do as he says."

The aunt is now rubbing her fingers against her thumbs. "Mikhail takes shiny round kind of button out of his pocket and says I am to put behind picture near Kalashnikov's desk. He hands me list of dates to put it in then take it out. 'What is this?' I ask.

"Mikhail shrugs like is not big deal. 'It listens to what is being talked about in the office. That's all. Kolya wants to find things out, and this is his way.'

" 'This is illegal to listen to people without their knowing it,' I say. 'He wants me to do illegal thing, or he will hurt us?'

"Mikhail hangs his head. 'Yes.' "

Susan is nodding. "You decided to do as you were told and insert the listening device rather than let your family get hurt?"

"Yes, ma'am."

Mack's voice softens. "She's coaching her. Good for Susan."

I nod. "Agreed, but skating close to unethical."

"Unusual circumstance. Susan can handle it," replies Mack.

Back in the interview room, Susan looks up from her notes. "Almost done. One last question. Do you have any idea where we can find your nephew *or* Kolya?"

Ms. Ivanicha's shoulders hunch, and she shakes her head. "I only know when Mikhail is home or at that nasty club place. He has not been home for two days, and club place is closed. The Kolya boy, I don't know and don't care what happens to him."

Susan stands. "Thank you again for your cooperation. We'll have your statement typed up and ask you to come in and sign it in the next few days. Can you wait for just a few more minutes?"

The aunt nods and relaxes as Susan leaves the room.

Susan comes into the viewing room and starts to speak when Bret pokes his head around the door jamb. "We found Mikhail. He was dumped at the entrance to the emergency room of New York Methodist Hospital about a half hour ago. He was beat up pretty bad. None of the kids who were seen dropping him off hung around."

Chapter Twenty-Eight

Rippa starts, her eyes wide. "What? We just saw him a couple of hours ago. How bad is he hurt?"

Bret looks at me. "Your niece?"

I nod.

He continues. "I don't know the extent. We were running a routine BOLO that includes canvassing hospitals. The admitting nurse in Emergency at New York Methodist said the boy gave his full name as he thought he was going to die and he wanted his aunt and mother notified."

Rippa steps back. "Die? It's that bad?"

"Got the stuffing kicked out of him," Bret replies. "But they haven't found any permanent damage so far. Plus, he's young."

She lets out a breath. "Good."

Heartfelt for someone she'd been standing on the sidewalk in the sun chatting with a short time ago. I pat her shoulder. "Do you want to go see him?"

Rippa steps toward the door. "Yes. Can we go now?"

I hold up a hand in her direction. "Seems like we might have to wait a while and get permission to talk with him."

Susan nods. "He'll need to be interviewed by us first. And his aunt or a legal representative will probably be with him. I'd wait a couple of hours.

Sounds like he's going to need some rest and is most likely overwhelmed."

Rippa's mouth is set downward in disappointment. "Okay."

I turn to Susan. "Are there any charges he'll have to answer to?"

She holds up the folder with the information Janean put together. "They're minor right now, but if it turns out he's part of this, there could be some major ones."

Red flags ride high on Rippa's cheeks. "Even with the extenuating circumstances we just heard?"

Susan lifts a shoulder. "Those, and him being only fifteen could go a long way toward leniency. Too soon to know. It may also depend on whether he has the guts to testify against Kolya."

Rippa sucks in a gasp. "Are you going to tell his aunt? I mean about him being in the hospital."

"Of course. She's been a big help, and she wants him out of the gang life. Maybe this is the wake-up call he needs."

I run my hand down Rippa's upper arm. "Late lunch and then we'll see if he's feeling well enough for a visit."

Susan's empathy is real. "I'll call and let you know."

"Let me know how it goes too," Mack volunteers. "I need to get back to my office."

****

Rippa and I go to lunch, but neither of us is hungry. A half hour after we return to the hotel, I get a call from Susan. "He's groggy but able to take visitors for a few minutes. I told the aunt about you, and she's protective

259

but willing to let you see him."

Rippa is all nerves again, rubbing the side of her nose and sighing.

"Going in there all wound up won't help, you know."

"I know."

An underlying fear or something not normally in Rippa's emotional makeup has colored her outlook. I give her a quick hug. "Hey. You still okay with this?"

She pushes out a breath and settles her shoulders. "The work we were doing back home. It never involved kids getting hurt, you know? Taking advantage of someone like Mikhail is just wrong. It makes me sad and angry."

"Me too. But this kind of situation is bound to crop up in investigation work occasionally. We just haven't experienced this kind of up-close-and-personal physical threat. If you want to back off and just be a technical assistant or spot me in the car for a while, I'm more than good with that."

Rippa is looking very young. She's almost eighteen and very mature for her age but doesn't always trust her decisions. "Can I evaluate a situation before I jump in?"

"Sure. You ready to visit Mikhail?"

"Yes."

****

Mikhail looks even younger without his gang clothes. He is eight kinds of a hot mess lying there, his skin splotched with bruises and abrasions. His aunt is in a chair by his bed, pulled up close and holding his hand. She doesn't look happy to see us.

I walk to her and hold out my hand. "My name is Julianne McCarren, Ms. Ivanicha. This is my niece,

Rippa. We're helping in an investigation. Detective Pavlycheva said you might allow us to ask Mikhail a few questions."

She doesn't take my hand and shakes her head. "You think my Mikhail steal necklace?"

"No, of course not. But he has been in close contact with Kolya Vladimirhoff, who is a person we and the police are interested in finding on a more serious matter."

A nurse is on Mikhail's other side, eavesdropping and checking his vitals. "Make it short. He's on pain meds and needs rest."

His aunt gives a curt nod.

One eye is swollen closed, but Mikhail peers through the other at us. "Do I know you?" Then a glimmer of recognition.

The nurse backs off but goes to stand by the door, unwilling to leave her charge. A she-bear guarding her cub couldn't be more wary.

"Hi. Remember me?" Rippa says. "I was wearing a pink wig and these." She pulls out her large sunglasses.

Mikhail makes a face, then sucks in air as if it hurts. "Yeah. You aren't really a student at NYU. What are you doing here?"

Rippa tips her head toward me. "This is my aunt. But you probably already know that. We've been working with a security agent to recover her stolen necklace. We think Mr. Kalashnikov and Kolya are involved."

If I thought he couldn't get paler, I was wrong. His good eye gazes at us, then looks away. "He wanted to know where you were going, who you were talking to. I didn't want to scare you."

I attempt a weak smile of assurance. "Did you lose us when we moved out of the hotel?"

He nods. "Kolya was mad." He remakes eye contact. "The police were here asking questions. Are they going to arrest me?"

"I think a good question is were you forced to do illegal things against your will?" I ask quietly.

The teen turns his head. "Yeah. At first, for me to prove I was worthy of being a gang member. Then I had to do some bad stuff, or my family would be hurt."

I make a decision based on pure emotion. Either Mikhail is an Oscar-performance-worthy actor, or he's been afraid of Kolya for some time. I speak to his aunt. "I'd like to pay for some really good legal representation for you and Mikhail."

She looks suspicious. "You don't know us. Why do you ask to do this?"

"Kolya's greed and need to be in control has hurt and maybe killed innocent people. I'd like to help someone he's hurt because I can afford to. And because I'm one of those people."

His aunt looks perplexed. "You have been hurt, also?"

I nod. "Inadvertently."

She looks at Mikhail. "If this will help keep Mikhail safe…"

"I'll leave you my card to think about it."

"I'm sorry this happened to you," Rippa says, sitting in the chair on the other side of Mikhail's bed. "I don't think you deserved it."

He tries to smile, but a tear leaks from the corner of his eye. "Me either. Stupid I guess."

Rippa gives him a break. "Not really. A bad

decision that seemed right at the time."

"Mikhail, can you tell us a few things?" I ask.

He tips his head as far forward as his injuries allow.

"Were your orders given by Kalashnikov or by Kolya?"

At the mention of our quarry's name, Mikhail stiffens. "I told the police we don't talk to Mr. K. It was Kolya. Always. He said orders were from Mr. K., but these last few months, we didn't think as much."

"Who's we?"

"The rest of the guys who hang around the club."

"Are they the ones who dropped you off?"

Mikhail tries to stifle a moan when his head falls back on his pillow. "I guess. I was pretty messed up. One minute I was being hurt so bad I thought I was going to die, and the next, Kolya was gone."

Rippa squeezes his hand, an action his aunt frowns at.

"Police already talk to him. He is in pain. Are you finished?"

"One more question," I say. "Did the police ask who hurt you?"

Mikhail averts his eyes and nods.

Rippa stands and pats his hand. "Thanks, Mikhail. Get better."

I hand my card to his aunt. "I meant what I said about helping. My number is on the back."

Chapter Twenty-Nine

Rippa and I are quiet after visiting Mikhail. We walk into the hall outside his room. Tangee is talking to the officer assigned to guard him. "Where to?" she asks.

My niece turns to me. "You never bought any souvenirs, and I'm sick of all my clothes. How about a short shopping trip and New York pizza? Please?"

Tangee jingles the car keys. "I live in Brooklyn." She hikes her thumb toward Mikhail's door. "If the guy who did this is the guy we saw earlier, no way he's all the way out there." She points at the cop on the door. "According to him, he hasn't been seen anywhere. Want to cruise my home turf? I can show you where to get some great tees and the best pizza ever."

Rippa answers for both of us. "We're in."

****

After touring Brooklyn, shopping, and eating with Tangee, Rippa and I decide on a cool room and showers. Tangee drives us back to Gramercy Park, "Summer in the City" playing low on the car's music system.

My short hair is low maintenance, so a wash and going over with a hair dryer for two minutes is all I need. I have just finished pulling on a new T-shirt when Rippa yells, "Jules! Come in here quick."

I run into our common room.

"Look," she says, pointing at the TV. "I was surfing and...look!"

I see the standard male and female news bots behind a desk. As the woman is speaking, the screen flashes a picture-in-picture mug shot of Kolya. "The body has been identified as Kolya Vladimirhoff, nineteen. He was found by a Crime Scene Investigation unit in a storefront that until recently was a decoy for a computer ransom ring. The unit was there on a tip that the location was the scene of a recent attack on another gang member. The building is owned by and also houses the office of a Russian businessman who is under police investigation."

I sit on the foot of Rippa's bed as the news moves on to other items.

"Wow," Rippa breathes. "Kolya dead. I can imagine the why, but I wonder how?"

"And who?"

She holds up a couple of fingers. "Someone who works for Kalashnikov or someone getting even for Mikhail's beating."

Another option occurs to me. "Or."

"What?"

My answer springs from a dark but legitimate knowledge. "I wonder if Ian somehow found out about Kolya's involvement with Timur's death. He has plenty of money and might have hired some anonymous thugs to take care of Kolya."

"That's sad to think of. I hope it wasn't him."

Remembering I had threatened Kolya with a beating just last week makes me shiver. "Me too." I retrieve my cellphone and call Mack. "Just saw the news about Kolya."

"Been in my office since the interview, but I took a short call from Bret. He told me about Kolya and gave me an update on Mikhail."

"Yeah. He looked pretty rough, but he'll probably bounce back."

He chuckles. "Since you're satisfied he'll be okay, you New York women have probably been shopping and seeing the sites."

The news clip keeps running a loop in my head. "We indulged a little after we saw Mikhail. Did Bret tell you Kolya's body was found in the empty storefront that had those heavily curtained windows?"

He whistles. "Bad luck for Kalashnikov, worse for Kolya. Although it will save the city money in prosecution and trial funds."

"Sad way to think of it, but yeah. Did he tell you if the police have any idea who did it?"

He makes a derisive sound. "Several candidates. He and Susan are getting their information from their Homicide counterparts, so they're left with suppositions until they hear more. Guessing Homicide owes them one since Bret and Susan turned over two cases that were already solved. The Homicide guys don't even have to build a case against Kolya.

"Good news, better news."

"You could've led with that. What is it?"

"Found Nadya."

I've almost forgotten about Mitch's manipulating ex-assistant. "Where?"

"Just as was suggested earlier—tucked away in an apartment McCarren Multinational has as a visiting client space. The building where the units were undergoing renovation. I talked to Fletcher, and he said the unit wasn't supposed to be occupied until the painting was done, but she convinced the painters she was allowed. Showed them the key."

"Gotta say, Nadya made good use of Mitch's key ring."

"She's not talking. She'd been there since Mitch bailed her out. They don't know if Mitch offered her the place and the key or whether she helped herself and had a duplicate made when she had access to his key ring. Her court-appointed attorney has been trying to contact your brother-in-law, without much luck."

Nadya strikes again. "What's going to happen to her?"

"Her passport is still with the police, and she missed her flight to Russia. Same song as before. She claimed she didn't let the court know where she was because she was in fear for her life. That Kolya was looking for her. The DA is working on the list of people involved in the death of Timur since we submitted Janean Barclay's reconstructions. Nadya's back in holding as a flight risk and may be spending hard time for her part in the plot that got Timur killed. And for instigating the theft of your necklace.

"Susan and Bret are going over your case tomorrow morning at nine. Bret said if you and Rippa are available, you're welcome to sit in."

"We'll be there."

Chapter Thirty

Mack and I are sitting in Susan and Bret's tiny office for the case overview. Rippa's here too. Bret tried to give her his chair, but she's fidgety from excitement and wants to stand.

Susan opens the file. "This is an interesting case, considering it started as a theft and ended with a gang bust and two murders." She glances at the closed door and smiles. "It wouldn't've gotten this far without your help, though. And again, we won't discuss how it sometimes skated on the edge of legal."

The declaration pulls at the corners of my lips. "Any solid leads on who killed Kolya?"

"Not a peep from one corner," Bret answers. "According to Homicide, although he had motive, and certainly means, Kalashnikov's lawyers have depositions that he was in meetings with his real estate partners and subcontractors all afternoon on the day the kid was beaten to death."

Rippa breathes a quiet, "Oh."

I rub my hands together. "We, um, didn't know that was how he died."

Bret ruffles the edges of the report. "Sorry."

Mack waits a beat, then taps Susan's desktop. "Kalashnikov also had access to, and control over, construction workers who depend on a paycheck, and kids who are on the fringe and want to prove themselves. However, during the little contact we had with him, he didn't strike us as a guy who hires out hits."

Susan nods. "That's the wrinkle. Kalashnikov's dirty, but it's white-collar dirty. We went through the documentation the gang unit had on him, and he makes most of his money in shady real estate deals and lately, in the computer-for-ransom gig, which may or may not net him short jail time. No hint of drugs, prostitution, white slavery, or gambling. Nothing as heavy-handed as taking over a rival gang's territory or having someone killed. Violence and murder just don't fit Kalashnikov's character profile. Something Kolya didn't understand."

"Yeah," Bret adds. "To him, being a gang member meant threats and thuggery, the way his father handled things. In the end, the way his father handled things is how Kolya died."

I lean back. "I thought he didn't know his father."

Susan nods. "Only that he died in Black Dolphin Prison. Kolya has lived on the streets, stealing and drifting in and out of gang situations for ten years, his head full of stories about his badass father."

I shudder. "He looked pretty fit. I'm thinking it took more than one assailant."

"And more than one weapon besides fists," Susan says. "No bullet wounds, but not an easy way to go."

I shake my head. "Neither is getting hit by thousands of pounds of steel and dragged on the asphalt. No sympathy here."

Susan lifts a shoulder. "Speaking of sympathy. I got a chance to talk to Mikhail and his aunt. The more I talk to them, the more sympathy I have. My gang unit experience and personal interviews convinced me he just wanted somewhere to belong. Kolya took advantage of that, and Mikhail was in over his head right away. Had Kolya been brought to trial, odds are he would have been convicted if Mikhail testified."

"You think my running into Mikhail at the messenger service office had to do with his beating?" Rippa asks.

I know she feels some of the blame for engaging in conversation with Mikhail while Kolya looked on, but my niece wants to be treated as a real investigator, and Susan obliges. "Partly. We think Kolya saw him as a liability, and his solution was to shut him up, permanently."

Rippa stiffens. "Kolya intended to beat Mikhail to death? That is so gruesome."

Bret holds his hand out. "Possibly. Here's what we know, and here's what we *think* we know. The Homicide guys, with our help, are piecing together a scenario. If we eliminate Kalashnikov as instigator behind the attack on Kolya, that leaves the possibility other gang members acted independently."

"His friends turned on him?" Rippa blurts.

Mack shakes his head. "I don't think Kolya had any friends. From what we've learned, he bullied and intimidated everyone."

"He was an outsider," Susan affirms. "Used to hang around another, larger gang, before moving in on the group at Club Bear. What he didn't figure on was Kalashnikov's business model. If that's what you want to call it."

Bret now holds up three fingers. "His organization might have looked like easy pickings. One big score for the boss and you're in the inner circle. He overhears Nadya's drunken bragging and decides Timur is his leverage against Nadya, who can get the key, and Ian, who can get to the box. But he can't carry off his threats against Timur without help, so he chooses the youngest and most vulnerable member of the gang. Mikhail."

Susan leafs through her folder to the picture of the badly beaten teen. "Luckily for Mikhail, the other gang members have adopted him as a sort of mascot. They don't interfere until things start to fall apart after Viktor's arrest. They can see Kolya's control is slipping and he takes Mikhail everywhere. They don't like it and keep close tabs."

I'm thinking some good came from all this. "You're surmising the boys without names who dropped Mikhail off at the hospital were other gang members."

Bret lifts a shoulder. "Could be they stopped the beating and a couple of them took Mikhail in while the rest took down Kolya."

All this talk about Kolya is giving my stomach the willies.

As the Russian gang unit liaison to the theft unit, Susan takes it more or less in stride. "It fits. According to Viktor, none of them liked Kolya. He just appeared one day and started taking over the younger crowd. After one of the regulars ended up with a broken jaw, Kolya wasn't challenged anymore. That and he probably thought he was smarter than any of them."

"None of them are talking," she says. "The gang unit rounded up a half dozen kids who are loosely connected and admit hanging out at Club Bear. Several had suspicious facial and body bruising but ready answers for the marks."

Rippa leans in. "Is Mikhail going to be okay? Legally, I mean?"

Susan pins me with a stare. "Mikhail and his aunt have somehow acquired a highly paid, top-notch defense attorney. Given that he's a minor and acted under duress, the kid'll probably be given a slap on the wrist, some community service, and his record sealed. His aunt will probably be given a pass too. You happy?"

Rippa jumps in. "I am. Jules is spending my inheritance, but in this case, I'm all for it. Just curious, though. What about Nadya?"

Susan's smile blooms. "Different story. Nobody has stepped up with a big-ticket attorney for her, but I'm guessing blaming the better part of the scheme on Kolya, now that he's dead, will be the strongest part of her defense."

Either Mitch has come to his senses, or Veronique has put her designer-clad foot down.

I hope Mitch has decided to do the smart thing, Cara.

Rippa rolls her eyes. "Finally. Uncle Mitch made a good decision."

My concern switches to Ian. He was such a vulnerable mess when I saw him last. I try to scoot forward, without much success. "I haven't heard anything about Ian Ward. I told the ADA in interview I wouldn't press charges, but he said that doesn't make a difference. It's a federal matter because a bank was involved. They're taking Ian's state of mind into account, but if they ever catch up with him, he *will* be charged."

Bret shrugs, his gaze on the paperwork. "His residence isn't in our district. Neither is his beach house on Fire Island, so we aren't privy to any sightings, but since his offense doesn't involve bodily harm or murder, I doubt he'll make the ten most wanted."

Some bit of my brain is happy their theories don't include making Ian a big target. Part of his life winked out in an instant because a narcissistic sociopath decided it would give him creds with the boss to use any means to get a hot necklace.

My sympathy goes out to Mikhail too, but he had choices and made bad ones.

Susan checks her watch. "Just about time for our mandatory attendance at the weekly staff meeting." She gives a Rippa-worthy eye roll. "Thanks to you we have some progress to report. Let us know if you need anything, and we'll do likewise."

She and Bret stand and hold out their hands. "We're still hoping to track down Ian Ward and get your property back," Bret says. "Looks like the last step to the recovery. Fortunately, your necklace is probably still in one piece. Something I would not have bet on at the beginning of this investigation."

I nod, and Rippa, Mack, and I shake their hands.

We descend the ancient stairs and arrive on the hot, muggy sidewalk.

"Next steps?" Mack asks. "Ian has disappeared, and if he does have your necklace, it's kind of a waiting game. You going home?"

Yes. Give yourself a break, Cara.

I release a deep, unsatisfying breath. "Bret and Susan assume so. I'll have a few days to think it over since the next available flight for Rippa and me to Atlanta is a couple days out."

Tangee Pike pulls to the curb, and Mack opens the car door. "She'll drop you at the hotel, then me to my office. Okay?"

I am distracted and not happy that this is probably the way my involvement ends and I still don't have my necklace. "Sure."

We are ten minutes into the drive when my cellphone rings. It's Ms. Barrick.

"Ian Ward has returned to work."

Chapter Thirty-One

The box is empty of my necklace. I'm cold and hot at the same time. For a futile half minute, I shuffle the contents with shaky fingers. The necklace is not here. As I move the papers around, a small, pale-blue envelope catches my attention. I didn't put it in here, and it has no name or information on it, so I slip it out, slide my thumb under the flap, and open it. There is a note.

Mrs. McCarren, my heart hurts that I took and held your beautiful necklace. It was an irrational thing to do. I'm returning it as I am more at peace now that Timur's death was changed to murder and his murderer is dead. I know you had a part in exposing him, and for that I thank you. I used the key Nadya gave me. It's on my desk under my employee badge. I will not come back to the bank, and I will not forget you as I know we share a bond of healing.

Yours, Ian Ward

Ian was gone when we arrived, and I'm happy to see he's finding peace but wonder if he realizes how much trouble he's in admitting to a federal crime in writing. Or if that holds any importance to him.

I glance in the box, tears banking behind my eyelids. Why would he leave a note saying he returned Angel Falls and change his mind but still leave the note? I don't know how he found out about Kolya's

275

murder or that Timur's death was changed from accidental to vehicular homicide, but I don't care. I take the envelope, close my box, and leave.

Mack and Rippa stand and take a step toward me, aware something's not right. I hand Rippa the note. "It's from Ian. He says he returned the necklace." I shake my head. "It's not here."

Mack's eyebrows draw together. "What the hell?"

The bank security man he's been working with, whose name is Comstock, has been called by Barrick and steps forward. "May I see the contents of your purse?"

Anger rises in me, but I realize it's his job and hand over my small crossbody. "Knock yourself out."

He makes short work of the inspection and hands my purse back, eyeing my T-shirt and cotton capris.

I hold my arms out wide. "Not on my person either."

His gaze slides away. "Policy for the security of our vault clients."

"So I can't claim the necklace wasn't there, then walk out with it. That's your job—I get it."

Rippa eyes Comstock as she passes the note to Mack. "Still rude."

I come very close to violating Comstock's personal space. "Where's Barrick?"

His cheeks fill with air, then he expels it, eyeing the note Mack is reading. "She was here until a few minutes ago. Would you like to talk to her again?"

A scenario is forming in my mind, and I'm too desperate to ignore it. "Yes. She said she'd be available."

He nods, then hesitates. "May I read the note?"

My turn to hesitate. I don't want to lose Ian's assertion that he left the necklace, but I need to keep bank security in the loop. Mack hands me the note and envelope. I turn it over to Comstock. "I'd like it returned."

"Thank you," he says and quickly scans it. When he looks up, I can see by his indirect glance that he didn't expect to find anything personal. He clears his throat. "Looks like it's pertinent to our investigation. I'll make you a copy."

Can't help liking this guy. Doesn't pander or genuflect at the mention of the McCarren name. Doesn't apologize for doing his job.

Mack rests his hand lightly against the small of my back, and my anxiety eases. "All right," I answer, and Mr. Comstock heads off.

Rippa leans in when he's out of earshot. "You think Ms. Barrick is involved?"

I lift a shoulder. "Not leaving till I get some answers. She's been privy to a lot of the information on the theft, and she's also known Ian the longest."

Rippa pulls out her cellphone, checks the time, and cranes her head toward the hallway Comstock is going down. "Somebody was very fast. The three of us got here about eleven minutes after she called you."

I tip my head. "*If* she was telling the truth about what time Ian left."

Mack starts to speak when Comstock returns accompanied by Ms. Barrick, who has the note in her hand.

Her color is not good, and her shoulders and mouth are stiff. "Mr. Comstock has given me the note that might have come from Ian Ward. Unfortunately, he can't verify that you didn't have the note on your person when you entered the bank." Didn't take long for her to come up with that plausibility.

I push down resentment at the implication that I'm a liar. "You're wasting my time. I want some answers."

She seems at a loss for a response, so I push my theory.

"First, I'd like to see Ian's desk."

Her mouth twitches as she cuts a glance at Comstock and back to me. "For what purpose?"

My patience has bottomed out, but I think I might be one step ahead of her. "According to his note, that's where Ian left the replicated key to my vault box."

This presents a crossroads for Ms. Barrick. The necklace is gone, presumably within the last fifteen or twenty minutes. Whoever took it was unaware of the note, or they would have taken it too. If the key is where Ian left it, either someone inside the bank took it, used it, and put it back, or another key was used.

Comstock and Barrick cut a quick look at each other, but neither claim the key has already been turned over to bank security.

Ms. Barrick has the added difficulty of dealing with the McCarren name. If she stays negative, she risks McCarren Multinational reducing or taking its business elsewhere. She huffs a breath and leads me, Rippa, and Mack deeper into employee-only territory. Comstock takes up the rear. She stops at an ordinary metal and Formica desk, its top containing a computer screen and keyboard, a wood pencil holder, Ian's badge, and underneath it, the forged key and another one, presumably the master used by the escorts.

Ms. Barrick sways a little, then tips her head

toward the desk. "This was Ian's."

I notice she uses past tense.

"Was there an escort other than Ian available this morning?"

Her gaze lands on the corner of the empty desk, her *I'm in charge* veneer slipping. "No, why?"

Anger brings back the edge to my voice. "Because I believe Ian's note. Which means my necklace was taken after he returned it and before I got here. That's a very short list of people who could have done it."

She lifts her gaze from Ian's desk and frowns. "You think Ian returned your necklace, then someone at the bank used the key to take it?"

"I think *a* key plus an escort master key was used after he left. Yes."

Comstock's on full alert. He glances at the employees at nearby desks. "We can continue this conversation in Ms. Barrick's office or a conference room."

Heads cant toward us, and Ms. Barrick agrees, some of her managerial spine returning.

Mack has stepped to one side and used his cellphone. He turns to the group. "The police detectives in charge of this case have been notified. They'll be here soon but are leaving it up to Mr. Comstock to notify the federal agents on the case."

Comstock nods and addresses Ms. Barrick. "Do you mind answering a few questions for them?"

She lifts a shoulder. "I'm sure we should help if we can." Her haunted eyes tell another story.

The five of us continue into the same small conference room across from Ms. Barrick's office. It's where Mack and I first interviewed Ian almost two weeks ago. Comstock closes, then stands by the door, and Ms. Barrick sits at the head of the table. I stand, too agitated to sit, my hands holding the back of a padded chair. Mack and Rippa sit, their chairs flanking mine.

I think maybe Comstock expected immediate denial of any involvement by bank employees at my earlier assertion, and his stiff body language intimates he is not happy.

My confidence is building that I'm right. I turn to Ms. Barrick. "Did you speak to Ian this morning?"

"Yes, of course. He came in a little early and filled out paperwork ending his personal leave."

"And you didn't notify Mr. Comstock or me?"

She studies her hands clasped on the table. "Technically, Ian hadn't broken any laws that I had been notified of as yet, Mrs. McCarren. I had no real obligation to notify anyone."

And a darn good reason to keep his return to herself for a while.

"Then why did you call me when he left?"

"That was unintentional," she responds, her gaze meeting mine. "You asked me to call you when he returned to work. I got busy compiling my weekly reports, and when I had a minute, I called. It was ringing when Ian tapped on my door and leaned in. He said he was sorry, he thought this would work out, but it hadn't. Thanked me for my help, then said he wouldn't be back." She shrugged. "Just like that. No paperwork. No exit interview. He just left."

I'm sure Ian had things on his mind other than giving an exit interview, but his abrupt vanishing act could be why she had sounded scattered when I talked to her. Or something else may have contributed to her state of mind.

"That's why I told you he had returned this morning but was now gone for good. I had no idea there was a note where he'd admitted taking your necklace." She tilts her chin up. "Or that theory was why you wanted me to call you."

One of several theories, but it's looking stronger. "Ian worked for you for five years. Was that his handwriting on the note?"

Her gaze skitters away again. "Yes, but maybe it was written under duress."

Rippa snorts inelegantly. "Right. By an imaginary bad guy."

Pale red flushes across Ms. Barrick's cheeks, but she still has enough grit left to shoot Rippa a look of censure. "I don't know what you want me to say."

I'm trying to fit all the pieces together. Barrick's a nice woman with a decent job who is supposedly not Russian or crazy. That passing assertion by Ian that her daughter had a serious and obscenely expensive disease just might be a piece. She is starting to fidget and could call a halt to what has turned into a personal interrogation, McCarren name or not.

I need to keep this moving. "I would like to see the digital recording of the vault access for the last hour."

Dulled eyes meet my gaze. "You needn't bother. I was the last person to go in."

"With a client?" I ask, knowing the answer already.

She shakes her head. "Ian's sudden departure scared me. His access was, I guess *trusted* is the word. Until he walked out."

Shining the light of suspicion on Ian. It's another good ploy. "You went into the vault to make sure there were no obvious signs of theft? Is that bank policy?"

Comstock interrupts. "You should have called security."

"I did when I came back out," she says, then turns to me. "No, it's not. It's a personal habit. Mr. Comstock and I hadn't even had time to go to Ian's desk when you arrived. I escorted you into the vault and went back to my office to call Human Resources."

She has answers for every step she took this morning, and I can't put my finger on why I'm not buying it. Maybe it's *too* smooth. My thoughts are interrupted by a squeaking, and I realize my fingers are digging into the chair back and the slight rocking motion is causing the seat to squeak.

Mack stills the chair by holding the armrest, then addresses Comstock. "When the report's written up, we'll need duplicate copies for McCarren Multinational, NYPD, and the feds on the case. It's still open, and I'm sure they'd like to investigate the details. Especially the timing involved."

Ms. Barrick blinks more rapidly than normal. "Timing?"

A light tap sounds at the door, and an employee leans in. "Ms. Barrick? Someone said they saw you come in here. I'm sorry to interrupt, but there is a Mrs. McCarren in your office. She insists you have a package for her and wants you to step out for a few minutes."

The room goes dead silent. Except for Comstock. He looks at me. "Is there another Mrs. McCarren involved in this?"

Rippa starts to giggle. Mack slaps the table and laughs. We are of one mind.

"Yes, there is." I look hard at Barrick. "Where is it?"

Chapter Thirty-Two

Faced with Veronique's presence in her office across the hall, the vault supervisor unravels. "In my desk." She puts her hands to her face. "Mia," she says, with a shaking voice. "I'm so sorry."

Comstock turns to the girl at the door. "None, I mean *none* of this is to be repeated. I'll be by your desk later to get a statement." He closes the door and turns back to the room. "Ms. Barrick, do not answer any questions without the bank's legal representation. Do you understand?"

She is shaking hard now but nods.

Rippa leans back to me, one hand cupped to her mouth. "Who's Mia?"

"I think I know. Tell you later."

"I'm going to need a quick rundown on the involvement of the other Mrs. McCarren," Comstock says.

I nod. "My sister-in-law, Veronique McCarren, is obsessed with my necklace. She had a copy made to wear to up-scale social events, intimating the original was hers."

He glances at the door as if he can see through to Barrick's office and the flaky woman within.

I continue. "I'm guessing Veronique cozied up to Ms. Barrick, waving a fat checkbook, on the off-chance that if the real necklace was returned, Ms. Barrick could obtain it for her. She either used her husband's key to my box or took it off his key ring and had her own copy made. And Ian Ward would end up being blamed for the whole thing. The catch came when Ms. Barrick overlooked Ian's note in her haste to take the necklace before I got here. She probably called Veronique the minute she had it, wanting it gone as soon as possible."

"She had a copy of a bank-issued key—a fake," Barrick says quietly.

Comstock stiffens. "Again, please don't speak further about any involvement."

Two key copies? Well, damn. That makes five keys. Good thing I'm going to take my box contents home with me.

"Fuhrman's been a busy boy," Mack murmurs.

Comstock holds up his hand. "I've heard enough to hold the other Mrs. McCarren for official questioning." He turns to open the door.

"Please," I say. "Let me tell my sister-in-law she's been sitting a few feet from my necklace since she got here."

"I don't think that would be a problem," Comstock says, a small smile hitching the corner of his mouth.

I nod and go through the door, cross the hall, and step into Barrick's office. "Hello, Veronique."

Epilogue

It's been a couple of months since New York. The pace and threats encountered there were short-term adrenaline pills that, when the effects wore off, left Rippa and me just plain tired. She and Ben both admitted they missed roaming around this big house, running the trail beside the lake, and raiding the fridge. That, and the relative quiet. Even quieter since Ben left for UC Davis ten days ago. Rippa starts classes at UW next week.

August means real summer here on Lake Sammamish, and that means the fragrance of warm pines and paddling my feet in cool lake water, which is what I'm doing. Hot sun on my shoulders and I tip my face up to soak in the warmth.

"You were right. This is a beautiful place. Parking sucks, though."

I nearly topple off the side of our dock as I twist toward his voice, my heart stammering. "Mack! What are you doing here?"

He leans to hold out a hand. "Had a week's vacation burning a hole, so I decided to surprise you. Fill you in on the latest."

His warm hand feels nice. And nice doesn't come close to describing the rest of him. He's got a little bit of sun himself, which heightens the color of his eyes, as does his gold T-shirt. His hair needs a trim, but I like the slight curl at his neck. I blurt a giggle-laugh as I grab my towel off the dock. "I'm back in New York in what, three weeks, for the McCarren Rescue Foundation Gala. And you're my escort."

This is great, Cara. The kids moving on has left you sad.

I tug Mack to the back deck. "Like a glass of iced coffee?"

He nods. "Can I help?"

I head into the house. "Nope. Back in a few."

Inside, I make sure Mack isn't watching and check my hair in the microwave's glass before pouring the drinks. It sounds like he can hang around for a couple of days, and updates on the case or not, I love it that he showed up.

Back outside, I sit. "Okay, what's happening?"

He takes a sip of the coffee and smiles. "Not a whole lot outside of the emails I've been sending, but there're a few things you might be interested in. And I really wanted to see your face when I told you."

I rest my chin in my hand. Hope this means good news.

"I know you have a soft spot for Ian Ward," he says. "Remember Comstock, the security guy at the bank? He's dealt with the same fed on another case, so he's been kept informed about the various players who had a part.

"As of yesterday, they'd interviewed Ian's parents and sister, and a number of friends on Fire Island, with no results. He'd already emptied his bank account and flown from New York to southern Florida. From there they think, with the help of friends, he got to Buenos Aires."

"Wow. Argentina has extradition, but I wonder, since this was a personal property crime that happened via a safety deposit box in a bank, if they'll spend much manpower on capturing him." Hopefully, Ian has friends there who can help him heal.

Mack leans in. "You already know Ms. Barrick was arrested, then fired. No large amounts of cash and a fast getaway for her. Unfortunately, she'll do prison time. The good news is The McCarren Rescue Foundation has accepted her application, and her daughter, Mia, will get the medical procedure she needs." He pins me with a look. "Seems someone with pull asked that the application get special attention. Ms. Barrick's sister is taking the girl to Switzerland soon. I'll keep in contact with Comstock to let you know how the case against Barrick turns out."

This news gives me a warm fuzzy. "I hope the judge will take into consideration the emotional duress she was under when she agreed to take Angel Falls."

"Mack!" Rippa bursts onto the deck and leans over to hug him. "When did you get here? How long can you stay? What are you guys talking about?"

Mack grins. "Today. A couple of days. The case."

"Oh, goody. I want to hear too. Which part are you discussing now?"

"I was about to catch Julianne up on your Aunt Veronique."

Rippa hoots and plops into a chair. "This I gotta hear."

I'm also eager to know more of the saga that is Veronique.

Mack mock frowns. "Sad days for Veronique. No blue diamond bracelet, for starters. Her friend Fuhrman is under investigation for more than the federal charge of duplicating safety deposit box keys. Remember his 'international diamond sources'? Turns out some of those unmarked stones he showed you may be part of an ongoing case in France. His business is closed while his stock is being audited. The pieces Veronique bragged about buying from him may contain some of them."

I suck air through my teeth. "Yikes."

He nods. "There's more. Veronique's arraignment judge had no sympathy for a woman dressed to the nines and whose prevalent attitude was that it was okay to *recover* a family heirloom. At first, Veronique claimed she was visiting Ms. Barrick as a friend she was taking to lunch. That didn't fly due to Ms. Barrick's deposition. Then Veronique's attorney paraded her memberships in several charitable organizations. That backfired. The judge smiled and told her, 'Glad to hear you believe in community service, Mrs. McCarren. I'll keep that in mind.' "

"Did any of that get through to her?"

His grin is wolfish. "Not really. And she has a bigger problem."

Rippa puts her hands to the sides of her face in a "I can't believe this is getting better and better" look. "Bigger than a possible federal conviction?"

I pull my lips in and out. "Mitch?"

Mack nods. "The absence of Mitch. Remember I emailed you that I didn't see him at Veronique's arraignment? He's since contacted me wanting to find out if the company security team could provide personal protection."

Laughing out loud wouldn't be nice, so I pose a

question. "From Veronique?"

"Divorce," he replies. "The tabloid-cover nasty kind. His mother had all but memorized the woefully naked prenuptial agreement Veronique signed. There was a tiny stipulation stating should she be prosecuted for a felony, Mitch could proceed with a divorce without financial penalty due to the damage it would bring to the McCarren name. Mitch hired a divorce attorney immediately."

Although it doesn't sound like she means it, Rippa responds, "Wow. Harsh."

Mack grins. "Yeah. And it's escalated. When Veronique received the papers, she threatened to set his library on fire. She'd already burned one of his most valuable Russian novels in a wastebasket. Now she has federal *and* arson charges pending. Mitch's attorney petitioned the judge to have her removed from the townhouse and a restraining order issued. She's free on a huge amount of bail and under house arrest. Doubt if any of her former socialite friends would visit someone wearing an electronic monitor ankle device."

I wince. "Yikes, I knew about the divorce. Mitch called and asked me to be 'a family character witness' at the divorce proceedings. I asked if he'd chosen a new assistant from the covey of blondes he was interviewing. His enthusiastic reply all but gave me her measurements. I told him I'd write a cautiously worded letter and hope not to be prosecuted for perjury."

Mack and Rippa laugh.

I shake my head. "No life lessons learned in either case, I'm afraid."

Rippa scrunches her nose. "Any good news? How about Mikhail?"

Mack grins. "He's doing well. Made a full confession to his part in the death of Timur. That high-priced attorney Julianne hired played Mikhail's sad family background, and it worked. He got a year's probation and is required to go back to school. He readily agreed. Seems he has a real aptitude for languages. Besides Russian and English, I told him if he learned German or French, I'd recommend him for a job at McCarren Multinational after college."

Rippa and I both clap. "That is seriously cool," she says.

He makes a modified bow from the waist. "You'll also be happy that I visited Rose and Frieda, as promised. They're the hot ticket in their building what with their stories of being involved with a criminal element."

I laugh and flap my hands at a bewildered Rippa. "Tell you later."

I want the latest info on one more person, knowing it's selfish in not wanting to hear good news. "How about Nadya, the girl who set the whole nightmare in motion?"

He takes another sip. "The prosecutor felt the same way about her plan. Even if it failed, she still had a fake key made to a bank box. A federal crime. Dragging a Russian gang leader into the fray and being indirectly responsible for two deaths didn't make her any fans in the courtroom. She was assigned a court-appointed defense attorney. Female, no less. Before being remanded to Rikers Island to await trial." He shrugs. "It's basically hell on earth, and I wouldn't wish it on anybody. Doesn't look like she'll be making a trip back to Russia any time soon either. And I'm guessing those heels she likes would be considered weapons in prison."

This produces a visual of Nadya, and maybe Veronique sometime in the future, in orange jumpsuits, with no access to blonde hair dye. Possibilities that spark a smile I can't suppress.

A word about the author...

DeeAnna is a freelance editor and travel agent for happy endings (romantic suspense, women's fiction, children's picture books, and mystery). She writes and teaches for the love of it, has never met a dog she did not want to pet or a pie she did not want to taste. She tries to live life without props.

~*~

Find DeeAnna online at:
http://deeannagalbraith.com

Thank you for purchasing
this publication of The Wild Rose Press, Inc.

For questions or more information
contact us at
info@thewildrosepress.com.

The Wild Rose Press, Inc.
www.thewildrosepress.com